Allah's Scribe:

The Woman in the Prophet's Shadow

Allah's Scribe:

The Woman in the Prophet's Shadow

J. Johannes

Fact or Fiction?

See appendixes for further information regarding
the historical facts which undergird this story.

Allah's Scribe:

The Woman in the Prophet's Shadow

J. Johannes

www.alevbooks.com

ISBN-13: 978-0-9881252-6-1
ISBN-10: 0988125269

Cover photo: Steve Evans

Books are not written alone, and I have been blessed by the input of many talented individuals.

I wanted to acknowledge a long list of women and men but they have all chosen to remain anonymous due to the sensitive nature of this story. (Remember what happened to Salman Rushdie after he published *The Satanic Verses*?) However, I thank all those from the Middle East who contributred valuable cultural insights, the editors, who drove me forward without driving me to discouragement, as well as those who traveled with me to the Middle East and made my travels exceedingly enjoyable. Finally, I want to thank the institution that made this possible. Salaam Aleykum.

Preface

The events described in this book took place in March, 2011. They are based on a series of interviews the author had with "Dr. Rauser", "Miryam" and "Omar" (for security reasons their names have been changed, though "Omar" is relatively safe in his prison cell).

A month after the events described in this book a revolution broke out in Yemen. The revolution led to civil war between the Shiite Houthis of the north and the central Sunni government. By early 2015 the Houthis had swept across the country and the central government had fled to Saudi Arabia. At the time of writing Saudi Arabia is engaged in a targeted bombing campaign on behalf of the ousted government-in-exile. The debacle is generally perceived as a proxy war between Iran, accused of supporting its fellow Shiites, and Saudi Arabia.

Because it became impossible for foreigners to visit the country, because several Yemenis who feature in this tale have been killed, and because the Yemeni House of Manuscripts has been bombed, there is some uncertainty at this time as to the whereabouts of the palimpsests and other manuscripts which led to the events described in this book.

Prologue

Yemen's House of Manuscripts, Sana'a, Yemen, 11:55 p.m.

Dr. Salim readjusted the Laser Raman Spectroscope and the faint lines of text sharpened on the computer screen. He leaned forward to scrutinize each Syro-Aramaic letter that came into focus. "Subhan Allah," he mumbled. It existed! He reread the text three more times; exhilaration and exhaustion coursed through his body. The evidence before his eyes was hard to believe.

He leaned back in his chair, his eyes aching but not leaving the screen. One last decision remained: when should he put into motion the plan to retrieve it? Ushering the Hafsah Quran onto the world stage - the only Quran known to have been unaltered by Uthman - would radically change the Middle East. It would either trigger a detente between warring Muslim factions or embroil the whole region in an Armageddon. Salim closed his eyes to focus on the future but to no avail. He was exhausted. It was time to go home and get some sleep. He stood up, turned and grabbed his brief case. That's when he noticed the man in the corner of the room.

"Salaam aleykum professor Salim. Enjoying your research?"

How long had the stranger sat there?

Salim's eyes shifted to the man's lap. The intruder's right hand gripped a pistol, his index finger on the trigger. Salim looked up and the man's lizard eyes blinked.

"The research is going fine." His throat felt tense.

"Tell me professor, have you been successful in uncovering the Hafsah clues?"

"What clues?" Salim noticed the tremor in his own voice.

Someone had betrayed him.

"Professor, don't be coy with me." The man's voice had a haughty lilt.

Salim's eyes shifted back to the pistol. It hadn't moved. He noticed the middle finger on the other hand caressing an elongated, brass box that dangled from a gold necklace.

"Salim, we want the Hafsah manuscript."

Salim's attention was drawn to the word 'we.' This man was part of a team, a team that had been watching him. Were the others in the museum?

"Unfortunately the Hafsah manuscript was burned by the Caliph Uthman 1300 years ago."

"Don't lie to me, Mr. Salim..."

"As Allah is my witness, I've never seen it."

The man smirked. He extended the arm holding the pistol and aimed it directly at Salim's head. "I didn't bring this to scratch my back Salim. Perhaps you want to change your answer."

Salim looked at the weapon and closed his eyes, inhaled and waited for the shot.

When he opened his eyes the pistol was back in the man's lap but the smirk was still scratched in his face. The young man addressed him condescendingly, as if he was his father.

"Salim." Their eyes locked again. "This is your last chance: where is the Hafsah Quran?" Salim's eyes again fell on the intruder's left hand. It still caressed the elongated box dangling from his neck. The pistol didn't move.

Salim hadn't moved since he had turned to get his briefcase. His back faced the large tables covered by manuscripts being augmented and reconstructed. The spectroscope still illuminated the Syro-Aramaic palimpsest.

"Professor, turn round and put your hands behind your back."

Salim turned and placed his hands behind his back. He looked down on the beloved manuscripts that had lain hidden for 1300 years, the ones the Yemeni government had told him to selectively reveal to the world. Was he willing to die for the truth these manuscripts hid? He swallowed. "What makes you think the Hafsah Qur'an was never burned?"

"Professor, we've followed your every move for the past few months, examined every file, looked at all your notes and know you're on the trail of the Hafsah Qur'an. We also know that you have your hopes and fears about its contents. I'm not interested in killing you, but don't mistake my patience with lack of resolve. This trip is part of my spiritual calling. So, for the last time, where is Hafsah's Quran?"

Only four feet separated Salim's back from the gun. He heard the fanatic's slow footsteps approaching him. He sighed a silent prayer: 'Allah please help me' and glanced at the window. The reflection of the wiry man showed he walked with a limp. He heard the box hanging around his neck swish against his white caftan.

"We have some clues," Salim suggested. He was too old for physical heroics. "I'm not one hundred percent sure where Hafsah's journal is hidden but I know some possibilities."

"You're stalling professor." An irritated edge had crept into the man's voice. "Have you forgotten that your mind was meant to be used in the service of Allah, not in collaboration with infidels against him?"

Professor Salim again glanced at the window. The reflection showed the intruder standing immediately behind him. His mind flashed back to his army days: one well-placed kick in the groin was all he needed—the man *did* limp.

The thought came too late. The intruder grabbed his index finger and shoved it into something. A sharp pain shot through his hand. He wheeled around to hit the man but was too late. He had stepped back. Salim froze when he saw the gun.

"Professor, you've begun your final journey. I predict it will end in hell." The man stepped back several more paces, the gun steady in his hands. "The pain now running up your arm is from the yellow scorpion." He pointed to the box dangling on the string. "I have the antidote. Perhaps you would like to reconsider your last answer regarding the Hafsah manuscript?"

The pain racing up Salim's arm was coupled by a sudden dizziness as the neurotoxins clouded his mind. He needed the antidote! But the price was astronomical: betraying all Sunni and Shia Muslims! And what would a terrorist do with a document that would prove beyond a shadow of a doubt the Prophet Muhammad's personal choice regarding his chosen successor? Use the information to blackmail one side against the other! And how would an assassin treat the world's only original Quran, hidden since the death of the prophet, the only one penned by the prophet's wife?

Yet, if he didn't cooperate, he would die—and face Allah's judgment. He wasn't ready for that. Salim took a deep breath, and slowly answered: "Search in the *Well of Souls*. Go to Al Quds."

"Thank you Dr. Salim," the attacker answered with a smile. "I knew you would see it my way. Your arrogant German colleagues have already confirmed your answer."

Salim flinched. What had this maniac done to them? The answer was immediate: "Yes, I disposed of them as well."

Clenching the small box that hung around his neck with his left hand, the intruder raised the pistol in his right. "Allahu Akbar," he shouted and headed for the door. The last thing Salim heard was the click of the door lock.

Alone, Salim turned his gaze to the manuscripts that hid the secret. He staggered, his eyes stung and his head swirled as he collapsed on the manuscript table. Somehow he had to make sure the secret would not die with him.

What can I do to make sure the right people understand? There's only one person left who would know what to do.

The next four minutes would change the course of Islam.

1

The Souk
Sana'a, Yemen

Rauser's lanky frame leaned back against the yellowed, plastic chair. Sharing a meal in Sana'a market with his childhood friend Habib had made him nostalgic. Around them people were negotiating carts piled high with fresh pita bread, bright tomatoes, shiny cucumbers, rolls of cloth or leather and a myriad of other goods and bawling the nature of their wares or crying "look out, look out." The noise made conversation difficult.

He pulled out his wallet, removed a picture and pushed it across the table to Habib. A smiling young woman dressed in an exquisitely scalloped floral dress with long embroidered sleeves held Habib's attention. Her head was wrapped in a maroon, silk headscarf. There was a smiling baby in a pink dress on her lap.

Habib smiled as his eyes lingered on the picture. "How's Fatma?" he asked over the din.

"Great. Mom's dotes over them like they're her own kids."

A year and a half earlier Habib had asked Rauser to help smuggle his seventeen year old sister out of Yemen. When pressed about the matter Habib had hung his head in shame: "She had sex with a boy in the neighborhood – she's pregnant."

Rauser knew Habib's father loved his daughter; he didn't want her judged and flogged. The family would have withered and died of social shame in their conservative Sunni neighborhood. Rauser had helped the girl obtain a U.S. student visa and now she was at a community college studying financial management. Her beautiful baby was a U.S. citizen.

Looking up from the picture, Habib's eyes glowed. "My father will be forever grateful to you – it transformed his perception of Christians – that the followers of Isa can be people of love."

Rauser felt uncomfortable under Habib's grateful gaze. Making the decision to help smuggle Fatma out of Yemen had been driven more by his mother's faith than his own. Since his wife's death in the explosion he hadn't paid much attention to God.

"He should thank my mother," replied Rauser with a grin. "Tell your dad to meet me here tomorrow and I'll update him on his daughter and grand-daughter. You have a wonderful family." Smuggling Fatma out of the country had been an adrenalin rush. The threat of Fatma's pregnancy beginning to show had meant hurrying all the paperwork. He had spent evenings on the phone getting Fatma to submit college applications, finding the necessary finances and pushing through the visa paperwork. All the while her family had kept her out of the public eye. When the six month pregnant Fatma emerged from Habib's home for the trip to the airport she was dressed in an oversized burqa, carrying an exquisite leather bag, which drew the attention from her belly. She had stayed close to Rauser's mother as they negotiated Sana'a international airport and finally boarded the plane. When they received the call that evening that she had cleared American customs, he and Habib's family had celebrated her freedom. The music, food and fun of the party was etched in his memory.

"So, what brings you back to Yemen this time?" Habib asked. "Things are a bit too politically unstable to be coming as a tourist."

Rauser had come with one goal in mind: finish his research before his university's seven year time limit for obtaining tenure ran out. Now, nearing that deadline, he was determined to finally finish what he hoped would be a foundational piece of historical reconstruction: *Was the prophet Muhammad a secret devotee of Jesus Christ?* He hoped that the answer to this question would redefine Christian, Muslim and

Jewish relationships and nurture greater peace and understanding between these three religious competitors.

"I'm on a sabbatical from the university to work on a research project that involves Professor Salim at the Yemen House of Manuscripts. You know him?"

"No, not really. Only foreign academics like youself take an interest in the old man and his documents." Habib took a sip of his coffee. "Old documents don't interest me."

"That's what puzzles me. I'm a Christian, yet these famous documents are more interesting to me than to you. Don't you want to know if these newly discovered manuscripts can shed fresh light on your faith?"

"You always liked to ask questions. You haven't changed since you were a kid," Habib responded. "When people ask me what you're like I tell them that I'm not sure. Sometimes I think you'd make a great Yemeni, and sometimes I think you're another spoiled American who likes to identify with us but can never be one of us." Rauser had to smile at Habib's unusually candid response. The Arab really thought of him as a friend. "I tell my friends that you either engender great love and loyalty, or you piss people off."

Rauser's smile opened into a grin. "Ah, what can I say to that?" Glancing to his left his eye fell on a waiter elbowing his way through the crowd towards their table.

"Salaam Aleykum. Are you Dr. William Rauser?"

"I am."

The man nodded his head towards the door. "There's a gentleman here to see you." Rauser glanced at the throng of people blocking the door but saw no one he recognized. "What does he want?"

"I'm sorry. He didn't say."

"Could you ask him? I haven't seen my friend here for almost two years." Rauser's hand lifted and fell on Habib's shoulder. "We have much to talk about. If it doesn't appear important, please apologize to the gentleman and tell him I'll be free later this afternoon."

The waiter left. Rauser wondered if this was yet another person wanting to thank him for his father's medical legacy in Yemen.

"Tell me about your research," Habib asked.

"I'm looking at palimpsests in the Yemeni House of Manuscripts about early stories pertaining to Muhammad."

"What are palimpsests?"

"Documents that have been over-written. In the past paper was expensive and so people would wash the ink from old letters and reuse the paper."

"Yemen's first recycling program," joked Habib. "Anything interesting come to light?"

"Yes. Salim said he discovered information indicating the Prophet Muhammad's personal choice regarding his preferred successor."

"Wow! *That* could have some political repercussions."

Rauser was pleased that Habib had caught the implications of the find. "Indeed. Imagine if this age-old question was definitively settled," he said. "What if all Muslims united behind one leader? Israel would terrified! No more divide and conquer!"

"Not only Israel. It would shake the world!" answered Habib. "Over one billion people suddenly taking orders from a single individual! The power this caliphate could have! Even the U.S. would live in fear." The political dynamics were, indeed, unfathomable, if Muslims agreed to unite behind one leader to form a new global hegemonic power.

Rauser did not mention the scan of the palimpsest Salim had sent him, a piece the old professor believed had been dictated by Muhammad to his wife Hafsah the week before his death. The old man suspected the section should have been in the Quran. It was the last part of chapter 2, verse 282. Salims' scan of verse 283 was different from the verse in today's Quran. It had amazed Rauser: *"But if ye fear the judgment of Allah, believe ye in the sacrifice of Isa son of Meryem, the one sent from Allah to reconcile the unworthy to Allah's favor. Follow him as ye have followed me."* If he could triangulate this piece of data with two other defensible pieces he would not only have tenure but international recognition.

"I need to publish something significant this year to get tenure. If I don't get my book published I'll lose my job. Every professor gets seven years to prove his mettle."

"Well, I wish you the best in your research then."

They both noticed the waiter angling back to their table, this time with someone carrying a blue binder tucked under his left arm. "I'm sorry Dr. Rauser, but the gentleman is very insistent. Allow me to introduce to you police detective Lieutenant Abdullah Hussein."

Rauser stood up to shake hands. The lieutenant had a firm grip. His deep set eyes looked intently into his own.

Why was a detective interested in talking to him?

Lieutenant Hussein came straight to the point: "I'm sorry to bother you Dr. Rauser, but my superior requested I contact you. We have a favor to ask. We are dealing with a murder investigation, and we feel that perhaps you can be of some service. Could you help us analyze some of professor Salim's documents? I don't think it'll take long."

"I'm not a detective; I'm an academic," Rauser replied. "This wasn't by chance Dr. Salim from the museum?"

"Unfortunately it was."

"You've got to be kidding!" Rauser exclaimed.

"May I sit down?" Without waiting for a reply the police officer pulled out another yellowed plastic chair, sat down, nodded politely to Habib and turned back to Rauser. "You don't know me, but I know your father. He set the broken leg of one of my cousins. How's your mother since your father's death? Many people in Yemen have fond memories of your father and we pray Allah has comforted your mother since his passing."

"My mother is doing O.K. -- still adjusting to life in America," Rauser answered while his mind processed the implications of Salim's death."

The detective continued: "It must be difficult after having been here for decades. Give her my condolences." Hussein paused briefly, then continued. "I'm sorry for insisting, but my captain really feels he needs your help. We noticed in Dr. Salim's agenda that you met him yesterday afternoon to discuss some manuscripts. Is that correct?"

"That is correct. We talked about his work on the manuscripts." The meeting had lived up to Rauser's expectations. Salim had shown him the alternate reading of 2:283 and they had discussed the theological implications. "This is nothing," Salim had said with a wide-eyed grin. "Tomorrow I'll show you something else. According to one palimpsest, which I believe was written by Hafsah, the Hafsah Quran is actually hidden away somewhere. And if I'm right, there are huge differences between today's Quran and the one that Hafsah had in her possession." Looking like a kid who just unwrapped his Idul Fitir present he added, "and can you imagine if the original Quran endorses Jesus as Muhammad's chosen leader, if it corroborates the verse I sent you! Just think of the repercussions between Christian and Muslims!"

"Where do you think Hafsah's Qur'an might be?" Rauser had asked.

"Let's talk about that tomorrow. That way I know you'll be back!" Salim had joked.

Sleep had been scarce last night. All he could think about was the Hafsah Quran. What if they actually found it? It would be like finding the Dead Sea Scrolls!

Lieutenant Hussein interrupted his thoughts. "This is how we found Dr. Salim a couple of hours ago." He pulled a photograph from the blue binder. It showed a man slouched over a manuscript table holding a dark light bulb in one hand. His other hand was painted with odd henna designs and was pointing at a pile of manuscripts at the end of the table.

Rauser's face turned pale. He looked more closely at the picture.

What's with the henna designs?

An apologetic cough interrupted Rauser's thoughts: "This photograph was taken in the *Yemeni House of Manuscripts;* we're not sure about the meaning of the henna designs."

Rauser scrutinized the image. There were no bullet holes and no blood. A flush of anger tightened his neck muscles. Why would anyone kill an old scholar who only prized his ancient manuscripts and his family? "Who did this?" He asked indignantly.

"We're not sure."

"I'm not sure what you think I can contribute," Rauser said glancing up at Hussein, "but if you think I can be helpful, I'm at your service."

Hussein moved his chair closer to Rauser, looked him in the eye: "We think it has something to do with the manuscripts he was studying."

Rauser's eyebrows shot up. He glanced down at the photograph. "And why is he holding a light bulb, and what would a man be doing with henna designs on his hand?"

"Mr. Rauser, there are many oddities pertaining to Dr. Salim's death. We believe they relate to his work; the light bulb, the painted hand, the position of the body, and no bullet wounds. We think you could be of help."

Rauser noticed Hussein now leaning slightly over the table; the detective's eyes probed his. The body language was clear: you'd better come with me! "How do you want me to help?" Rauser handed the photograph back to the policeman.

"Maybe you can help us to understand the henna design on his hand."

"I can try," Rauser said as he stood up to pay the bill.

2

Yemen's
House of Manuscripts

"Excuse the mess," Lieutenant Hussein said. "The boss likes to eat while I drive." Rauser watched as Hussein wiped some crumbs off the Toyota pick-up truck's passenger seat, then sat down. Hussein turned on the siren and the vehicle sped along the narrow Sana'a streets.

Rauser loved these bustling streets: the goats, the veiled women, the men chewing qat and the vehicles careening like bumper cars on steroids past brightly painted adobe buildings. The place had a vibrancy he missed in his sanitized, suburban, American commute. Here you lived history. His mind shifted to the murder investigation. How could his knowledge of palimpsests, culture and history be a help – he was hardly the CSI type. Perhaps the cops were interested in the knowledge he had picked up when he worked for the Saudi embassy during his time in the military. Did they even know about that?

Hussein drove like a NASCAR racer, but with bikes, carts, chickens and children dashing out of their way. It was like being in a video game, only more exciting. "I think you'll be interested in what you'll see," the lieutenant shouted over the noisy siren.

"Uh-huh." Through the side mirror Rauser noticed an Arab giving an obscene gesture at the receding police car.

"The boss doesn't like waiting," Hussein grinned, looking in the rearview mirror. The radio crackled and a commanding voice broke through the static. "How long before you get here?"

Hussein grabbed the receiver. "We'll be there in 30 seconds." He looked at Rauser. "Fouad, the boss, takes life too seriously. He needs someone to inject a bit of humor into his life."

"And that's your calling?" asked Rauser with a smile.

Hussein smiled and nodded as he yanked the steering wheel to the right and pulled the vehicle through the museum's high gate. Hussein scanned for a parking spot when Rauser noticed a short, barrel chested officer step through the front door. The man approached their slowing vehicle and when it came to a stop, opened Rauser's door and stuck a chubby little hand out in greeting.

"Salaam aleykum. You must be Dr. Rauser."

"Aleykum issalaam." Rauser stepped out of the car while shaking the hand. "Yes, I'm William Rauser. How did you find me?"

"I checked with the visa office," Fouad replied smiling. "Your application mentioned which hotel you would be staying at. Finding you after that was easy. I suspected you'd hang out somewhere non-touristy yet lively; the market was my first guess. I am pleased that the son of the great surgeon is willing to help us."

Rauser smiled. This Fouad fellow was smooth, a good read of character, he thought. "Excuse me," he asked, "but I didn't catch your name."

"Oh, I'm sorry. My name is Captain Fouad. Your Arabic is very good, just like your father's."

Dad's shadow followed him everywhere...

They left Lieutenant Hussein with the car and walked toward the museum. Fouad opened the door. "Lieutenant Hussein showed you the photograph." The statement was meant as a question.

"Yes."

"You`re probably wondering why we asked you to come."

"Hussein mentioned something about henna," Rauser answered.

"That's right. Our investigators are used to working with clues that relate to the 21st century: blood analysis, DNA sequencing and stakeouts." Fouad's hands were in constant motion as he talked. "This killing is different. The clues seem rooted in ancient Yemen. We hope you can help us with Dr. Salim's eccentricities, as well as what may be some critical evidence. We need to isolate the clues pertaining to the nature of Dr. Salim's death from oddities that may have been part of his character and unrelated to his death."

They walked partway down a hallway when Fouad opened another door into another hallway. Pocket Hercules, thought Rauser as he followed from behind. *He looks like a hobbit on steroids.*

"So you had an appointment with Dr. Salim?" Fouad asked.

"Yes." Rauser had decided to take the airport-immigration-approach: answer all questions with short pithy answers; no point in forming hypotheses that weren't grounded in facts.

"When did you meet?"

"Yesterday."

"How did Dr. Salim appear when you met him?"

"Fine." Rauser didn't want to overstate the excitement of Salim's new findings. He feared it could implicate Salim as a sympathetic Shiite in a nation where that could cause considerable problems.

"What was your meeting about?" Fouad probed.

"I was interested in Dr. Salim's work; we talked about the Sana'a manuscripts."

There was no point in discussing the 'new Quranic verse' or the traces of Muhammad's last will and testament in the palimpsest. That was meant to happen today.

"Have you known Dr. Salim a long time?"

"Yes. My father knew him. We talked at conferences and were in email contact."

Fouad gestured with his hand as he led Rauser down another corridor. "Did you or Dr. Salim set up the appointment?"

"I did."

"Have you read any of Dr. Salim's work?"

"Yes. His work is well known among German historians. I read German."

Fouad's barrage of questions never let up: "What was Dr. Salim's response to your request to see him?" he asked as they passed a display of ancient manuscripts.

"He heartily agreed." Rauser did not mention the fact that they were more than e-mail acquaintances, that they were part of a secret working group set up at an international academic conference which had published some articles under German pseudonyms.

"Why do you think he was interested in seeing you?"

"We had some shared research interests." Suddenly Rauser became somewhat apprehensive.

What if Fouad had learned about the secret working group?

"Salim had mentioned that he was working on some new hypotheses," Rauser said nonchalantly. As soon as the words left his mouth he regretted the offered information.

Captain Fouad raised one eyebrow. "What were these hypotheses?"

"He had found some palimpsest that appeared to indicate that Muhammad may have left a last will and testament. That's what we were going to discuss today."

"Why didn't you discuss them yesterday?"

"I had another appointment, and so we decided to continue today."

"So what did Dr. Salim know about you?"

Rauser was beginning to feel like he was being interrogated. "He knew my father and he'd read some of my articles. Last year I sent him a copy of something that I was thinking of publishing."

"What was the topic?"

"I'm researching a book on Islam. My sources included some of the manuscripts here at the museum."

"How did you get access to the museum manuscripts?" The questions kept coming, and Rauser was irritated at being treated like a suspect.

"Some of the older ones are available through a CD produced by the United Nations. Others are in private collections. Salim promised I could take a look at some of the ones here, ones not yet made public. That's why I'm in Yemen."

Fouad pulled a pen out of his shirt pocket and started to twirl it between his thumb and index finger. "And Dr. Salim is an expert on Islamic history?"

"World class." Dr. Salim had deduced that the oldest versions of the Quran were not even written in Arabic but in Syriac, and that at its inception the Qur'an was drawn from Christian Syro-Aramaic texts, in order to evangelize the Arabs in the early 8th century. Clearly Fouad had no idea how famous a figure Dr. Salim was in the world of Islamics. The pseudonyms had worked.

"Did your research promote or undermine Dr. Salim's work?"

The question made Rauser uncomfortable. Was this Fouad actually suggesting he had a motive to murder the man? "I'm a researcher. We develop hypotheses and try to prove or disprove them. We academics usually don't engage in feuds."

"What were your hypotheses about – the one's Salim may have found interesting?"

There is no way, Rauser said to himself, that I'm going to expose my hypotheses to the charge of blasphemy. No one here need know I'm writing a book meant to prove the Quran was not written in Arabic, and that the best scholarly research actually indicates Muhammad may have been a misguided Christian.

I'll baffle him with bullshit.

"My hypotheses are very tentative at this stage. I'm convinced we can better understand the worldview and hermeneutic of the modern Qur'an by examining the suppletion and morphophonemics of the underlying proto-Arabic forms which appear to have been Syro-Aramaic and which have embedded in them the essence of the underlying form of the subsequent Quraish dialect spoken by Muhammad."

"Sounds interesting," Fouad mumbled looking over Rauser's shoulder. His eyes brightened when he saw Lieutenant Hussein re-appear. The lieutenant approached and whispered something in Fouad's ear. The Captain nodded. A hand motion told Rauser to follow him. "Let's go to the crime scene."

Rauser followed Fouad to a door guarded by a policeman. Above it was small black sign with white, flowing Arabic letters: *Labaratorium.* Fouad muttered something and the policeman opened the door. Rauser's gaze fixed itself on Salim's corpse hunched over a manuscript table. He was surprised to see that it had not yet been taken away.

"Let's take a closer look at the body, Dr. Rauser." Rauser sucked in a deep breath of the cool, air-conditioned air. I'm going to be here for a while, he thought.

3

The Crime Scene

Dr. Salim's body was slumped across several conservation tables that had been pushed together. Pressed between one table and the body, Rauser could see several old manuscripts. There didn't seem to be any blood. What made Captain Fouad think the old man hadn't just died of a heart attack or stroke?

Rauser recognized the assortment of chemicals—soluble nylon, gelatin and methylcellulose—used in manuscript preservation lined up in neat little jars beside the body. Dr. Salim must have been reinforcing manuscripts when he died. The sink and countertop along the far wall were also covered with beakers and various types of paper used to augment and reconstruct ancient manuscripts. Across the room were several more large tables on which the ancient Sana'a manuscripts were either drying or kept in presses. The cool dry air meant to preserve the manuscripts made the lab feel like a morgue.

As Captain Fouad led Rauser towards the sagging body Rauser noticed the Laser Raman Spectroscope. Salim must have been analyzing the ancient pigments; odd... the machine was still on. He wondered if the palimpsests were being analyzed with the black light on the far table. He felt the policeman touching his elbow.

"I'm surprised there's no blood anywhere," Rauser whispered quietly and wondered why he had whispered as soon as he voiced the question.

"That's not the only thing that we find surprising," answered Foaud.

"How do you think he died?"

"We're not sure."

"How long was he dead before you found him?"

"The coroner thinks it was about eight hours. You ask a lot of questions."

Not as many as you, thought Rauser.

Fouad thrust a short, handwritten text under his face. "What do you make of this? We found it beside Salim's right hand." Rauser looked at the text. The script was angular, yet not unlike Arabic. "I'm not sure," he said. "May I take a picture of it with my cell phone? Then I can analyze it later."

"No problem professor."

When Rauser zoomed in on the text he suddenly recognized the language. "This is Syro-Aramaic," he exclaimed and snapped a picture.

"What does it say?"

Rauser slowly translated: *Namhtu's planned destruction is seriously in doubt. The widow's conservation was actually carried out 15:80* and *60:2:6-8.*

"What do you think it means?" asked Fouad, his voice sounding more and more like an interrogator.

Rauser felt pressured to say to something but wasn't sure what: "I'm not sure. I've never heard the name Namhtu before. Perhaps Namhtu was a historical figure whose military campaign was foiled by a widow, but that is just an educated guess."

"What about the numbers?"

"I have no idea."

Fouad walked around to the other side of the body and pointed to a light bulb on the table near Salim's other hand. "He was holding this light bulb when we found the body. It had been dipped in some kind of dark ink. Why would a curator dip a light bulb in ink?"

"Strange," answered Rauser moving to pick up the bulb.

"Don't touch it!" commanded Fouad. "We haven't examined it for fingerprints."

"Perhaps, the bulb refers to something that light uncovers?" Rauser suggested, trying to cover up his near faux pas.

"Could be," Fouad nodded. "What does that machine do?" he asked, pointing to the Laser Spectroscope.

"It reads palimpsest."

"What are palimpsests?"

"Older text over-written by newer text. Some of the old Sana'a manuscripts Dr. Salim was examining were palimpsests. Perhaps he found something interesting in his research."

"So what do you think he may have found?"

"That's what intrigues me as well. I was hoping to find out by working with him on some manuscripts today!"

Rauser had read the article which Salim had recently published under a pseudonym in a German academic journal. Based on palimpsest data from the Sana'a manuscripts, Salim had convincingly argued that the Caliph Uthman, one of the early Muslim empire builders, had one primary, overarching fear after the death of the Prophet Muhammad: disunity within the military. Many of his soldiers were tired. They also felt guilty about killing Christians, whom they considered 'fellow believers'.

Not only was there disagreement about Muhammad's true wishes, Uthman's generals argued incessantly over whose memories of Muhammad's actual words were correct. Accusations and denunciations of heresy and truth-twisting was undermining the unity of his army and left it vulnerable to the Byzantine forces just north of the Arabian Peninsula. His solution? Create a Qur'an that would support his political ends.

After he'd compiled his version of the Qur'an he had all competing versions burned or laundered, thus eliminating all rival claims to be the inspired word of Allah. His Quran was now the only true Quran.

The brilliant move had unified his army. It had identified those potentially disloyal to him and forced everyone to line up with his new religio-political manifesto or face the consequences: being condemned to hell by Allah. If people did not follow him he could take any action he wanted against them because they would not only be against him but against Allah's revelation. And he was eager to serve as the sword of Allah.

According to Salim, Caliph Uthman's handling of the conflicts over Muhammad's revelations was pure genius in terms of empire building. His Qur'an defined the sacred space of his subjects. He now controlled their eternal destiny—meaning he could make them do anything he wanted. After all, it was all in the book of Allah.

There was one problem: Caliph Uthman never anticipated that 1300 years later people would be reapplying the ink from the manuscripts he had laundered and rereading the original through a Laser Raman Spectroscope. Dr. Salim had reversed Uthman's dry-cleaning efforts, and the original non-politicized Quran was waiting to be revealed to the world.

Dr. Salim's article had made a clear-cut case for the political manipulation of the Quran's final edits. He had included several photographs of the palimpsest proving that through these edits Uthman had sabotaged the possibility of detente between the expanding Muslim empire and Christian Byzantine Empire.

After reading the article, Rauser had written the curator. Salim's reply had intrigued him:

Hello Dr. Rauser, and thank you for the compliments.

You might be interested in knowing that I have found the fragment of a letter signed by Uthman stating that under threat of death, all instances of the prophet Muhammad, peace be upon him, affirming the resurrection of Jesus were to be removed from the final version of the Quran. He also commanded washing the ink off any Quranic document that mentions Muhammad's last will regarding his chosen successor – the eternally living prophet who was bodily raised up from the dead to heaven (which I presume to be Isa al Masih, or Jesus the Messiah). I have attached a scan of the palimpsest, Quran 2:283 that proves such verses were laundered.

Another intriguing yet frustrating find is that some of the oldest palimpsests appear to hide not just two layers of text, but three. Initial fragmentary evidence suggests that the palimpsest with three layers of text may have been written by Hafsah, Muhammad's wife. Since my technical 'know how' is limited, I'm having trouble getting an undisputed clear reading of the third layer. My hesitant hypothesis is that they allude to Hafsah's assertion that her Quran was never burned, but that it was hidden by her father at a sacred site. Further analysis is ongoing and the only impediment right now appears to be my abilities with the sophisticated German equipment. I would love to uncover where the Hafsah Quran is hidden.

Just think of the implications! Imagine Muslims striving together to assert their presence into the farthest reaches of the globe! I doubt if this last sentence thrills you, but as a Muslim who has been humiliated through colonialism and been forced to submit to foreign powers this idea thrills me. At the same time, however, we would be joining hands in helping to usher in the coming of the Messiah – your Jesus!

Sorry, I digress. I look forward to seeing you next week and hopefully you can help me with the German scanners.

Salaam,

Salim.

"Dr. Rauser," Fouad interrupting his thoughts. "Why do you think 'Hafsah' is written on his side?"

The question jarred him back to the present. Fouad unbuttoned Dr. Salim's shirt and Rauser glanced at the deathly pale flesh. Fouad took a tissue paper and peeled a yellow sticky note from the far side of the corpse. The word "Hafsah" was written in red ink.

"That's odd. How did you find that?"

"Dr. Rauser," said Fouad, "it's our job to inspect a crime scene; we may not be academics but we do know how to find and piece together evidence."

Rauser smiled wanly. "Perhaps the note was meant to reinforce the meaning of the Syro-Aramaic text." Rauser turned his eyes from the corpse; he felt there was something disrespectful about handling a half-naked body like a sack of potatoes.

"Any suggestions why *Hafsah* may have been written in red?" asked Fouad, one hand still holding up Salim's shirt while the other braced the lifeless head.

"Red often relates to blood or ancestry," said Rauser walking back to where he had left the Syrio-Aramaic text.

"So you think this relates to *Namhtu's* blood from the Syro-Aramaic text, or perhaps Namthu is an important ancestor?" Fouad asked incredulously.

"Maybe."

Fouad laid the corpse back on the table and slowly stood up, signaling to the back of the room. Lieutenant Hussein turned off the lights. He then gestured for Rauser to look under the Laser Raman Spectroscope.

Rauser walked over to the spectroscope and looked through the eye piece at a palimpsest. The faint shadow of the ancient text, covered by the dominant surface text drew Rauser's attention.

"Dr. Rauser, can you help us understand the meaning of this text?"

Rauser recognized the script; it was Aramaic. Strange. He was hesitant to venture a guess; he needed more time. "I'm sorry sir, but the script looks like Aramaic, not Arabic. The text and the quality are such that I can't make out what it says. Perhaps, when it's adequately restored, I'll be of more help."

Fouad once again signaled to the back of the room and Lieutenant Hussein turned on the lights.

Rauser's eyes shifted once again to the corpse and he wondered aloud to Captain Fouad: "Where is the murder weapon? What motive would someone have to kill Dr. Salim? Perhaps he died of a heart attack."

'Let me ask you something, Dr. Rauser. How many people do you know who might write a girl's name on a piece of paper and then put this paper under their shirt before they die of a heart attack? We also know that he called his wife, telling her he was dying, just before he passed away."

"Did he tell her who killed him?"

"His wife said he appeared incoherent on the phone. He slurred his sentences. He said something about the manuscripts, but his speech was so incoherent that she couldn't make out what he was talking about."

Rauser looked up at Fouad and felt he was being visually dissected. His concern increased when the captain winked at Hussein, who smiled in return.

What was that all about?

Fouad knew Hussein had interpreted his wink correctly. They both had misgivings about Rauser and had included him as a likely suspect. It was the note taken from Salim's schedule book that had raised their suspicions. Beside Salim's 3:00 p.m. appointment with Rauser—

yesterday's last appointment—Salim had scribbled: *"Don't get caught discussing something you'll regret."*

"Dr. Rauser," probed Fouad looking intently in Rauser's eyes, "is there anything in the work that you and Dr. Salim share that could lead to regrets for Salim?"

Fouad looked intently at Rauser's face trying to discern how the American responded emotionally to the question. Rauser's eyes momentarily widened. He looked surprised, taken off-guard. Fouad quickly followed up with another question: "Perhaps something that, if publicly known, could cause you problems in this country?"

"I'm not sure what you could be referring to?"

Salim waved his hand in the direction of the manuscripts on one of the tables: "Suppose some of these documents undermine the legitimacy of our Sunni government, especially in regards to suppressing non-Sunni religious minorities. Suppose the two of you found something in these documents challenging the legitimacy of the Saudi regime and its support for our government."

"I really don't know what Dr. Salim may have found here. In any case, how would an ancient document threaten the present government?" Rauser shrugged defensively.

"Dr. Rauser," Fouad said condescendingly, "you're an intelligent man. You're aware of the historical roots that form the primary sources of political instability in this region: fights over the prophet Muhammad, praise be upon him, and his chosen successor. Are the Iranian and Syrian Shi'ite's correct or the Sunni Arabs? The wars in Syria and Iraq are ultimately about this issue, as are the tensions between the Iranians and the Saudis." Pointing at the documents he continued, "Suppose Dr. Salim found something that settles this question once and for all with great historical certainty. Then, suddenly, we have winners and losers—and not every loser is a 'happy loser.'"

"Captain, what you are saying makes a certain amount of sense," Rauser nodded, "but it presupposes that such a document actually exists, then finding it, and then deciding who the potential winners and losers are."

"True. But there could be another possibility. Suppose the document proves that both Sunni and Shia are wrong, who then would have the most to gain in such a scenario?"

"That is an interesting hypothesis. I'm not sure I can venture a guess."

"Those who want to keep the Muslim world from uniting into one big, united force. Those who fear Islamic global domination, a new hegemonic power able to establish a new international world order, based on Sharia law."

"And who would that be?" Rauser anticipated Fouad's answer.

"The Jews and the Americans. Even with their nuclear weapons the Jews would be unable to protect their speck of land. As for the Americans, they would be confronted by a new world order imposed by a united Islamic Caliphate."

"That's quite the conspiracy theory," Rauser smiled with eyebrows raised. Fouad's conspiracy theory was typical of the perfected Middle Eastern art of blaming their failures on the U.S. or Israel or both. He had heard hundreds of these theories before. "To prove it you need to find some supporting documents."

"That's why we asked you to come, Dr. Rauser."

4

Salim's Lab

Rauser felt uncomfortable under Faoud's gaze and turned his eyes to Salim's corpse. His eyes were drawn to the man's other hand—not the one that held the painted light bulb but the right hand—the one painted with the strange henna design. Rauser recalled the photograph Lieutenant Hussein had shown him at the restaurant and noticed something oddly familiar in the design, something he'd seen before, something from his childhood. But where?

He bent forward, moving his head from side to side as he examined the hand from different angles while trying not to touch it. "So Dr. Rauser, what do you make of the hand? You can pick it up if you want. Dr. Salim won't object," Fouad chortled.

"It intrigues me," Rauser said.

"Have you ever seen such a henna design before?"

"It looks remotely familiar."

"Any guesses as to what it may mean?"

Rauser picked up the hand. It felt stiff and cold. Rigor mortis was setting in. "It's an odd, very poorly executed design. There appear to be four different sections, which is really strange." One line ran down the middle finger to end in a diagonal line that appeared to cross the thumb, while another began where the two lines intersected, and ran diagonally to his wrist. "It doesn't look like a typical henna pattern at all. Perhaps it's a map. Who do you think painted this?" Rauser turned over the pasty hand to see if the lines went around to the other side.

"We think Dr. Salim painted it on himself." Fouad pointing to the sink. "We found a wet henna brush with the same tint over there."

"That explains why it's such a poor job." Rauser let go of the hand; it fell stiffly back on the table. Walking over to the sink Rauser examined the brush. "He's probably never painted henna on himself, let alone with his left hand."

"So what do you think it means?"

"I have no idea," answered Rauser still looking at the brush. His photographic memory sifted through his research on Middle Eastern henna but no mental picture fit the design he saw before him.

This was never meant to be henna.

"I thought a man of your intellect would be able to figure this out Dr. Rauser." The sarcastic barb was well placed.

"Well, my intellect will be your big disappointment of the day Captain Fouad." The man's pushiness began to irritate Rauser. "Do you mind if I take another picture for subsequent analysis?"

Fouad smiled. "No problem," he answered while Rauser took a picture, "Perhaps I should show you the rest of the clues we're trying to decipher. Remember how we pulled a sheet of paper from Dr. Salim's back that read 'Hafsah'?"

"Yes?"

"Take a look at the other side of the body."

Rauser walked back to the corpse. Fouad grabbed Salim's palled shoulders, rolled him over and pointed a finger at the stomach. "Look at the art work on his stomach. We found the hand painted with henna pointing to his left nipple." Fouad placed the hand to its original position.

Rauser suddenly realized he was reading text. Under Salim's left nipple was the Arabic word *qambus*, and under his right nipple the Greek word κατερίνης. Finally, there was an arrow pointing downward towards his navel. "Any idea what this might mean Dr.

Rauser?" Fouad's repeated use of the word 'Dr.' began to irritate. It was said more in mockery than respect.

Rauser looked at Salim's eyes. They were frozen in place but seemed to communicate an unspoken message: *please solve my death.* "I'll do everything I can to help you my friend," Rauser said to himself. He turned to Fouad.

"The Greek word means 'Catherine' and you'll recognize the Arabic word *qambus.*"

Fouad nodded as if he already knew this information. He signaled for Hussein, standing at the back of the room, to come over. "Any word from forensics?"

"I expect them shortly," Hussein replied.

"Who is helping you analyze the clues?" Rauser asked.

"I have taken a few pictures on my phone and sent them to some scholars we found listed in Dr. Salim's contact list. I also have a local officer working on it." Fouad stopped to jot something down in his a little notebook.

"Would you mind sharing their findings?" Rauser sensed a deepening commitment to solving this case. It was not just the growing anger of seeing a colleague murdered for no apparent reason, but also the mysterious clues that intrigued him. Salim obviously wanted to communicate something before he died. Rauser wondered if the murderer was a fanatic who had uncovered some of Salim's theological assertions.

Fouad was holding a piece of paper in his hands. "Dr. Rauser, can you tell me anything about the German scholars listed on Dr. Salim's contact list?"

Rauser's eyes skimmed down the list. "They're from a variety of academic disciplines but they all have one thing in common: they're Middle East experts focusing on different aspects of early Islamic history. Have you contacted them?" He didn't mention that several had published journal articles under pseudonyms with himself and Salim.

"We have not been able to reach them in person. We sent voice mails, faxes and e-mails asking them to contact us as soon as possible."

"What have your local forensic experts found so far?"

"I'll introduce you as soon as the officer arrives. You may want to compare notes with her."

'Her'? This Fouad has a female on his forensic team? I would not have guessed him to be so open-minded.

Rauser nodded. He looked again at the scene and wondered how Fouad was trying to piece together the puzzle. "You mentioned 'many oddities' that made you suspect foul play. But maybe it was just a bizarre suicide?"

"What makes you think that?" This time Fouad raised his eyebrows.

Sweeping his hand around the room Rauser answered: "I'm no forensic expert, but in the field of anthropology we're trained to analyze cultural and historical clues. Look how clean the place looks. If I was examining this site like an anthropologist, I would conclude that there's not enough evidence to assert a life and death struggle."

"Why?" asked Fouad, hands now on his hips. "He's dead, phoned his wife and said, 'they know about the manuscripts' which appears to indicate that there were people in the room."

"Maybe. However, if Dr. Salim was murdered, the attack must have been relatively quick. There is no evidence of a fight. The attacker must have left before he died or else he wouldn't have called his wife. Perhaps his attacker thought he was dead when he wasn't. He must also have known he was dying or else he wouldn't have left all these bizarre messages."

"So why do you think an academic would leave bizarre messages?" Fouad looked straight at Rauser. His hands remained on his hips.

"Academics can be strange," said Rauser holding the phone list. "Freud took cocaine to understand the drug; Timothy Leary took hallucinogenics to ascertain their properties. Perhaps a drug was mentioned in one of the ancient manuscripts – like soma – and Salim experimented with it. Maybe he was forced to take it by whoever killed him."

"Is this a joke?" Fouad asked sarcastically.

"I agree it sounds far-fetched." Rauser paused briefly, then he went on. "Suppose he did die of chemical poisoning; his clouded brain may have encouraged him to write their names down in a way that seems bizarre to us but perfectly normal for someone on drugs. Perhaps the names 'Hafsah' or 'Catherine' were his killers. I'm sure you're checking out the names in your hotel registries."

"Don't worry. I'm following *all* leads,"

5

Yemen House of Manuscripts

A loud knock on the door reverberated through the lab.

"That must be Maryam," Lieutenant Hussein announced.

"Tell her to wait a few minutes." It'll remind her who's in charge. Fouad knew she was struggling with the recent loss of her uncle, but she often got on his nerves. The female detective was brilliant, he had to admit, but she often forgot that this was Yemen. Here women reported to men. Here Allah had ordained men to be in charge.

Fouad turned to Rauser. "So you think drugs may have been involved? Made him act strange?"

"Hi Hussein!" A woman's warm voice cut Fouad's train of thought. She tossed a mischievous smile at the lieutenant as she pushed through the door and marched into the lab. Self-assurance radiated from her eyes as she strode up to Captain Fouad. Fouad threw an angry look at Hussein, who rolled his eyes behind her and affected a helpless shrug.

"Captain Fouad!" she exclaimed, "it's so good to see you again. Your office sent over the blood samples and the photographs and we were pleased to help your forensic team. We have some preliminary findings which you might find interesting."

She acts like one of those Western feminists, thought Fouad. Big ego, self-centered. "Maryam," Fouad said with restrained politeness. "I'm busy right now. Please join Lieutenant Hussein at the back of the room. As soon as I have a minute I'll be happy to take a look at your analysis." He was telling her she was on his leash. She was expected to come and go when he said so. This was Yemen, not France.

On the one hand she intrigued him. Also, her European education in forensics and ability in French and English provided him with expertise he badly needed. On the other hand, he was irritated that she'd decided to work for the *Coordinating Office for Security*, the new department designed to coordinate information pertaining to terrorist activities between the U.S. and the Yemeni governments. He felt she had wormed her way into the department just to further her private crusade of empowering women in Yemen.

Rauser interrupted his thoughts. "What's her background in forensics?" The American was looking with interest at Maryam.

"She's good. Trained in Europe. Works for an American-Yemeni intelligence department meant to track terrorists. Their department has the best technology so I sent the blood samples and pictures to them for rapid analysis."

"Lieutenant Hussein did indicate I should stay out of the room, but..." Once again Maryam interrupted him.

"Thank you Maryam," Fouad nodded condescendingly, "I'll be with you in a moment." Maryam turned obediently and walked towards Lieutenant Hussein at the back of the room. Just as Fouad opened his mouth to continue his conversation she piped up again: "You were right about the henna design."

Fouad and Rauser looked at her back. "It appears that Dr. Salim drew a map on his hand." Her tone was a balance between anger and defiance. Fouad didn't know what to do. Should he call her back? Should he ask her what the map revealed?"

"Thank you Maryam..." He turned to Rauser. "So, Dr. Rauser, perhaps you're interested in what Inspector Maryam found?"

"Very much." Rauser looked at the woman in the khaki colored uniform now standing beside Lieutenant Hussein. Pretty, about twenty-five years old. A fashionable veil emblazoned with olive swirls hid her hair. Spirited, pitch-black eyes radiated from her face.

43

"Maryam, meet Dr. Rauser."

She approached Rauser with extended hand: "Pleased to meet you Dr. Rauser." Her tone was firm. There was something vigorous about her. Turning to Fouad she continued. "The henna design on Dr. Salim's hand appears to be a poorly drawn map of the Arabian Peninsula, from the southern coast all the way to Palestine. There were three markers on the map and we're still correlating it with the other evidence."

"Thank you Maryam," said Fouad, adding quietly, "I'm sorry for your loss. I know you must feel very committed to this case." Fouad noticed Rauser's furrowed brow turn in his direction and answered the question on his face: "I'm sorry to say, Dr. Rauser, but Inspector Maryam was closely related to Dr. Salim; he was her uncle."

"My condolences inspector," said Rauser somberly, "I'm extremely sorry at the loss of your uncle. He was a great scholar and many have praised him as a man of impeccable character."

"Thank you Dr. Rauser," she answered. Sadness clouded her eyes. "He was a good man, dedicated to his family and his work. He touched many lives." She paused for a moment. "He touched me deeply."

"If there is anything I can do for you…" Rauser asked hesitantly.

Maryam briefly glanced downwards before answering: "I'm sure my aunt would be honored if you were to join the funeral to represent my uncle's international colleagues. As you know, we bury our deceased as soon as possible, preferably within 24 hours. The funeral will be held tomorrow if Captain Fouad completes his investigation and releases the body."

"I think that's possible Maryam," answered Fouad, "there are no external wounds and we have enough blood for a toxicology analysis."

This will also give me a chance to keep an eye on Rauser, Fouad thought.

"I would be honored," Rauser said. "Where should I go, and when?"

"If Captain Fouad approves I could pick you up at your hotel at 10:00 a.m. tomorrow morning."

Glancing at Fouad and seeing him nod Rauser pursed his lips and nodded as well. Maryam nodded back at the two of them, then turned and strode towards the back door.

"Seems like a confident person," Rauser commented after Maryam had left the room.

"Women who go study abroad come back different from the way they went. Her family has had their share of public notoriety. Her father was an Islamic scholar who used Western forms of literary criticism to analyze the Quran. He published some blasphemous articles that suggested the Quran had been changed over time, which resulted in him being charged by a fundamentalist imam and convicted as a heretic."

"That must have affected the family terribly."

"The aftermath did. Some clerics asserted that according to Yemeni law heretics were not allowed to remain married to Muslims. Since her father was now considered a heretic they again took him to court. This resulted in the court demanding her father and mother divorce."

"What happened?"

"They moved overseas. They loved each other and didn't want to abide by the ruling. Maryam joined them in France, where she studied forensic science."

"Is she married?"

Fouad shook his head. "Only to her work."

I think he's intrigued by her, Fouad thought.

6

Ghamdan Palace Hotel

Sana'a, Yemen

Light flooded through the window of Omar's hotel room. A cricket chirping in the bathroom penetrated his consciousness. He must have over slept. He looked at his watch and was surprised to see it was almost noon. "Forgive me Allah for missing my prayers, and thank you again for enabling me to eliminate the heretic."

He felt conflicted, torn between exhilaration at the successful completion of his mission and a dark, heavy-heartedness. He had killed three men, one a great scholar. By the end of the day Salim's murder would be public knowledge. Then what?

He took a quick shower and said his noon prayers. He was hungry. He left his room, walked down the hallway, descended two flights of stairs and exited through the heavy doors of the Ghamdan Palace Hotel.

He felt the familiar pain in his chest. "Allah, I'm ready to die for you" he whispered, "and yet I feel compelled to ask, 'have I sinned against you in any way, O merciful God?'"

There was no response.

He wandered down the street, then sat down on the stool of a street restaurant. An Audi careened over a racetrack on the flickering television overhead. "Comfort, Power, German reliability!" The voice was loud, oily, and had a Saudi accent

He nodded to the approaching waiter. The man nodded back. "Salaam Aleykum," he said. "What would you like?"

"Shawarma and tea." As the man shuffled off Omar went over the previous day in his mind. Thank God there had been no blood. A clean kill was like a smart bomb: it depersonalized things; you didn't personally do it -- something he had learned from the enemy: a smart bomb from a drone, a mere machine, and two friends dead. No guilt, no shame for the pilot.

The television caught his attention again as news headlines flashed by. The anchorman looked down at him: "Dr. Salim, chief curator at Yemen's House of Manuscripts was found dead in his laboratory this morning by his staff," the man announced. "Police have not ruled out foul play. Dr. Salim was known as a dedicated scholar who played an important role in the preservation of the manuscripts found in the attic of the Sana'a mosque in 1972."

Omar's eyes flitted over the restaurant. He felt as if everyone followed the anchorman's gaze at him. He gulped down his shawarma and tea, left money on the table and hurried back to the hotel. He tried to look casual as he walked past the concierge's desk. The slender box around his neck swayed erratically and he grabbed it to keep it from swinging. "I'm walking too fast," he muttered to himself.

This box was his own sinister invention. He called it the "Assassin's Assistant." His little assistant inside the box, Yigal, was named after the orthodox Jew who had assassinated Yitzak Rabin, Prime Minister of Israel. "Yigal," he whispered, "you must be hungry. Let's get you some food."

He walked up the stairs and down the hallway leading to his room, and fumbled with the lock until the door opened. He kicked off his sandals, walked across the room to the bathroom and stepped into the shower. Using the door key he popped off the drain cover, put his fingers down the drain hole, and pulled up a wad of hair swarming with life. He extracted a cockroach, slid open the small cover on the Assassins' Assistant and shoved the cock roach through the hole. The sound of a brief commotion came from inside the box.

"Sahtayn u afiye, Yigal," he whispered. He felt better for Yigal. He looked up at the ceiling: "Bless my humble efforts ya Allah. I have fought for your honor and the honor of our beloved prophet, peace be upon him. May my efforts bring you glory and advance your kingdom."

He examined his surroundings. Could the police have been here while he was out? Everything appeared untouched. The garbage had not been emptied and a towel was draped where he had left it. His small backpack leaned against the foot of the bed, the Quran lay open on the small dresser, right under the mirror he'd covered with the other towel. Mirrors were distractions for true warriors of Allah.

Allah blessed me last night. I should thank him.

He reentered the dank bathroom and washed his face, hands and feet. His thoughts shifted to the Imam who had revolutionized his life: "If we take the time to wash before visiting friends," the Iman had blogged, "the least we can do is wash before we come into Allah's presence."

He left the bathroom, hands, feet and face dripping, dried himself, looked out the window to orient himself towards Mecca, and began his prostrations. He recited the standard "Allahu Akbar" sections, then found his throat tightening over the next Arabic phrase: "*Astaghfurul laha rabbi wa atoobu ilaihi* -- I ask Allah, my Lord, to cover up my sins and unto him I turn repentant." He stopped. Was there a need for repentance?

He needed perspective. He needed Siddiqi. He stood up, unzipped his backpack and pulled out a cell phone. He dialed the number from memory.

"Salaam aleykum," a male voice answered.

"Siddiqi, I have finished the work Allah has asked me to do."

"Has Allah blessed you with success?" The voice was intense.

"The godless Germans and the infidel Salim are standing before Allah's judgment seat."

"Subhan Allah," the voice responded excitedly. "Did you obtain the information?"

"Yes. They all said the same thing."

"You're *sure* of that?"

"Yes."

There was a pause on the line and then Omar heard it again: "Subhan Allah." The voice had become a worshipful whisper. Omar`s heart soared. Siddiqi understood. He too saw these kills as worship. There was another pause before the voice said: "You have done a great service for Allah and his people; may Allah bless you for your efforts, my son."

"Siddiqi," continued Omar enthusiastically, "the enemies of Allah are incompetent dogs. I threatened them with a toy gun and they thought it was real. Then when I offered them the antidote they immediately sacrificed their secrets. The enemies of Allah are weaklings!"

"Was Dr. Salim in the museum?" Omar was pleased Siddiqi probed for more details. He was emotionally invested in this mission.

"Yes," Omar answered, proud of what he was about to report. "It was just like the informant said. Salim left the *Yemeni House of Manuscripts* at closing, taking some of the Sana'a manuscripts with him. He then returned after having gone home for supper. I hid in the back of his minivan while it was parked at his home and he drove me straight through the security gate into the museum compound an hour later. I waited a half hour before slipping out of the car and found him in the lab."

"Anything out of the ordinary happen?" Siddiqi probed.

"I don't think so. I left quickly." Omar knew Siddiqi was concerned someone would trace him and expose everyone.

"Did anyone see you leave?"

"I don't think so. The informant said there was a gardener at the museum but I didn't see him. He was probably home already. The place was empty."

"Did Salim say anything about the Hafsah manuscript?"

"He appears to believe it exists."

Siddiqi took a deep breath. "We can use this to strengthen our case with the Saudis, the Iranians and against all those who have undermined the work of Allah's holy family. Do you have it?"

"No." Omar was silent for a moment. How would Siddiqi react to the next piece of information? He paused before he spoke: "He said it was in the *Well of Souls* in Al Quds."

"Al Quds!"

"Yes."

Omar waited, wondering what Siddiqi's reaction would be. "That's the place where Hafsah's father, the Caliph Umar, prayed and which he cleansed. Garib.... Strange..." The sound of Siddiqi's tongue tapping against the roof of his mouth told Omar a plan was being formed. Again he waited.

"Omar, go to Al Quds, to the *Dome of the Rock*, and retrieve the manuscript." Omar's heart sank. "When you arrive," Siddiqi continued, "Allah will have prepared the way. Remember how he was with you in Germany."

Omar was silent. A wave of doubt washed over him. He would go anywhere but Jerusalem. "I don't know," he stuttered. "I don't know if I can do that. Al Quds... I don't think that's possible."

Siddiqi pressed him. "Remember your namesake, the Caliph Umar. Remember the message in his ring which I had engraved in yours: 'Enough is Death as a Reminder to You O 'Umar.'"

50

"I don't know..." mumbled Omar. Tension spread across in his neck and his head began to throb. He hated Al Quds and every memory associated with it. Nothing good had ever happened there.

"Omar you have evaded death because Allah's hand is on you! And should it strike, you'll be counted among the great warriors in Allah's presence. Allah's blessing awaits!"

"I'm a *persona non grata* in Jerusalem. Getting into the Dome of the Rock will be almost impossible," Omar dared to protest.

"I'll guide you," Siddiqi said with the confidence of a politician. "I have contacts in high places. The Saudi Royal family are with us. You need not fear."

Siddiqi left the airport prayer room. He walked briskly towards the gate of his next flight. His right hand fiddled in his pocket with a key chain emblazoned with the emblem of the *Palestinian Islamic Jihad* (PIJ) on it: a map of Israel over which the Dome of the Rock and two fists holding AK-47s were superimposed. Siddiqi and the PIJ had one primary mission: the destruction of Israel and the establishment of a Palestinian Islamic state. They were pro-Allah, pro-jihad and pro-Palestine.

As recently as three months ago it looked like the PIJ would be choked of funds. New legislation prevented U.S. and European financial institutions from doing business with any bank which transferred funds to suspected terrorist groups. This had been a cause of great concern among his supporters, and he had prayed fervently and daily for financial resources. In the pit of his stomach he had believed Allah would not allow the PIJ to die.

Allah had heard his prayers. First the Iranian Minister of Defense had promised to continue supplying weapons and financial resources, and now the news from Omar. The PIJ was again ready to pounce from its lair to strike at the Jewish Zionist oppressors. They now had the potential of unlimited resources.

He felt his cell phone vibrate in his pocket. "Not now," he thought, "we're about to board."

"Salaam Aleykum?" he said hastily.

"Aleykum Salaam" a voice replied. "Has Omar tracked down the manuscript?"

"Yes, it's at the *Dome of the Rock.*" The voice made Siddiqi nervous; it always made him feel like a school boy in the principal's office. He had never met its owner.

"Great news," the voice said. "We need to move quickly. Can I count on your assistance?"

"God willing, I will do what I can. I've already asked him to go to Jerusalem. It may take several days before he finds the manuscript."

Siddiqi listened carefully and then closed his cell phone. When he looked up he realized he was the last passenger to board the plane. From the plane he sent a quick text message to Omar: Go to Faizal in the Arabic quarter. Can't miss the house. He recently went on the hajj.

7

Salim's Funeral

Rauser walked from the mosque to the grave site with a crowd of several hundred men whose lives Salim had touched. The pallbearers walked ahead, down the center of the street, each holding the leg of what looked like a single, brown bed frame on which lay Salim's corpse. The corpse was wrapped in a white shroud and draped with the Yemeni flag. The Minister of Religion had endorsed the flag to honor Dr. Salim's contributions to the preservation of Yemen's heritage. If the man had known what Salim had published under his pseudonyms, there would have been no flag.

The thought of Salim's pseudonyms triggered a wave of fear through Rauser. Somehow he had to get to Salim's museum computer and erase any files linking his name and those of the research team to the pseudonyms under which they had published.

The mourners approached the cemetery and made their way through the tall, wrought-iron gate and followed a row of small, rounded headstones towards a hole flanked by a pile of dirt. They congregated around the hole while the imam said a few words. This was followed by a shovel of dirt signaling the start of Salim's new eternal existence. Rauser looked around. He did not recognize any one. People didn't linger. Someone offered to take him back to the mosque where he had left Salim's car.

He was surprised when Maryam had offered him the use of the car, but she said her aunt had insisted on it. "We need to honor Salim's foreign friends," she had told her. "We can't treat them like a Yemeni camel herder."

On his way back to Mrs. Salim's home he again thought about the computers. If he managed to get access to the computer and erase the pseudonym file, he would also look for the palimpsest scans of the Hafsah Qur'an which Salim had mentioned. He wondered if Fouad or Maryam would give him permission to access the computer.

He pulled into Mrs. Salim's driveway. Maryam met him at the door. "I'm sorry you had to go alone, Dr. Rauser," she said.

"I felt honored to represent your uncle's colleagues." He knew women were not permitted to join the funeral procession to the grave site.

"This may seem like a strange request at this time," she said, "but I wonder if I could examine something."

The question caught Rauser by surprise. "What might that be?"

"Oh, I'm just testing a hypothesis." Before he could respond her hand dove into his suit jacket and pulled out a piece of plastic the size of a large button.

"Interesting," she said. She turned the button over in her hand and put her fingers to her lips, ensuring Rauser didn't say anything. Then she winked at him and continued speaking. "Sure, the bathroom is over here, let me show you." She waved him in the direction of the hallway.

They walked to the bathroom and Maryam put the button on the vanity and signaled for him to leave. Then she closed the door, leaving the button in the bathroom.

"I think it's an electronic bug," she whispered, "give me a few minutes to see if it's just a tracking device or also a listening device." Without waiting for a reply she disappeared into the bathroom.

Who in the world would want to track me?

He heard the toilet flush and Maryam re-emerged.

"It's just a tracking device," she said with a smile. "At least our conversation isn't being recorded."

"Did you flush it?"

"No. I left it on the vanity."

A flush of anger surged through Rauser. "What's going on?" he demanded. "Who here is monitoring me?"

Maryam held up her hands in mocking self-defense. "Try to see this from Captain Fouad's perspective. Dr. Salim has been working at the museum for years and no one had ever tried to kill him. He had an impeccable reputation and no known local enemies. Then, right after you meet with him, he drops dead. You don't know this yet, but we just learned that three of his closest colleagues in Germany, the men with whom he works on the manuscripts, are also dead. So... who wants all these academics dead?"

Rauser turned pale. The academics in Germany she was referring to must be the colleagues he and Dr. Salim were working with. "I have no idea," Rauser's voice was shaky. Then he became angry. "My family served this country for decades and suddenly, I'm a murder suspect!"

"You flew in from Germany didn't you?"

"Yes."

"Weren't you ready to publish something on the manuscripts?" Maryam then looked Rauser straight in the eye. "Fouad sent Salim's computer to the lab and he had tech comb the hard drive and email folders for anything related to the crime." Rauser dreaded what was coming. "Oddly enough," she went on, "they found a file squirreled away in a subfolder called *Pseudonyms*. It connected a list of pseudonyms with email addresses. Guess whose names and addresses were on the list?

"Everyone who is now dead," he whispered.

"That's right," she paused, "except you."

Rauser didn't know how to respond. He could not deny anything she had said. The whole pseudonym affair had started at an academic conference in Amsterdam. Around lunch the discussion had turned to the murder of the Dutch cinematographer Van Gogh by a Muslim fanatic. Salim had commented that if the imam at his mosque knew his positions on the Quran and some of his other convictions he would be joining Van Gogh before the week was out. In the end the group of friends had agreed to start using pseudonyms and create email addresses dedicated to their correspondence with Salim. "No point in endangering anyone's life," Rauser had said.

Rauser looked up at Maryan. The silence hung heavily in the air.

"Could you tell me the names of the Germans who were killed?" he asked.

Maryam was silent for a minute before she murmured: "You probably have some idea."

"Yes." Rauser glanced at the floor. "Sadly, I do." He looked up at her. "I just wanted to be sure..." He paused again looking into her eyes. "So that's why I'm suspect?"

"Correct." Maryam pursed her lips and nodded. "The common thread between all of you is that you were members of a clandestine group of academics interested in the Sana'a manuscripts. All are dead," she paused for a moment, "except for..."

"Me," Rauser finished the sentence. "Why does Fouad think I would kill my own colleagues and friends?"

"Academic rivalry." Maryam's voice possessed the quality of a prosecuting lawyer.

Rauser looked at her stunned. He shook his head. It was as if a judge had brought down his gavel and passed an unjust sentence. Killing for academic rivalry? Absurd! He finally found his voice. "That thought would never even occur to me!"

"You need tenure, right? Fouad had Hussein question Habib. Didn't you tell him at the restaurant that you needed to get your book finished this year or your deadline for tenure would pass? That your job at the university would end if you didn't publish something soon? Not only that; Fouad found email correspondence between Salim and the Germans in which they had decided to keep you out of their next publication, something on Muhammad's, peace be upon him, last will and testament. Perhaps you found out and got angry. You felt cheated, robbed, stabbed in the back. Your honor would be tarnished and you wouldn't receive tenure. That's reason enough to kill – at least in Yemen."

"I'm not Yemeni," he protested.

"Maybe not in your passport," Maryam responded slowly, "but what about in your head?" That was not a new thought for him; he did feel part Yemeni in his mind. "If you have Yemeni culture in your veins," she continued, "honor and prestige is a value you highly cherish, and is something for which a real Yemeni would kill."

Rauser took a deep breath then shook his head. Her "Yemeni theory" caused a tightening of his chest. "This is absurd," he muttered, as his mind looked for loopholes.

"No, Dr. Rauser. This is not absurd. A thief would've taken something, but nothing appears to have been removed. The computer, his wallet, his phone were all there. If it had been an angry relative, we would've known about it through our interviews with family and neighbors. We've ruled that out. Dr. Salim was well liked by everyone. You are the prime suspect. If the pattern continues, you are either the killer or you will be killed..."

"Then why don't *you* take me in?" Rauser now looked the woman in the eye.

Maryam paused and looked straight back. "Because I don't think you did it..."

Rauser raised his eyebrows. He let out a long breath of air and smiled wanly. "What do you mean?" He was confused.

Maryam motioned for Rauser to follow her down the hallway towards the living room, away from the courtyard where people from the funeral were beginning to congregate. She motioned for him to sit in an overstuffed chair.

"Let me tell you why," she began. "You are five years older than I am, so you don't remember me. However, my childhood home was just blocks from yours. Before we went to France my mother worked in your father's hospital. She often talked about your father's selfless service: how he would stay on after every doctor had left the hospital to review patient charts and check their prescriptions. I broke my ankle once and he treated me. I'll never forget him asking my mother if he could pray for my healing."

Maryam paused briefly. Rauser noticed her eyes begin to water. She glanced away. When she met his gaze again it was as if she was looking through him at someone else. "He prayed as if he knew God ... and God knew him... he talked to God in the same manner I talk to my mother." She paused. "I'd never heard prayer like that before... there was no formality or tradition... he expected God to heal me... and I *was* healed."

Suddenly the room fell silent. Rauser's heart stirred as it had not since the death of his wife. A spiritual homesickness washed over him. He took a deep breath to control his own emotions.

"You look like you just saw a ghost," Maryam said, brushing the corner of her eye.

Rauser took a deep breath. "I did. You brought my father back into the room – along with his God." Rauser looked away. After a moment he refocused on the present. "So why don't you think I killed Salim?"

"A man like your father couldn't raise a killer; a boy who heard his father pray like I heard your father pray would *never* be able to become a killer. Allah wouldn't allow such shame."

Suddenly Rauser felt the reach of his father's prayers from beyond the grave. Prayer, he suddenly realized, was not bound by time and death.

Prayers of long ago could reach into the future. "So now what... what do I do?" he asked emboldened.

"Go to Najran."

"Why?"

"As Fouad told you, Salim phoned his wife – my aunt – just before he died. According to her, Salim was pretty incoherent on the phone. He stammered, almost incomprehensibly, over and over, 'Go to Najran, trust Rauser, just trust Rauser, no one else, not even the police – go to Najran.'

"Did she tell Fouad what you just told me?"

"No. My aunt would not betray my uncle's last words," Maryam said. "The week before he died," she continued, "Salim had insisted she prepare for the trip by having her hands hennaed and to pack her ancestral henna bowl, paints and brushes. They had planned to take *you* along."

"Me?" Rauser asked surprised.

"My aunt asked him why, and he told her it had something to do with your shared research project. They were going to find Muhammad's chosen successor and the true Quran."

Rauser's fingers played with the armrest on the chair. Maryam wanted him to go on to Najran. Logically it didn't' make sense. The risk was enormous. "Let me get this straight. You're suggesting I take Dr. Salim's wife over to Saudi Arabia to Najran? I'm Fouad's prime suspect! If I was him and my prime suspect runs off to a neighboring country my suspicions would just be reinforced."

"That's one way of looking at it."

"And what are you going to do?"

"Go with you." The woman was full of surprises! He was not ready to make a dash for Saudi Arabia with the police after him. Traveling with an officer who believed in his innocence, however, was a viable option, especially in a nation where one is treated as guilty until proven innocent. But was this his only option?

"I think I'll opt for the next flight out of here; I don't mean to insult you and your offer or to be disrespectful to your aunt, but I think I'm best served by the Yemeni legal system if I don't become part of it."

"True. If you're serious about leaving on the next plane, let's go to the airport; we'll leave the tracking device here at the house and I'll drive you to there; I presume you're carrying your passport?"

"Yes. I should probably pick up some clothes and my computer at the hotel."

"All right," she shrugged, "let's go." She turned and headed for the car. Rauser looked out of the window as they drove to the hotel. He felt torn. He wanted to get out of Yemen, but didn't want to do so under a cloud. Leaving probably meant the end of his tenure and the end of his academic career.

Maryam waited in the car while he ran into the hotel and up to his room to grab his suitcase. She popped open the trunk when he re-emerged. He dropped the bags into the back of the car and slid back in the passenger seat. As they merged into traffic, Maryam kept looking in the mirror.

"What are you looking at?" Rauser asked.

"I think we're being followed. There's been a black Toyota minivan behind me for about four minutes." She suddenly increased speed, then took a quick left turn into an alley. Looking in the mirror she answered Rauser's question: "It passed."

"Look out!" The alley came to a dead end meters ahead of them. Maryam jammed on the break and angled the car to a stop. "Let's just wait and see if they back up and come down the alley," she said, and shifted her eyes back to the mirror.

"Why would Fouad put a tail on us if you're with me and he has me bugged?"

"He suspects you of killing four men. Maybe he's concerned for my safety. He may also be afraid you're going to make a run for it after having discovered the bug. In that case he could grab you."

Rauser began to feel claustrophobic. Turning around he saw no one. "I think we've waited long enough. Let's go."

Maryam backed the car into the traffic. Rauser looked up and noticed an airplane climbing over the city. He wondered if he would be able to get a ticket at the last minute.

"We're being tailed again," said Maryam as she took the exit for the airport. Rauser turned around and noticed the black Toyota minivan. "The Sana'a police force owns five of these exact minivans. If we see another one at the airport they're probably waiting for you."

As they approached the departure level drop-off zone they both saw two black, Toyota minivans with three police officers walking nearby.

"Shit," Rauser said.

"Fouad expected you to run."

"Keep driving," commanded Rauser. He was no longer just a suspect. Fouad was putting things into place to ensure he stayed in Yemen until a good case against him was finalized.

When they exited the airport grounds Maryam broke the silence which had enveloped the car. "Dr. Rauser, since you seem unsure of what decision to make, allow me to make one more comment. Your father left us all with the impression that Christianity meant loving your neighbor as yourself. If you carry his mantle, then you'll go to Najran with my aunt and me. You'll be showing my aunt that you care for her by carrying out her late husband's final request, just as she carried out his request by not informing the police of what he told her about you."

Rauser's mind teetered between his options: run from the law or confront it. His father had taught to never run from the law, while his military experience in the Middle East had taught him to be suspicious of the Middle Eastern version of 'due process.' He could confront Fouad with the list of pseudonyms and explain its purpose. He shouldn't have to be afraid of confronting the truth; after all, he had *not* killed anyone

He stared at the passing cars. 'All truth is God's truth' was his father's favorite phrase. Another phrase from the Bible flashed through his mind: "the truth shall set you free." Should he stay and trust God and Fouad's evidence collecting process to set him free? Even if he was exonerated from the murder charge, the charge of blasphemy hiding in the computer files would eventually implicate him.

Maryam was waiting for an answer. "I'm concerned about the impression I would leave if I took off for Najran with Salim's wife. It's only been a day since her husband was buried. In my country this would raise suspicions that I had more than a casual relationship with her."

"We know you never had an affair with my aunt," Maryam answered. "Your willingness to honor my late uncle's final wish by following up on his request would mean so much to her. I have a hunch that whatever is in those manuscripts—and they must be important for people to kill over—can best be revealed to the world by someone raised in a family that didn't just talk about the importance of character but actually lived it."

Maryam's speech brought a wan smile to his face. It touched him that she thought him worthy of her uncle's work. He was also moved by the fact that she was willing to stake her career and future on her knowledge of his family.

I should be more like my dad. "I don't have much of a choice do I? I'm doomed if I stay, and doomed if I run. I may as well run, but how? Fouad's tracking device lets him know where I am. If we leave together you'll be a suspect as well."

"You're right. Here's what we'll do," the woman responded decisively. "I'll drop you off at our house while I get my aunt ready for the trip to Najran. That may take some time—we'll need to wait until the guests leave. Then I'll come back and get you."

"All right..." Rauser wasn't at all sure if he was all right. As she wove the car through the chaos of Sana'a traffic he wondered where Maryam lived, and with whom. They pulled up to a traditional style four story, brownstone apartment with white, stone arches accentuating each window.

Maryam told him to walk up four flights of stairs and knock on the door. As she drove off he wondered about the wisdom of her proposed course of action. His father had always maintained that an innocent man had nothing to fear.

He walked up the stairs and knocked on the door. An old man wearing a white and black kaffiyeh opened up; he seemed to be expecting him. The man nodded, gestured for him to step inside, and led him to an overstuffed chair beside a window. "Tfaddal. U'ud," he said kindly. "Welcome. Sit down."

The man shuffled off to return a few minutes later with a glass of water. "Tisrab kahve?" he asked. "Would you drink a coffee?"

Rauser nodded. He suddenly felt tired and lost; an urge to talk to someone who truly understood him coursed through his veins. A thought flashed through his mind: "Pray." It was as if someone was speaking in his head. He sat in the chair by the window and wondered what to say. He hadn't prayed since they'd buried his wife. As they lowered her body into the grave he'd told God that he needed time to think. That was two years ago.

"God," he whispered, "I've been absent for a while, but I need your help. Should I run or try to work with Fouad. I really need some wisdom." He leaned back in the chair, his eyes still closed. He should get outside advice. He stood up, pulled his cell phone from his pocket, searched for the number of the U.S. embassy, and dialed. The receptionist picked up on the second ring. Rauser explained who he was and quickly told his story. She told him to stay on the line while she contacted a consular officer. Within seconds a man with a southern accent addressed him.

"Dr. Rauser, I'm glad you called," the confident drawl on the other end of the line began. "We've tried to reach you several times but were unsuccessful."

"Is there a problem?"

"We understand that you've been identified as a potential suspect in the death of a Yemeni citizen. Is that true?"

The soothing southern lilt emboldened his honesty: "I know that the police have me under surveillance, but I'm innocent."

"I don't mean to alarm you Dr. Rauser, but I think it may be wise if you come to the embassy as soon as possible. Where are you now?

"At a private residence. I just got back from a funeral."

"We understand that Dr. Salim is the man you may be accused of murdering. I hope you didn't go to his funeral."

"Why?"

"Because if I was a Yemeni, I would take great offence if the man accused of killing someone in my family had the gall to go to the funeral and gloat over his body as it was being lowered into the ground."

Agh shoot! Rauser paced the room, his eyes darting yet not looking at anything. "I'm sorry but it *was* Dr. Salim's funeral. His wife asked me to represent his foreign friends." He swallowed. "What do you think I should do?"

"Give us the address where you're staying."

"I'm not sure. I'll check." He noticed a pile of letters on the coffee table, paged through the stack until he saw one addressed to Maryam. He read the address: "224 'Aladi St."

"What I want you to do," the man said gravely, "is stay where you are. We will send someone. When they arrive they'll give three quick knocks, followed by a pause and then two more. They'll help you get to the embassy. Then we can address your situation without the police making things difficult. What we don't want is you getting into Yemeni police custody. We want to avoid working through Yemeni legal channels because it'll mean you'll have to wait in a Yemeni prison cell while things get cleared up."

"I should probably tell you that I found a tracking device in my pocket," Rauser said.

There was a brief pause before the cool voice responded. "That shouldn't be a problem. Let's proceed with the plan I just told you. It isn't recording right now is it?"

"No."

"O.K. Wait a few minutes and someone from the embassy will come and get you." Rauser was ready to hang up the phone when the officer continued: "Dr. Rauser, don't worry; we're committed to helping you in any way we can."

"Thank you. I appreciate that." Rauser turned off his phone, walked to the window, and exhaled a nerve-calming sigh. *It's good be American*, he thought. *I should never have gone to the funeral. Nice guys finish last! Hopefully the American cavalry comes soon.*

His thoughts were interrupted by the old man. "Here's your coffee; I'm not sure how Americans like their coffee so I'll let you add your own cream and sugar."

Rauser looked up and saw the old man put the coffee cup on the brown wooden coffee table in front of the dark green overstuffed couch. "Thank you very much – it's just what I needed."

The old man smiled and a shining gold tooth could be seen in the corner of his mouth. "One of the tastier gifts of Allah," he said, "I hope it relaxes you."

It was less than ten minutes before he heard the knocks: three short ones, a pause, and then two more. Rauser turned the lock and the door was pushed open. There before him stood Maryam looking like an angry mother ready to kick her lazy son out of bed.

"What are *you* doing here?" Rauser exclaimed suprised.

'You're an idiot," her voice had a sharp edge. "You shouldn't have called the U.S. embassy on your phone. You think Fouad was dropped on his head as a child? Your phone is monitored."

Maryam walked down the hall and shouted over her shoulder, "Get ready to go; I'll be with you in a minute," and she disappeared down the hall. Within a minute the door opened and she reemerged. "Come on," she commanded tucking a loose hair under her veil. "We don't have much time before Fouad gets here. Grab your passport and your stuff; my aunt is in the car downstairs."

"Wait, how did you know about the secret knock? Are you working for Fouad or for the U.S. embassy?"

"I'll tell you later; we don't have much time!"

"What about the tracking device? Should we leave it here?"

"Of course not! He's expecting you to move. Leaving it there would just raise suspicions. Remember, Faoud probably listened in on your phone call."

8

Police Station, Sana'a

"Where has he gone?" Hussein asked standing behind Fouad holding his mid-morning coffee. "Did he go to the funeral?" Fouad was hunched over a computer monitor.

"Yes. He didn't stay long."

"Is he still there?"

"No. He went to Maryam's house and now he's beginning to move," Fouad said. "He has Salim's car. It will be interesting to see where he goes."

Fouad didn't hate Americans; he just distrusted them. "You can't trust them," he'd say, "They're the only people in history to use atomic weapons to kill their enemies. They're full of talk about human rights but don't practice what they preach. Just look at their unqualified support of Israel!"

"Lieutenant, get the car and follow him. I'll radio you directions"

"Yes boss."

Even after 15 years on the job Fouad still enjoyed the rush of the chase, whether on foot, by car or on screen. The best part of his job was the sense of competition between himself and his suspect. This time the contest was international: Yemen vs the Unites States.

He glanced out the window and saw Hussein climb into an unmarked car. Fouad turned back to the computer screen. "Rauser seems to be heading out of town. Follow Zubayri Street east." Two minutes later the dot on the screen made an erratic move: "Hussein! He's taken an odd turn. He's heading north. Going slow, strangely slow considering the low volume of traffic. Head for the *House of Folklore*."

All right American, thought Fouad looking intently at the screen, lead me to your contacts. You can run but you can't hide. He reached for his radio to check with his men at the airport.

"Nothing to report sir," the voice at the other end stated. "A car looking like Salim's was spotted by one of the other teams but it never stopped here. It must have been another car of similar make and colour."

"OK. Keep your eyes open." Fouad had been impressed by Rauser's ability in Arabic and his unflappable responses when pelted by questions at the crime scene. This was going to be a fun match of wits.

"He's turned again," Fouad gripped the microphone. "Turn east again and head towards the Sheraton. Perhaps he's meeting another friend." His phone rang.

"Yes?" he barked impatiently.

"Captain Fouad, this is Maryam. I thought I should tell you that I'm with Dr. Rauser. We're taking a quick tour around the city."

"What's going on?" Fouad asked suspiciously. The woman had lost all sense of Yemeni propriety running around with an unmarried man and no escort.

"After the funeral he requested I show him around town. He wanted to visit some haunts from his childhood."

"O.K...?" Fouad's voice was caught between a question and a statement.

"Thanks, Captain. I'll keep you informed."

Fouad hung up the phone and turned to the radio. "Hussein!"

"Yes chief."

"He is touring the city with Inspector Maryam. Keep following them; my gut tells me they're up to something. I'm still not sure Maryam is to be trusted. Have you seen their car?"

"No. So where do I head to now?"

"Keep heading in the direction of the Sheraton. "

"O.K. chief."

"If there are any changes in direction, Fahmi will let you know. I'm going to say my noon prayers."

"O.K. chief."

Fouad walked across the courtyard to the masjid. Some had already finished the first rukuat of prayers. After completing the prescribed routine Fouad added a personal note: "Thank you, ya Allah, for the great colleagues you have given me, and a wonderful job. Help me find Salim's murderer. Please."

"I sure hope Fouad can take a joke," Maryam's twinkling black eyes shone above a big grin.

"What do you mean?" Rauser glanced in her direction.

"His tracker is taking a trip through Sana'a's sewer system! I'd love to see his face when he finally figures that out," she laughed.

"Are you crazy?!"Rauser exclaimed. "When did you do that?" He noticed a dimple as she smiled before responding.

"Remember, I went to the bathroom just before we left my dad's place ... remember I told you to hurry up and get ready to go and that we shouldn't leave the tracking device in the house?"

Rauser couldn't help but smile. "Crappie idea," he joked wanly, "but I'm not sure I'd want to be there when Fouad figures out you didn't leave it at the house... What's this going to do to your career?"

Maryam turned serious. "I've thought about that," she said. "It'll depend on how this ends. Family is more important than career."

"How does your family fit into this decision?"

Maryam smiled enigmatically. "At least I have a chaperone this time," she said, nodding towards Salim's wife gazing from the back window.

Rauser fell quiet, his mind flitting from one thought to the next. The view reminded him of the Arizona desert: dry, rugged and rocky. He wondered what the woman next to him was thinking. Was she thinking of him as he was thinking of her? The intriguing mix of clashing Yemeni and French cultures she displayed prompted another thought: she's a third culture kid – just like me and Ruthie had been.

A whirling sand devil in the distance reminded him of the explosion in front of the hotel. Ruth's dismembered body was the last time he had seen her—it had been a closed casket funeral. That was also when he'd quit praying. How could a good God allow his Ruthie, someone who'd exemplified the life of Christ, die like that?

"Dr. Rauser?" Maryam broke the chain of disjointed thoughts.

"Yes?"

"We need to bring you in on the bigger picture." Twisting her head towards her aunt in the back seat she continued, "My aunt has something to show you, something her husband said was very important."

Dr. Salim's wife reached into a leather bag, pulled out a brass henna bowl and passed it over the front seat. Rauser took it from her and examined it with the eye of an art appraiser. The cusp was inscribed with beautiful flowing Arabic letters: *"O Mary, worship thy son devoutly."* The initials HBU were inscribed on the bowl's bottom. "This bowl has been in our family for as long as we can remember. It dates back to the time of Muhammad, peace be upon him," she said.

Turning to Maryam's aunt in the back seat, Rauser smiled: "I'm honored to hold this valuable link that you have to the prophet Muhammad, peace be upon him. Could you tell me about its history?"

"This bowl has been in our family for centuries. The story passed down in our family is that the *HBU* inscribed on the bottom stands for Hafsah Bin Umar, the name of Muhammad's wife. Your father opened my husband's eyes to the possible meaning of the words inscribed on the bowl. He pointed out the only Mary he would have known that would worship her son was the mother of Jesus Christ." Sounds like dad, Rauser thought. Then he saw the woman's eyes fill with water. This must be tough on her, he thought. His own depression after his wife was killed had been horrible. If she was experiencing the agony of spirit that he had experienced, she would be in great turmoil.

They drove in silence for several kilometers, leaving the last suburb behind them. Finally Maryam's aunt took a deep breath and continued speaking. "He was in Germany in the 1980's as a graduate student looking for a topic for his Ph.D. dissertation. His advisor, a man who had been key in finding funding for the Yemeni House of Manuscripts, showed him some photographs he had taken of the more sensitive documents from the old Sana'a mosque." Interesting, Rauser thought. He wanted to ask for the name of Salim's advisor but hesitated when he noticed the old woman wipe her eye. Let her speak without interruption. It'll do her good. The woman took another deep breath. "His advisor had been hesitant to proceed with a detailed publication of a certain palimpsest because he was concerned about offending Muslim sensitivities. He was, however, happy to turn the manuscripts over to a Muslim scholar. He felt Salim was more equipped to negotiate the cultural and political minefields these documents might demand." Rauser nodded. He knew the rest of the story; Salim had discussed it with him via an e-mail exchange the week before.

9

Fouad's Office

Fouad turned to the file of printouts which the computer tech had recovered from Dr. Salim's computer. He opened it and gasped. "What in the world!" A full page picture of a bloody, mutilated torso minus the head stared up at him. It was emblazoned with the caption, *'Don't Mock the Prophet.'* He took a deep breath and turned to the next photograph. This time there was a grainy picture of a group of men holding up different body parts with the same caption. The snapshot answered how the men got the body parts: it showed an industrial paper cutter with a hand being severed. This time the caption was different: *"Technology Serving Those Who Dishonor the Prophet and the Quran"*.

This is sick, Fouad thought. Was this sent to Salim or did Salim send these? He flipped to the next page where his eye fell on his techie's neat handwriting: *SMS exchanges between Salim and Rauser from the last seven days.*

Rauser: How long have these manuscripts been laid aside?

Salim: About 15 years.

Rauser: So you knew about these documents in 1987. Why haven't you released them?

Salim: Too sensitive.

Rauser: Can you explain?

Salim: I found clear evidence of Muhammad's last thoughts (Peace Be Upon Him) when he knew he was poisoned and about to die. The palimpsest indicated Muhammad's greatest fear (PBUH) at the end of his life was that God would send him to hell for beheading the 700

Jewish men in *Banu Qurayza*. In the palimpsest he recants his office of prophet and pleads for redemption through the sacrifice of Isa Al Masih. It also mentions that in the last week of his death he instructed his wife Hafsah to hide her Quran at a location of her choosing after his death; it appears he had no intention of ever wanting to create 'another Bible.'

Fouad was stunned. He quit reading. The Quran was the divinely inspired guide for a billion people! Allah must have over-ruled Muhammad to ensure it came into being. He leaned back in his chair, drew a deep breath and glanced out the window. Never in his wildest imagination had he pictured Muhammad wanting to be redeemed through the death of Jesus Christ. This was blasphemous heresy!

Fouad looked around the room, uncomfortable, afraid even. He felt as if he had come into contact with a dangerous, spiritual virus. He sensed it already infecting his thought-processes as his mind locked onto the implications of finding the original Quran: what if it proved everything he believed was wrong? He must not let his mind go there! He took a deep breath and continued reading.

Rauser: What did you do with this palimpsest?

Salim: I got some advice.

Rauser: From whom?

Salim: I hypothetically raised the idea of finding such a document in a private meeting with the Saudi Minister of Religious affairs at last year's AABA conference.

Rauser: What did he say?

Salim: He said that if such a document was ever found it would be best to burn it. There was no way it could be true, and even if it was, it would be better it never surfaced if I wanted to stay alive. Too many powerful people had too much invested in the existing world order to consider changing anything (i.e. Saudi Royal family, The Iranian,

Sudanise and Pakistani regimes, the Muslim Brotherhood, Hamas, ISIS, Al Qaida, etc.)

Rauser: So is that the end of the story?

Salim: No. The minister must have talked to someone because we began getting threatening phone calls, letters and emails.

Rauser: Like what?

Salim: Pictures of mutilated bodies accompanied by messages stating this would be my fate and that of our grandchildren if any documents ever emerged from the Sana'a mosque which shamed the prophet Muhammad (PBUH) undermined the Quran or challenged any Muslim government.

Rauser: How do you know they weren't bluffing?

Salim: One of my assistants went missing. We received a picture of his mutilated body with the caption, 'This is what happens to people who use their intellect to insult the prophet Muhammad (PBUH).'

Rauser: Did you go to the police with the letter?

Salim: No. We received a phone call. The voice on the other end asked if we'd received the recent warning. The man then thanked me for not publishing any blasphemous material from the Sana'a documents, and that Allah had blessed me for my commitment. I was to check my bank account.

Rauser: And...

Salim: 21,000,000 Rial had been deposited into our account.

Rauser: Wow!

Salim: Yes, a lot of money. But I refuse to sell my academic integrity. I would like you to take a look at the documents next week. Help me come up with a plan.

Rauser: I'll try. See you next week.

Fouad's mind was churning with the implications of what he was reading. The people that killed Salim were brutal, rich and connected to the highest religious and governmental structures of the Middle East. He picked up the phone, called tech, and left a message on his answering machine: "Hi Yusuf, please keep all information you pulled from Salim's computer to yourself; I'm sure you realize why."

He put down the phone and leaned back in his chair. Why would someone like Rauser kill Salim? Perhaps the man worked for a Saudi-U.S. hit team; the relationship between those two countries was very deep. Or maybe Rauser was blackmailing Salim, trying to get access to the documents without Salim being aware it was him. And then there was that message by Salim: *"Don't get caught discussing something you'll regret."* Perhaps Salim told Rauser something that triggered the American's anger. Perhaps it was Salim's reluctance to publish the blasphemous manuscripts because he sensed it would be too destructive to people's faith. Rauser had to be interrogated. He could always be charged as an accessory to promoting blasphemy and defaming religion. He swung his chair to face the window and stroked his chin. He needed to check the veracity of Salim's claims in the email exchange with Rauser. Was the man actually being pressured by a foreign government? He could contact the Saudi Minister of Religious Affairs, but that would be a bureaucratic nightmare. Another option would be to analyze the palimpsest, but with the exception of Rauser the people most qualified to do that were dead. The most hassle-free approach would be to bring in Rauser and lean on the man.

The call to prayer rang out. Fouad stood up and walked to the bathroom to wash his hands and face. He returned to his office and stood at the foot of the small rug in the corner of his office and went through the ritual. Then prayed, *"Allah, please give me wisdom to pursue justice, recognize the righteous, and pursue with diligence your glory in all I do. In no way do I want to blaspheme you or bring dishonour to your name."*

10

Border Crossing

"We're about to cross into Saudi Arabia," Maryam said. She turned to Rauser. "Women are not allowed to drive in Saudi, so you move into the driver's seat. Get your passports ready." They stopped along the side of the road to change seats. A few minutes later Rauser pulled the car up to what was clearly a little used border crossing. He inched the car under the green sign that arched above both lanes: "Welcome to Saudi Arabia." As he pulled up to the booth he wondered if Fouad had already alerted the border guards about him.

The officer reached through the window and took his passport. "Do you have a visa?" The man's voice was condescending.

'I was hoping to get it here."

"We don't issue visas for Americans at the border. You need to apply at the nearest embassy."

"Is there any way that we could work this out?" Rauser implored.

The guard flipped slowly through the pages. Then he stopped and looked intently at the document. "You've been here before," he said without looking up. The flipping began again. Rauser hated these power games.

"One of your visas is still valid." The official looked up. "If you process some paperwork inside, we may be able to let you through." He handed Rauser the passport and pointed to a building. "Park along the building on the left. Someone inside should be able to help."

Rauser exhaled a slow sigh of relief and smiled at Maryam. "There's hope," he said as he parked the car near the grey, marble clad building.

"Do you want to come," he asked glancing at Maryam while parking the car, "or do you want to stay in the car?" Before she could answer there was a tapping on his window -- a customs official had followed him to the parking spot: "Could you please open the trunk?"

"Sure," replied Rauser.

The customs official walked to the back of the car and Rauser turned to Maryam: "Do they usually check the trunk?"

"No, never," muttered Mrs. Salim.

Unfamiliar with the car, it took Rauser a minute to find the trunk button. He popped it and unloosened his seat belt and got out of the car.

As Rauser closed the car door he noticed the agent by the trunk holding up a paper tube used to transport paintings, posters and large manuscripts: "What is this?" The agent asked.

"I'm not sure, sir."

He poked his head into the car. "Does either of you know what's in the cardboard tube?"

"I don't know," Maryam replied and turned to her aunt: "Do you know what's in the cardboard tube auntie?"

"I have no idea what Salim has in his trunk. Perhaps it has something to do with his work."

Within minutes another customs official showed up. "Mr. Rauser, our computers indicate that you are not the owner of this car. Is that true?

"Yes, that's true."

"Then why are you driving the car?"

"Because women aren't allowed to drive in Saudi Arabia." *Careful, don't sound like a smart aleck!*

"Do you have an international driver's license?"

"No, sir. It's an American one."

"Please follow us inside."

Rauser followed the officers and Maryam also got out. They walked to the Customs and Immigration building, trailing the officers about ten paces. "What do you suggest we do," he whispered to Maryam. "Are we going to get stranded here at the border?"

"Let me handle this."

The officers moved behind a counter and towards a computer terminal. Maryam approached the counter and tilted her eyes meekly downwards: "I'm sorry officers for the inconvenience we have caused," she said demurely. "I know you must be very busy and we have wasted your time. You are absolutely right concerning the car; it belongs to my uncle but he gave permission to Dr. Rauser, one of his esteemed colleagues from America, to use it to follow-up some research in Najran. Dr. Salim's wife is sitting in the car and she can verify this information. In order to help you verify our story, here's my identity card," and she passed her ID card to one of the customs officials.

The customs officials scrutinized the card and looked at each other. They asked Rauser and Maryam to wait in some chairs along the wall. They confered for a few minutes, and then one of them walked out the building towards the car while the other keyed Maryam's ID card number into the computer.

"I see you work for the *Coordinating Office for Security*," said the officer looking intently at his screen. "Isn't that the American funded office on counter-terrorism?"

"Yes," replied Maryam, eyes still tilted to the floor.

"We have one here too."

Rauser scanned the office and wondered if they had lock-up cells in this immigration office. Perhaps they were down the hallway. If he was apprehended, would he get a free phone call? Who would he call?

"Excuse me Mr. Rauser," said the officer who now reentered the building, "but these manuscripts were in the trunk of your car. They look very old. Could you tell us anything about them?"

Rauser looked nervously at Maryam and then back at the officer: "I'm not sure, but perhaps my friend here can help you – I presume they belong to Dr. Salim." He looked expectantly at Maryam.

Maryam smiled demurely, eyes still pointed to the ground. "Oh, those belong to my uncle, Dr. Salim at the *Yemen House of Manuscripts* – I'm sure you've heard of him; he's a great scholar of Islam. He probably left them in the car – he's your typical absent minded professor."

The immigration officers looked at one another and began to whisper. The officer behind the computer suddenly looked up and addressed them: "Why don't the two of you help yourselves to some coffee; I'm sure this won't take long but we just have to check on a few things."

From his time working for U.S. intelligence in Saudi Arabia Rauser knew how the game was played. The customs officers would go to their superiors to get some advice. Their superior would then call a Yemeni embassy official or the Sana'a police department to verify their story and the veracity of Maryam's identity card. Then, within ten minutes, one of them would be on the phone with Fouad. Once Fouad discovered their ruse, the hammer would fall. Within twenty-four hours all of them would be sitting in a Yemeni jail waiting for the Yemeni justice system to roll – and that could be weeks.

Maryam's face tilted upward although her eyes never met those of the immigration officer. "Excuse me officer, but I'm sure Mr. Rauser can clear up any misunderstandings. It might be beneficial if he could speak to you in private. Do you have any private interview rooms where he could talk to you?"

Rauser turned to her with questioning eyes. What in the world was she doing? Was she ditching him? It would be helpful if she would look at him so he could at least try to read her eyes!

The officers smiled and nodded. "Please," said the older one, extending his hand in the direction of the hallway at the back of the office, "why don't we go to one of the rooms we have at the end of the hallway – feel free to take your coffee." He smiled at Rauser. Rauser grabbed his coffee, glanced at Maryam, whose eyes were still looking at the ground, and followed the officer around the corner.

Rauser wanted to say something but didn't know what. He glanced once more over his shoulder hoping to catch Maryam's eye but she was still looking at the floor. "Mr. Rauser, sorry for the inconvenience," began the officer as they walked down the hallway, "but we need to do our job – I hope you understand."

"No problem." Rauser wondered what he meant by 'having to do his job.'

Opening the door, the officer pointed to a chair across the table that faced the door. Rauser sat down and the officer got straight to the point: "While my colleague is checking out your visa situation, I'd like to ask you a few questions. I'm a customs officer and took the time to check your car while your visa paperwork is being verified. I'm wondering if you would be so kind as to tell me about the old manuscript we found in the trunk of your car. What is its value and are you planning to import it into Saudi Arabia?"

"I'm a researcher from the U.S." replied Rauser, "interested in research that is going on at the *Yemeni House of Manuscripts*. The document you saw from the packing tube must have been used by Dr. Salim, who must have left it in his car." The officer scribbled notes on his writing pad and Rauser looked around the room. There was only one small window, and it was in the door behind the officer.

"It seems odd," said the officer, "that you would be taking it across the border. Isn't it necessary to keep such valuable manuscripts in the museum? Don't they have some kind of policy on releasing documents?"

"I agree sir, but I had no idea it was in the trunk," said Rauser. He had committed himself to telling the truth.

"Perhaps if you would give me the phone number of the curator. That will help us corroborate your story and we can solve this dilemma quickly and you can get on your way." Rauser was about say that he did not know Salim's phone number when he saw Maryam peeking through the door window with her index finger pressed to her lips.

Rauser realized he hadn't answered the officer's question yet. "I'm sorry sir, but I don't have his phone number. I'm sure his wife in the car will have it."

"OK," said the officer and pushed back his chair. Before he had gotten fully out of his chair the door opened and Maryam was ushered into the room by the other officer. The two officers looked at each other and Rauser noticed the one who had just arrived wore an expression of concern. Looking at his colleague, the officer nodded his head in the direction of the door and said, "We need to talk." Turning to Rauser and Maryam he added, "you two wait here; we'll be right back."

As the two officers left Rauser looked at Maryam. "You know what's going on?"

"I think they're going to close the border. I heard the officer get a phone call that a bunch of Yemeni separatists had run across the Saudi Border and that Yemen had requested Saudi help in chasing them down."

"Well, at least we're on the other side of the border, even if we're still holed up in a customs cell." Rauser then paused before continuing. "So what do you think will happen?"

"We may be here a while. I would guess it's going to be an "all-hands-on-deck" type situation. They'll just leave us until they get these more urgent matters settled."

"How urgent you think it is?"

Maryam paused and Rauser noticed the corners of her mouth crease into smile. "Well, since I made the call, I think they'll be busy a whle."

"What?" exclaimed Rauser, "when did you make the call?"

"When I excused myself to go to the bathroom."

Who did you pretend to be?"

"I noticed their operational chart at the back of the main office. There was a name of a woman about three rungs from the top of the chart. I just impersonated her and told them that the Yemeni government had notified immigration that a bunch of people with automatic weapons and grenade launchers had been chased and that they crossed the border from Yemen into Saudi Arabia just ten kilometers to the east of here. I told them to secure their office, close the border, grab their weapons, and to head east and join the police and military who had already been dispatched to the area as well."

"So... are you thinking what I'm thinking?" he asked raising his right eyebrow.

"Yes. Let's wait another minute or so and go." They heard a door slam and smiled. Two minutes later they walked past the computers. Maryam tossed him a walkie-talkie left by the guards on a table. "It may be helpful to listen in on the action," she said as she grabbed the manuscript tube left on the counter.

"It sure took long," Mrs. Salim said as they opened the car door. "It was getting hot in here. Any problem with Salim's manuscript?"

"Everything is fine, auntie," Maryam smiled. "Let's get going to Najran; I'm ready for some refreshments."

Fouad entered the communications room. ``Where's the American?" he asked Fahmi.

"East end of town. There's something strange going on. He sometimes moves to odd locations and then just waits there for a long time. This has been going on all afternoon and into the evening."

"Have you copied down the addresses where he stopped?"

"Of course."

Fouad grabbed the microphone with one hand while the other held his coffee: "Hussein, what do you see out the car window? Any sign of Rauser?"

"No sir. I'm at the sewage treatment plant."

"Stop trying to be funny! Do you see any people? Anyone that looks like Rauser or Maryam? A car?"

"No sir. Haven't seen their car in hours. I think Fahmi has been chewing too much qat.

"Quit joking. What do you see?"

"I'm not being funny. I just passed the guard office to the sewage treatment plant."

"Ask him if any other cars entered the compound recently. They've got to be there!"

"I have sir. He said that the only vehicles that passed through the gate within the past two hours have belonged to the sewage plant."

Fouad's face grew hot and the veins on his short neck began to protrude. Rauser had made an idiot out of him. He'd shamed him in front of his men. "Good work Hussein," he said with forced calm, "but I think we're on a wild goose chase. They duped us. They must have flushed the tracker down the loo. The rats escaped this time, but the cat's not finished hunting." Time for a plan B, he thought as he walked to his corner office and turned off the lights. He thought better in the dark.

11

The Road to Najran

Rauser's driving fatigue evaporated just before sunset. That was when he noticed a black BMW following them. He realized that that set of headlights had been trailing them from several miles after the Saudi border. When he slowed down it did too, and when he increased speed so did it.

"Why are you driving so erratically?" Maryam asked.

"Someone is following us."

He'd slowed down again while Maryam turned to look at the car. She reached for her purse and dug around for her phone. "I'll take a picture of it and have my secretary trace it—if I'm still in the office's good books." Just as she pulled out her phone the BMW sped by.

"Let's see if they pull up behind us at the next turn off," Rauser said. Maryam was no longer listening but was engrossed in her phone's pictures, scanning through the ones of Salim's crime scene.

"I forgot to tell you," she said looking intently at the small screen, "but there was a file in Salim's office with some photographs in them. On the file there was a yellow sticky note with your name on it."

"What did it say?"

Reading from her screen she replied: "Query Rauser about the murder threats before publishing anything."

"Probably relates to the death threats he'd received."

"That's not how Fouad will interpret it."

Rauser suspected she was correct. It would only add to Fouad's mounting evidence against him. He was alive while Salim's pseudonymous German friends had died in mysterious circumstances. "Any other pictures on your phone from the crime scene?" he asked.

"I don't know if this is of any help," Maryam said scrolling through her pictures. "There were a series of numbers on a page. They look like they could be identification tags."

"Read me the numbers."

"CODEX DAM 01-27.1; CODEX DAM 02-32.2; CODEX DAM 03-15.5 and several others."

Rauser searched his memory for any reference to the numbers. "Interesting," he mumbled after a few minutes.

"What do you mean 'interesting'?"

"These sound like the identification tags used for some of the manuscripts found in the Sana'a find in the late 1970's. These numbers were used when some of the manuscripts were sold at auction; they were pre-Uthmanic pages of the Quran." If Salim was closing in on the location of the Hafsah Quran, he conjectured, perhaps these pages could be used to authenticate Hafsah's original Quran. But there was another question: why did he insist, on his deathbed, that his wife go to Najran? "Mrs. Salim," he asked, "Why did your husband want us to go to Najran? What did he hope to find here?"

"Our family has always asserted that we are related to Muhammad's wife Hafsah, just as the bowl I showed you proved," she replied. "Over many generations secrets have been passed down orally in my family. The problem is that different members of the family have been privy to different parts of our Hafsah history. Salim's study of the Sana'a manuscripts validated certain aspects of our family history."

"Does my father know some of these family secrets?" Maryam asked.

"Oh yes, but he wondered how to pass that history on to you. He was hoping the tensions between you and him would ease so that he could bring you in on the family secrets." Everyone fell silent. Rauser wondered if he had stumbled onto some dark family secret. Then Mrs. Salim broke the silence: "Do you want to know what your father was working on with my husband Maryam?"

"Yes and no..." Maryam responded slowly. "On the one hand dad's work brought a lot of pain, and with uncle Salim's death it just seems to never end. However, if I'm part of this story, I should probably know."

"He should have told you years ago, but he wanted to wait till you were older," Mrs. Salim said. "What I'm about to tell you stays here in the car. The information could get you killed." Maryam nodded affirmatively.

"Your father and my husband come from a family that held the keys to the Sana'a mosque for hundreds of years. You know that Muhammad himself, peace be upon him, commissioned the building of the Sana'a mosque and gave the keys to our ancestors. There is legend in our family asserting that the Hafsah Quran was hidden by Hafsah and that its location would be revealed by those holding the keys of the Sana'a mosque just before the second coming of Isa Al Masih."

"That's fascinating," Rauser mumbled.

"Salim and your father were in the process of finding clues in the palimpsests that legitimate our family legend. Furthermore, your father thinks the original Hafsah Quran may have been buried in Najran. When found, he believes it will be significantly different from the modern Quran."

"What makes him think it is buried in Najran?" Rauser asked.

"First of all, Islamic tradition mandates that old Qur'ans should be wrapped and buried. Burning is a last resort. If Uthman had burned the best record of Allah's revelation, the one that Hafsah would have had verified by her husband the Prophet, peace be upon him, the public response would have been disastrous for him. Uthman's career would have ended right there. In other words, it would have been illogical to burn such a document. Furthermore, there is a hadith which states that Hafsah got her Quran back after Uthman was finished with it. In fact, she insisted she get it back. There is no record she ever burned it." The older woman's voice trailed off.

"Is there anything else," Maryam asked.

"The stories circulating in our family. We have always named our women *Hafsah* because our family believes the Hafsah Quran was not burned and that it will be found one day. We believe the tensions in the Middle East and the immorality in the world point to the end of the world. Your father and Salim believed that if they could find the Hafsah Quran we could speed up the coming of the end of the world."

Rauser listened quietly. It all added up. He knew old Qurans were often wrapped in cloth to protect them and buried like people on the grounds of a mosque or cemetery in specially chosen places where people didn't walk. He too had questioned Uthman's alleged destruction of the only true Quran, a hunch bolstered by the legends circulating in Salim's family. The subject of oral history intrigued him.

"Suppose we find the Hafsah Quran, then what?" Maryam asked.

Rauser felt compelled to share what Salim had told him about Muhammad's deathbed renunciation of his prophetic office and his hope for salvation through Jesus Christ. "What if there was proof that Muhammad saw himself as nothing but a tribal leader used by God?" he asked quietly. "What if he had renounced his prophetic office before he died, and prayed to be forgiven through Jesus' redemption because of the guilt he experienced for beheading the 600 men at *Banu Qurayza?*"

Several minutes of silence passed before Maryam's subdued reply. "It would change everything."

Rauser hesitated but knew it needed to be raised. "How do you think people would react to *you,* if you were the one who provided convincing proof to the world that the Quran they held to be the infallible word of Allah had errors in it, and that the prophet they emulate never wanted to be emulated?"

She didn't answer. Mrs. Salim finally who broke the silence. "I think a Muslim fanatic killed my husband," she blurted out. "Salim sensed he was being spied on but could never prove it. He had his German colleagues photograph all the manuscripts because he believed spies were looking for them and wanted to destroy them. Dr. Rauser, if you can, please find my husband's killer. Help bring justice to his work."

Rauser didn't know what to say. The silence enveloping the car made it feel like a morgue. He thought about the implications of such a commitment. On the one hand he was afraid about committing to a task that had already resulted in several deaths. Yet, how could he say 'no' to a woman whose husband was killed while working on the same project he had been involved in? She deserved justice—no matter where that led to.

They neared the outskirts of Najran. "I had to think about your question," he said as he squinted into the lights of an oncoming car. "I'm not a policeman or a detective, but I will help as best as I can." There was a ring of determination in his voice.

12

Najran

The late evening call to prayer rang from the mosque. Rauser wondered if it would awaken the women asleep in the car. He glanced into the rear-view mirror and saw Mrs. Salim change her position but her eyes remained closed. He looked back at the road. The moon, now just a sliver, was about to disappear behind the horizon. The two lane highway had broadened to four. It was flanked by the dark silhouettes of palm trees. Glowing street lights welcomed him to the outskirts of Najran.

His thoughts drifted to an article he had written as a grad student seven years ago. It had been on Najran's Christian community during the time of the prophet Muhammad. The article had concluded with an unsettling question: Was it possible that orthodox Christian teaching had been manipulated by military leaders like Uthman, the editor of the modern Quran, and by men like Ibn Ishak who wrote 150 years after Muhammad, to nurture their political and military ambitions? If that was true, was it possible that the religion of the original Muhammad had been nothing more than another Arab Christian sect? Had the original community which had formed around Muhammed actually been nothing but misdirected, Messianic Muslims who believed in Jesus?

The article had been published by the *Christian Science Monitor.* Once on the internet it had caught the attention of Aljazeera. After they gave it airtime the threatening emails started to arrive. He had had to change his email account, and the strong reaction had made him more circumspect in what he would say under his own name in the future. It had also made him sympathetic to the pressure Salim and his wife must have felt when they had been threatened.

He heard movement in the back seat, looked into the mirror and saw Mrs. Salim adjusting her veil. "Dr. Rauser, please turn left at the next light, we're almost at my sister-in-law's home."

He turned into a dimly lit street bordered by high walls and steel gates and saw several parked cars but no pedestrians. As they neared the end of the street Mrs. Salim indicated he turn into a narrow lane. He parked the car along a wall behind a two-story house. They got out, stretched, and Mrs. Salim rang the bell by the gate. A light turned on over their heads, and a Filipino-looking guard asked who they were. Minutes later the gate opened and an older looking woman wearing a traditional black abaya but no veil came walking towards them. She exuded self-assurance. When he saw her up-close Rauser realized she must be Salim's sister. Maryam embraced her aunt and started weeping with the other two women.

The old lady looked at Mrs. Salim, tears moistening her eyes: "My heart is weeping with you," she said. "And may Allah, the compassionate one, be your strength during this difficult time. Thanks for blessing me with your visit during this time of mourning."

Rauser stood silently to one side. Then Maryam released herself from her aunt's embrace. "Aunt Hafsah, this is Dr. Rauser, a friend of uncle Salim and a friend of our family." Rauser bowed slightly. The old woman took a step towards him, reached out and took hold of his hands, holding them gently in hers. Slowly she nodded her head. Rauser was struck by the fact that the woman felt comfortable holding his hands. Then he noticed the henna painted design on her hands. *Strange. I've seen this design somewhere else, but where?*

"I'm sorry for the loss of your brother," he said solemnly. "Dr. Salim was not only a great scholar in his own country, but a man of integrity and honor. May Allah be with you during this time of sadness."

"Thank you, and may Allah be compassionate to you during this time of mourning," the woman said as she released his hands. Rauser felt the chatter of the woman lifting the atmosphere. No matter where he had ever been, recounting the life of the recently departed brought comfort to the bereaved. Aunt Hafsah led them past a covered patio with a large ancient copper pot. A fountain of pink bougainvillea flowers cascaded from it, contrasting sharply with the dark brown door, which was opened as Maryam's aunt led them into a room lit by several floor lamps. Rauser noticed the beautiful Persian carpet on the floor. Smaller copper pots and an array of other artifacts were on display on shelves along the walls. One corner had been turned into a sitting area covered with maroon colored pillows.

"Cozy," he thought. Then he saw the large wooden screen designed to separate male guests from the females and wondered if he would have to sit by himself. However, the women were so engrossed in conversation that the screen was not used. While they talked he had the opportunity to look around. To the right of the door through which they'd walked was what looked like a checkerboard of framed family pictures. He looked until he found Salim. Then his eye roved over the many unique artifacts on the shelves. Suddenly he noticed the qambus on an end table, under a picture of the Ka'aba.

Was this the reason Salim had sent them here? "That instrument has been in our family a long time," a voice said over his shoulder." It was aunt Hafsah.

"Do you know how to play it?" Rauser asked, unsure whether he should touch the ancient looking instrument.

"Our family has played the qambus for generations," their host replied, eyes twinkling, "though not always legally; it was illegal to own one for many years."

"I know," said Rauser with a smile. He wondered if the clues Salim left related to songs played on this qambus. "Do you think it might be appropriate for us to sing a song that Dr. Salim enjoyed?"

The old woman's head bobbed up and down. "My brother used to love to sing our family song. It goes back to the dawn of Islam and the early believers." She glanced briefly at the picture of Salim. "Sometimes I wonder if my brother and I are the last ones who remember it."

"Could I video you singing it on my cell phone?" Rauser asked. A digital record would allow for careful analysis later.

"Certainly. Just let me cover my face." The old woman adjusted her veil, picked up the qambus, tightened a few strings, strummed a few chords and began to sing in a remarkably clear voice.

Rauser focused his phone on the hennaed hands plucking the strings—he knew they'd object to him filming their faces. Although there were old Arabic words he didn't recognize, he understood the song's broad outline. It was about pilgrims and caravans traversing the vast desert. The tune was haunting. Each stanza described a different place the pilgrims passed through. However, there was something different about this traveling song. It began in Mecca and recounted a journey *away* from there. It moved north, towards Palestine.

"Strange," Rauser thought. "Each stanza ends with an oddly familiar refrain:

> *Uthman's planned destruction,*
> *Is seriously in doubt,*
> *Hafsah's conservation,*
> *Was actually carried out.*

Still videoing, he scrutinized the hennaed hands strumming the qambus. The design appeared to extend past her hand and onto the instrument. It seemed like one continuous pattern moving from hand to instrument. When the song ended everyone clapped their appreciation. Mrs. Salim wiped away a tear from the corner of her eye. "You all look a little tired," their host said, looking at Mrs. Salim. "I'll get you all something to eat and then I'll show you to your rooms."

The three women followed her out of the room to what Rauser presumed was the kitchen. He reached for his phone and began to scroll through the pictures he had taken of the crime scene. He stopped at the note Salim had left in Syro-Aramaic: *Namhtu's planned destruction, Is seriously in doubt. The widow's conservation was actually carried out 15:80 and 60:2:6-8.*

"Namhtu," he now realized, had been rewritten from back to front to reconstruct the name "Uthman." The widow had also been identified: *Hafsah*. However, there were no numbers in the song.

A Filipino maid arrived with a selection of olives, cheeses and meats. He ate by himself, after which the maid showed him his room. He lay on his bed, physically tired but his mind was racing. If he was tracking Salim aright he would have to review the video to see what stops were mentioned in the song. These could identify where Hafsah's manuscript, or parts of it, could be hidden. *All right Salim, I'm catching on. We're going to finish your work and leave you the legacy you deserve. I just need some time to figure out your clues before Fouad and the Saudi police catch up with us.*

And then he fell into a deep sleep.

13

Sana'a Police Station

It was midnight when Fouad received the phone call from Hussein: "We found the bug in the secondary filter, Captain. It was wrapped in plastic. That's why it kept functioning."

Faoud tried to hide his anger. "Good job Hussein. Go home and get some sleep. It's been a shitty day." He dropped the phone into its cradle, locked the office, walked down the lonely corridor, greeted the man on duty, and stepped outside. A hot dry breeze was blowing in from the Hadramaut. He walked to his car. Where would they have gone? Would Rauser kill someone and then take a police inspector hostage? Unlikely. Were he and Maryam in cahoots? Possibly. If they were, how had Rauser convinced her in such short order to throw in her lot with him? A well trained inspector like her would never fall for some fast-talking American.

He pulled out of the station's parking lot and onto the street. Say Rauser discovered the bug. Why did he flush it down the toilet wrapped in plastic? He would have thrown it in the garbage. Wrapping metal objects in plastic and throwing them down the toilet wasn't normal. This was a deliberate set-up. Maryam must be helping him. If so, she had become a traitor and this had become a national security issue. He did a sudden U-turn, sped back to the police station, nodded to the surprised duty officer, stomped up to his office and dialed the *Coordinating Security Office*. "This is Capain Fouad al Yamani from the major crimes office. I'd like to speak to officer Maryam bint Ali," he demanded.

"She's not in right now sir. It's after hours," the receptionist replied. "You'll have to wait till morning."

"Morning!" Fouad shouted into the phone, "You find her and get her to call me here at my office even if you have to turn over every rock in Yemen!"

"Yes sir, but what if we're unsuccessful?"

"Call me and let me know!"

He flicked on his computer. There was a message from one of the computer techs: "Rauser called the American Embassy yesterday. Will provide transcript in the morning." Probably wants the embassy to intervene, Fouad thought. I'll post some men at his hotel as well as at the embassy to intercept him before he disappears inside.

It was after 1:00 a.m. when the receptionist called again. They were very sorry, but they could not locate Inspector Maryam. "Your bloody department is good for nothing!" He slammed down the phone, picked it up again and dialed the American Embassy. An answering machine informed him that office hours were from 9:00 a.m. - 5:00 p.m. I may as well go to bed, he thought bitterly. I'll think clearer in the morning."

Next morning at precisely 9:00 a.m. he called the American Embassy. "No." the receptionist said, "we have no contact with an inspector Maryam from the *Coordinating Office of Security*. He asked about William Rauser. "Sorry," said the receptionist, "but American privacy laws don't allow us to answer any questions about specific individuals."

It was time to lean on the Americans: "Excuse me ma'am, but what is the point of the *Coordinating office for Security* if it isn't a two way street. We believe we have evidence that Mr. Rauser may have killed one of our most esteemed researchers and taken one of our female inspectors hostage. I don't want this to become an international incident, but it will if we cannot iron out our differences quickly. Let me remind you again that this is a murder investigation and you're a guest in our country."

"That's a serious charge captain, and we want to help you in any way we can. We will check our phone records and get back to you as soon as we can." Fouad sensed the person on the other end of the line was stonewalling. The embassy staff would get together, discuss whether to share information or stall and delay assistance. He wondered how long this would take. Would they put their own citizen ahead of Yemeni justice? He was pleasantly surprised when a consular officer phoned back in less than ten minutes. This had risen up the diplomatic rank and file in record time.

"Captain Fouad?"

"Yes."

"One of our embassy staff talked to Mr. Rauser yesterday. He informed us that he had gone to the funeral of Dr. Salim." That piece of information was confirmed. It appeared the Americans were actually trying to work with him. Imagine that!

"Did he tell you anything else?"

"He told us he might have landed in an uncomfortable legal situation regarding his work and personal life and asked for our assistance. We told him to stay where he was until we sent someone to help him."

"Did you send someone?"

'Yes."

"Who?"

"We called the *Coordinating office on Security* and they sent a certain Inspector Maryam. She usually works for us in such matters."

"Thank you for your assistance. You've been very helpful."

"Glad we can work together."

Fouad now needed concrete proof that Maryam had not only gone to see Rauser but had teamed up with him. After calling Maryam's home and office without getting an answer he decided that perhaps Dr.

Salim's widow could help. He drove over to the house and found it empty. *Strange; I wonder if the neighbors know anything.*

Checking with the neighbors he received different answers: "She left quickly" or "we didn't even see her go." Several of the neighbors saw Maryam arrive in uniform. Of course they had all expected her to grieve for three days. No one understood why she suddenly left the house.

Fouad needed to think. He went back to his office and reread his notes from the crime scene. *If Rauser and Maryam are working together I need to know what they know so I can anticipate their next move.* He listed everything they might have known about the case on the office whiteboard. Then he stood back and looked at the data. Suddenly he realized a piece was missing: *Who in the Coordinating Office of Security had sent Maryam to the crime scene?*

"Hussein!" he yelled down the corridor. "Did you specifically ask Maryam to be involved in the investigation?"

"No sir," Hussein shouted back.

"Then who did? If you never asked for her how did she get assigned to our case? Everyone knows she drives me nuts." He folded his arms over his chest and resumed staring at the whiteboard. "I need to think," he said to Hussein who was now framed in the doorway, "and that means breakfast. Let's go." He quickly erased the whiteboard, grabbed the file and signaled to Hussein to follow him. They walked out of the police station and across the street. Fouad ordered hummus and fuul—chickpeas and broad beans—for them both. Rather counter-intuitively, a full stomach seemed to energize his neurons.

Fouad could flare up easily, but could just as easily poke fun at himself—a quality that had greatly endeared him to his men. Over breakfast he and Hussein had a good laugh at their own expense at being fooled by the American. Then they talked strategy. After their third cup of coffee it was time to move on.

"Ready for another round with the American?" Fouad said standing up and mimicking some boxing moves. "Let me get this bill," he added with a smile, "its my token of repentance for making you dig through shit yesterday."

"Boss, when the gecko drops its tail, the wise hunter brushes it aside. I'm ready for another chase."

"Right. First we need to know who sent Maryam to help with our investigation. Perhaps she's working for the Yanks. I'm going to swing by the American liaison to *Coordinating Office on Security.*" He lowered his voice as they walked onto the street. "In the meantime you read everything tech is finding on Salim's computer but do not, under any condition, tell anyone what you find. From a couple of email exchanges between Salim and Rauser I've read it seems they were about to find the prophet Muhammad's last will and testament as well as the Hafsah Quran!"

"Wow!" Hussein's eyes grew big. "That... that would be earth-shaking...!"

"Keep your voice down, stupid! Yes, it would be—but not everyone likes earthquakes," Fouad whispered hotly. "You'll see that when you read the Saudi reaction. I'd like you to give some thought into who would win and who would loose should Rauser find Hafsah's original Quran and Muhammad's last will and testament."

"How can I do that if I don't know what they actually say?"

"That's why I want you to look at all the research on Salim's computer. I'm sure he's thought about it—those academic types think best when they write down their thoughts. In the email exchange between him and Rauser they list a bunch of governments who would be affected, but they don't say how. There's bound to be a file on this somewhere."

'O.K...'

"Let me know if you find anything unusual."

"Yes sir."

"And keep yesterday's little goose chase between the two of us."

"What goose chase?" Hussein grinned as they headed back to the station. Fouad signed out an unmarked car and Hussein made himself comfortable in front of the computer.

The nondescript office of the *Coordinating Office of Security* was right beside the American embassy. Fouad parked his car, approached the security agent at the front gate and presented his police ID.

"I'm here to see Mr. Shepherd," he said.

"Just a minute, I'll page him. Please walk through the metal detector and be ready to present your ID once again." As he walked through the metal detector Fouad took in the men working the scanner, the lady checking people's bags and the plain-clothes policeman at the back of the room as well as the unobtrusive little mirrored glass bulbs hiding rotating cameras. Difficult place to break into, he mused.

Shepherd had been the chief American liaison officer to the Coordinating Office of Security since it had been established two years ago. The office provided training and consultant help in complex terrorist and forensic matters. Their high-tech abilities in tracking money and people had proved to be very beneficial. Fouad had had opportunity to meet Shepherd several times. He liked the man, even though he was a typical American: straightforward and to-the-point. The subtleties of language were foreign to him. He said what he meant and meant what he said. Unlike the people in his department who were masters of nuance, one and all. Except maybe Hussein.

"Captain Fouad! Salaam Aleykum!" Shepherd greeted him with a strong American accent as he entered the waiting room with extended hand. His booming voice, drawling Arabic and big smile brought a smile to Fouad's face.

"Why don't you come down to my office? How's your family?" Fouad noted that instead of being ushered into the man's presence by some secretary, Shepherd had come down to the waiting room to meet him in person. He wondered if he should feel flattered. He noticed photographs of American presidents lining the hallway. Shepherd's office was the last one at end of the corridor. The American beckoned to a leather chair. Fouad sat down, and after some initial small talk got to the point.

"I want to thank you for the close cooperation we have had over the past few years with respect to security matters. We appreciate your government's continued anti-terrorist training. However, we have a situation with one of our citizens working here who, it seems, has given some assistance to an American who appears to have disappeared. Perhaps you can help us."

"And who might that be?"

"Maryam bint Ali."

"Maryam bint Ali? She called to tell us that she would be busy for the next few days in the murder investigation of Dr. Salim. We were under the impression that you had assigned her, and so we never interfered since we view her as a professional, trusted by both our offices. Is there a problem? Did you assign her to the case?"

"No, I thought you had."

"Well, we didn't..."

Time to probe, Fouad thought. "So, do we have a communication breakdown?"

"Perhaps," the American responded. "Do you think Maryam can be trusted?"

He's trying to ascertain whether Maryam is a spy, Fouad thought. If she is not I need to be able to cover myself. "I have no reason not to trust her, although her assistance outside of normal protocol has me confused." Fouad paused, leaned forward a bit and looked Shepherd direct in the eye. "Unless, of course, you give us a reason."

Shepherd smiled knowingly at Fouad's question. "We still have confidence in her," he said, "but if we have any concerns, you'll be the first to know."

I think he's saying she's not spying for them. "I would appreciate your confidentiality in this matter," Fouad continued. "We have a few back-channel means of contacting Inspector Maryam. We'll get back to you if need be. If anything comes up with respect to Mr. Rauser we'll be sure to let you know as well."

"I appreciate that," Shepherd nodded his head, "and if there is anything we can do, don't hesitate to ask. Please let us know, and if we have any leads on Professor Rauser, we'll contact you."

Really? Fouad stood up, thrust out his hand to close the conversation and left the office. He thought about Maryam as he walked towards the exit. She had obviously gotten herself into this case without anyone's authority—but then, did *he* have authority over an agent in the *Coordinating office of Security*? If he was going to bring Maryam to task he'd better have a water-tight case; he did not want to be shamed by a woman or by the Americans.

"What are you doing here"? Fouad asked Hussein when he exited the embassy gate. "You think I need an escort back to the office? I got my own car."

"I have a break," Hussein answered. "I checked on Salim's car. It wasn't at his house. I put out a bulletin asking everyone to keep an eye out for it and ran the licence plates through the computer. It crossed the border near Najran."

"You sure it was their car?"

"Yes! And you'll never guess what happened. Two Saudi customs officers were about to charge Rauser and Maryam with antiquities smuggling when, unfortunately they were briefly directed to another concern. It seems our two favorite suspects waltzed out of customs as the officers were called away to attend to another matter. The two fit the description of our Maryam and Rauser."

Fouad felt both an adrenalin rush and frustration. He now had a solid lead and was sure the Saudis would cooperate: they were now chasing criminals who had broken Saudi immigration and customs laws. However he didn't like having to defer to the Saudis. He leaned his back against the patrol car. "Good work," he said. "But this changes things. We now have an international incident."

"What do we do next?"

Fouad thought a minute before answering. Time was running out. The first day someone went missing was crucial. Fugitives always needed the same things: money, a place to hide, and transportation. Perhaps it was time to contact Interpol. They now knew their suspects were in Saudi Arabia as well as the make and number of the vehicle. Interpol could monitor their financial transactions—anytime they bought food, gas, plane tickets, or a hotel room on credit, they would be monitored. "I'm going to contact the Saudi police," he responded slowly. "We'll get them to trace the car; in fact, they may already have done so. I want you to go to the office and stay close to the phone. Be ready to involve Interpol as soon as I call. We cannot let them disappear in some sandstorm."

"Yes boss."

"In the meantime continue reading whatever tech finds on Salim's computer. My gut feeling is that there should be something about the political ramifications of finding the Hafsah Quran, and politics means people, and people can be tracked down.

15

Sana'a Airport

Omar paced restlessly around the airport. Trying to find a way to Israel had taken longer than he'd anticipated. There were, of course, no direct flights between Yemen and Tel Aviv, and all the flights to Amman, Jordan for that day had been booked full. Spending an extra day watching news reports while lying low in the Ghamdan Hotel had done nothing but heighten his apprehension about going to Israel. Things were never good there—but then things were not getting better in Sana'a. Salim's suspicious death had been mentioned several times on the news and this morning it had made the newspapers.

He looked out the window into the darkness and realized it would be close to midnight before he would enjoy freedom from the snooping Yemeni police. He was glad for the hotel arrangements Siddiqi had booked in Amman.

The thought of Siddiqi made him think of his zanjir. It was one of the few things in life that rooted him to his secret ancestral history: a Palestinian Shia hiding in a sea of Sunni Muslims.

Finding the zanjir had been predestined by Allah to help him find his true calling as a jihadi. It happened two months before the explosion. As a bored ten-year old he had climbed into the crawl-space below the roof. There he discovered a small leather bag. He remembered how his heart thundering in his chest. Was it treasure? Slowly he had opened the draw string and found the several pieces of chain dangling from the tip of a short wooden handle. He immediately thought it was a weapon made for hand-to-hand combat.

He remembered his dad's shining eyes and big smile when he brought the bag downstairs. "Well, son, I guess today is as good as any other day," he had said. With eyes still shining, his father had explained that the zanjir had once been used by Imam Jafar al Sadiq, one of the greatest imams in Shia history, a man descended from the very bloodline of the prophet himself.

"Can I show my friends?" he had asked.

It was as if he had just called his father a pig. "No!" his father had shouted. "We have enough problems without bringing another divisive thorn into this community." Under oath he had been forced to never reveal the family's Shia roots to his Sunni friends. Now he understood why.

Unfortunately the zanjir in his suitcase wasn't his father's. It had vanished in the explosion. But this gift from Siddiqi had been the surgeon's scalpel for his tormented soul — the pain it inflicted always helped purge his guilty conscience. He remembered the first time he'd felt its expiation, during the life-changing celebration of *The Mourning of Muharram*, the feast celebrating the death of Ali, the grandson of the prophet Muhammad, peace be upon him.

His new friend and mentor, Siddiqi, had asked him to join him on a clandestine trip to Iran to raise funds for the PIJ. One evening, while sitting on the floor of the mosque after everyone had left, Siddiqi had entrusted him with his own great secret: he too was a secret Shia and had grown up in northern Palestinian in the town of Saliha, the same town in which his father had lived. That evening Siddiqi had regailed him of experiences he had shared with his father: sneaking off to Beirut to enjoy the delights of the big city; spying on the Jews who had opened a kibbutz; stealing a rifle belonging to a Jewish farmer. But it was the story of how they had hid under a pile of corpses as the Israeli government massacred 94 people in their town center that had bonded Omar and Siddiqi as father and son. It was that massacre that had been the genesis of both Siddiqi and his father's commitment never to make peace with the Israelis' and to fight them from inside Israel instead of fleeing to Lebanon.

Siddiqi had filled in the emotional and religious fissures that had plagued him since the explosion. It was Siddiqi who had helped him finally understand the meaning of his father's smile when he had come down the stairs with the zanjir. The zanjir had been the root that tied their family to the imam, and the imam was descended from the very bloodline of the prophet himself!

The revolutionary power of the zanjir had filled him on that clandesting trip to Iran. His mentor had taken off his shirt, along with hundreds of other celebrants in the mosque square and with his own zanjir flagellated himself till rivulets of blood coursed down his back. The experience of the men, all beating themselves and shouting "Allahu Akbar, Allahu Akbar" as if in a trance, had sent shivers up Omar's spine. Everywhere he looked he saw red. The shirts of the men were red, their trousers were red and the ground was red, blood red. Blood coursed into pools that attracted flies, only to be shooed away by men with long handled squeegees paid to clean up after the flagellators.

Omar had been hesitant to join in but after watching for ten minutes or so a spiritual presence had come over him. Before he knew it he too was beating his chest with the same blind abandon as those around him. It had been exhilarating. For the first time in his life he felt as if he had become a true jihadist. Allah himself had unified the spirits of the men in the square with the kind of unity that must have been felt among the warriors of the prophet Muhammad—the warriors who had changed the world. He loved to grip his zanjir's short wooden handle from which the five short lengths of chain hung. His blood was still smeared on the links of the chain. It was the blood of true devotion; the blood of the coming revolution.

Omar sat down and looked around the waiting room. A young man with close-cropped hair and faded jeans was looking in his direction. Only police wear hair that short, he thought and stood up to move to another chair when he heard the announcement: "All passengers on Royal Jordanian Airlines flight 637 to Amman, Jordan, please prepare to board." As the crowd congregated around the counter he instinctively felt for the little wooden box hanging under his robe: "Let's go Yagil" he murmured. "We've got to get you through security."

Then he lined up with the other passengers waiting to go through security.

It took about ten minutes before it was his turn to pass through the metal detector. A dour looking official waved for him to proceed. He put his suitcase on the belt leading through the x-ray machine and approached the metal detector. He hated airport security. It made him feel like he was stripped naked.

"Excuse me sir," the x-ray technician said after he had passed through the metal detector, "is this your bag?"

"Yes."

"Please open it." Omar clenched his teeth as he unzipped his bag. The agent probably had concerns with the zanjir.

The agent rummaged through his suitcase and found the zanjir. "I'm sorry, but we cannot let you take them on the plane," the agent said shaking his head.

"So what can I do?" Omar asked.

"What we can do is put your carry-on with the strollers and car seats under the plane. You can pick them up at the gate when you touch down in Amman. You'll be able to find them along with the baby stuff."

"That would be great sir."

Subhan Allah.

16

Allenby/King Hussein Bridge

It was late by the time Omar's plane landed in Amman, and even later when he checked into the Asri Hotel behind the King Hussein Mosque. Nevertheless he woke up at 5:00 a.m. to join the congregants for early morning prayers. He took extra time to pray for smooth passage through Israeli immigration. He decided his best chance of entering Israel with minimal hassles, was the Allenby/King Hussein Bridge.

Only one more border to cross before I'm back in Israeli hell. Nervousness gnawed at his stomach during the long shared taxi ride to the border. When he got out at the bridge a shiver ran up his back in spite of the hot, humidity of the Jordan River valley. He hated the computer screens of the immigration officers. He wondered how much of his past those screens revealed to the uniformed Zionist who revelled in making him squirm before passing final judgement on whether you were good enough to be allowed into a country that they'd stolen from his people. Stay calm, he told himself once again as he lined up to have his bags scanned.

"Please remove your necklace and put it in one of the bins by the scanner," a female officer said. "And please give me your passport."

Ya Allah, he should've tucked Yagil under his robe like he normally did. He took off the necklace slowly. "Please Allah," he silently prayed, "protect Yagil and me." He put it in a bin and watched it disappear into the scanner as he handed his Israeli passport to the officer. Then he walked through the metal detector towards the officer on the other side. He glanced back to see if Yagil had been noticed. The officer at the scanner had stopped the belt and was looking intently at the screen. Then she glanced at the officer standing in front of the metal detector and raised her eyebrows.

"Excuse me sir, but we're going to have to ask you a few questions," the officer facing him said. "Please follow me." Another male officer joined them as they went down the hall and entered a small interrogation room. Looking at his passport the officer addressed him: "Have a seat Mr. Omar." He sat down while the officer continued paging through his passport. The other officer closed the door behind them and put the necklace on the table, "Sir, would you please open up the little box."

Omar hesitated. If he opened the little box, the scorpion could escape. If he didn't their suspicions would increase even more. "It won't open sir," he bluffed, looking straight into the eyes of the immigration official.

"Shall I try?" the officer said. He slipped on some plastic gloves

Ya Allah, irrhamni! Oh God have mercy on me! Before he could respond the officer slid back the top cover. Omar held his breath. There, with tail raised, ready to strike, stood Yagil.

Curses exploded from the customs officials and everyone backed away from the table except for Omar. The immigration official by the door yelled in Hebrew and an armed soldier burst through the door. "What's going on here?" The soldier's eyes fastened on the scorpion. Without waiting for an explanation, he raised his rifle. Omar closed his eyes. He heard the rifle butt hit the table and felt Yagil's guts splatter on his arms.

"You stupid *ibn-himar*, son-of-an-ass," Omar shouted. Immediately he knew he had overstepped the parameters of immigration protocol but didn't care. "What the hell has that little creature ever done to you?" Before he knew what had happened one of the agents had put him in a half nelson and crushed his face into the table. Another officer grabbed painfully twisting his other arm behind his back. A pair of handcuffs were slapped on his wrists.

"You'll be sorry you tried this," someone whispered menacingly into his ear. They threw a black, puke-smelling hood over his head, grabbed him by his collar and pulled him upright. They thrust him forward. He took a hesitant step fearing an obstacle. He couldn't see anything. They pushed and shoved him down a hallway and around several corners. He heard a door open and close, and then he was yanked down onto a chair.

He knew the grilling was next. He waited for the questions to start but all he heard was the door close. The room was silent. Was he alone? Was there someone in the room? How big was the room? He sat there for an eternity. He was not tied to the chair, but was afraid to get off it. He breathed through his mouth so the putrid smell of the hood wouldn't trigger his gag reflex. Finally he could hold it no longer; he had to go to the bathroom. "Excuse me," he said into the hood, "I have to go to the bathroom." There was no reply.

What were they doing? They would know he had just come from Yemen and Germany. They would also know his previous criminal record. What would happen if they figured out he had killed Dr. Salim and the Germans? The thought sent a shudder up his spine and he opened his eyes. All was darkness.

He couldn't stand it any longer. He tried to stand up, unsure if someone might be in the room but everything remained silent. The urge to go to the bathroom was getting stronger and stronger: "Excuse me," he yelled. His voice was muffled. "I have to go to the bathroom!" Again, no answer.

He couldn't hold it any longer. He moved away from the chair. Then he inched backwards. Where was the wall? He stretched his cuffed hands back as far as he could. He felt something brush his shoulder and stopped. It was the wall. I'll follow the wall, he thought, and took his first hesitant step. Was this the direction to the door? He took three hesitant steps along the wall.

Suddenly someone shoved him from behind. He took two quick steps to regain his balance but to no avail. He felt what must have been another chair and tried to fall into it. It tipped backwards and he crashed to the hard concrete. A sharp pain shot up his arms. Then the final humiliation: warm urine flowing down his leg.

"You're all the same: bed-wetting babies," a gravelly voice said sarcastically in fluent Arabic. Omar felt his face flush with embarrassment as the warm urine caused his pants to stick to his leg. He felt his heart pounding, but said nothing. "So bed-wetter, what's with the scorpion? You want to sit down and continue the conversation?" the voice asked. He said nothing. He squeezed his eyes together. He was dizzy. He determined not to cooperate.

"So you don't want to talk... Perhaps you need to wet yourself some more," the voice said. A few seconds later he heard the door open and close.

"Zionist pig," Omar mumbled.

"Really?" said the voice. Someone struck him. Excruciating pain flashed through his head. They were playing head-games, never letting him know whether or not he was alone. "Perhaps we should begin this conversation again. Why did you try to bring a scorpion through customs?"

"I'll tell you if you help me sit back in the chair," Omar said. He was hanging on to his dignity and negotiating for self-respect.

"We can accommodate that," the gravelly voice said. Someone grabbed his arms, pulled him up and led him back to the chair. "Sit down," the voice said.

"I was hoping to bring the scorpion home," said Omar. The hood reeked.

"Where did you get it?

"I got it in Yemen." He heard pages turning.

"Do you know you can't bring animals into Israel without a permit?"

"I thought that referred to cats, dogs and other zoo animals."

"Liar!" a different voice shouted. He ducked automatically but the punch struck him in the stomach. He doubled over in pain. I'm going to throw up, he thought. He needed to stay calm if he was going to avoid doing something stupid.

"So, tell me, why we should let you into Israel?" the gravelly voice asked.

"Because I have an Israeli passport," Omar mumbled.

"Israel is not interested in Palestinians who break the law... and that's something you're good at." Omar remained silent. He knew better than to argue. Someone opened the door and he heard some whispering. Then the door closed again. Everything went silent. He lost all track of time. His wrists and arms burned and his stomach churned. Was he alone? Would they hit him if he moved? What would happen next?

Finally he heard the door open. "Get up," a new voice said. Someone grabbed him by the arms and led him away. Another door opened and a cool breeze blew against his face. Someone removed his handcuffs and lifted the hood off is head. "Here's your bag," said the officer dropping it next to him. "Next time keep your animals in Yemen."

Omar slumped to the ground and sat there, breathing in the cool, fresh air. Finally he stumbled to his feet and walked to the public bathroom. He washed up as best he could and put on another robe. He threw his filthy one into the bin.

It was dark. Hopefully he could still get a bus to Jerusalem before the Israelis or Yemenis traced his recent travel itinerary to the dead Germans and the murdered Salim.

17

Visiting in Najran

Rauser was dog-tired when he finally tumbled into bed, and he slept in the following day. When he finally got up the two older women were in the kitchen. He looked around the screen separating men and women and saw Maryam sitting in an armchair. "So, Dr. Rauser," she said smiling, "you feeling at home?"

"Getting there. A good night's sleep helps. So does being out of Fouad's reach." He paused. "Also, I really appreciate being with someone who enjoys Yemen and also understands the West." Before the words had left his mouth he suddenly realized that he was attracted to Maryam. It made him feel guilty vis-à-vis his late wife, and he quickly changed the subject. "Have you given any thought as to what Salim thought we might find here?"

"Not really. Have you?"

"I think there may be a connection between the last song your aunt sang and one of the words Salim wrote on his torso, although I haven't been able to make the connection yet."

"Let's check the crime scene pictures." She picked up her cell phone and started paging through the pictures. Then she stopped and pulled the phone closer to her eyes. "It's hard to read these small screens" she said, "but I think it says 'qambus' under one nipple and under the other – I don't know."

"What can you tell me about your family's qambus?"

"Our qambus has a hinged neck. It allowed the instrument to be folded and hidden in the folds of people's clothing while walking outside, leaving everyone on the street with the impression it was the Quran."

Rauser's thoughts turned to the song. "I noticed your aunt's hands when she was playing the qambus. The design on the qambus and the design on her hennaed hand almost appeared to be woven together. We should compare it to the map Salim hennaed on his hand."

"Let me ask my aunt." She got up and went to the kitchen. As the minutes passed Rauser's mind flitted from one thought to another. Qambus, henna, Catherine? Why had Salim directed him to this home? Just as he was becoming vaguely impatient with being left alone, Maryam and her aunt walked through the kitchen door carrying trays of the coffee, fresh bread, hummus, zeit and za'tar, jams and cheese. He didn't need the aunt's urging to enjoy the food.

Then, sipping her coffee, the aunt answered Maryam's question. "The henna pattern and the music contain codes in which we hide our family's history. The problem is, we have forgotten the codes. Salim was working on sorting this out."

"I wonder how we should proceed," Rauser mused. "We cannot return to Yemen and the museum. There must be a way to pick up the trail of clues Salim felt were here..."

"Perhaps one of the black sheep in my family can help us," Maryam's aunt said, "He's the bastard son of a family in Riyad, but lives here in Najran. He is knowledgeable about the early years of Islam and has many connections; he really knows the history of Najran. You may even have heard of him. His name is Abdullah Saud."

"Abdullah Saud?" Rauser exclaimed. "Of course I do! He's not a recognized scholar but he knows what he's talking about. When could we see him?"

"Let me call him."

"That would be great." Rauser turned to Maryam. "You never told me you had connections to the Saudi royal family!"

"He's not on the royal 'Most Loved' list," she smiled.

18

Rauser Meets Osama

Something made Rauser look up, and when he did he saw a young man in Saudi robes and sporting a neatly trimmed beard standing on the far side of the room. His black eagle-eyes shifted suspiciously from one person to the next. The man's hands were clasped in front of him, and Rauser noticed a large gold ring on one of his fingers.

Must be family, Rauser thought. How else could he have entered the room unannounced? The others still did not seem to notice him. Rauser stared back without saying a word. After a minute Maryam's aunt looked up and saw him.

"Ahlen wa sahlen, ya Osama" (Welcome, Osama), she said. In response the man thrust his chin in Rauser's direction and asked Maryam's aunt something; Rauser was too far away to hear what he said. He saw her put a hand on his shoulder as if to soothe his concerns. "Everyone, I would like you to meet my nephew Osama," she said. She then turned to the young man. "Osama, these are family and friends from Yemen. You know your cousin Maryam. The Westerner is Dr. Rauser, the son of a surgeon who worked for years in Yemen. He is a professor." She turned back to everyone else in the room.

"Welcome to my home Dr. Rauser," Osama said. "Do make yourself at home." He looked around as if he was going to say something else, and everyone fell silent. After an awkward pause Osama continued mechanically: "I'm sorry, but I have to excuse myself. I have to go to the mosque." Then he bowed his head slightly towards Rauser, turned and left.

"Not too interested in extended family is he?" Rauser said quietly to Maryam. "Or do you see him all the time?"

"He's a bit like the other Osama – the Bin Laden one. He views life through the lens of hatred: hatred of westerners, hatred of moderate Muslims, hatred of Shia Muslims and especially a hatred of Jews and Americans."

Oh great!

"He's off to the mosque," his aunt said with a smile. The smile appeared a bit forced, Rauser thought. "He spends most of his time there. I don't think we'll see him for the rest of the day."

While the women picked up the thread of their conversation Rauser sipped his coffee. He'd no sooner finished the warm, energizing liquid when the door opened with a flourish and a man in flowing white robes and matching caftan entered the room. He had a regal presence and confident smile. "Salaam Aleykum," the man said brightly while nodding at everyone in the room.

"Aleykum Salam," everyone replied in unison.

The man turned to Rauser and extended his hand. "It's a privilege to meet you Dr. Rauser."

Rauser grabbed the man's hand in both of his and noticed Saud's firm grip. "The honor is mine. And let me thank you up front, Mr. Abdullah, for running to aid a struggling academic." The man's smile revealed an impish spark in his eyes. He turned to greet the others in the room, made some small talk, and then sat down beside Rauser.

"I understand you are puzzled about something. I'm sure any unsolved clues will probably be beyond my humble abilities, but perhaps if we work together we'll be able to make some progress. What do you say in English – two hands make light work? So what's puzzling you? Is it cultural, theological or something else?" There was something about this man, other than his sense of humor, which led Rauser to believe he could be trusted.

He explained the nature of how his visit to Dr. Salim was meant to secure his tenure, and what he knew about Salim's murder, adding how they were now following up on some of Salim's research. He decided not to share the fact that he was the primary suspect in Salim's murder. "What we're looking for is a connection between the qambus, some hennaed designs which we believe are unique to Salim's family—and which we think may hide a map—the name *Katherine* in Greek as well as some ancient Arabic documents that Salim thought may have been here in Najran," he concluded.

 "So what makes you think these are clues in Salim's work? What was he trying to uncover?"

At this point Maryam entered the discussion. "My uncle phoned me before he died and we talked about these clues. He also mentioned them to my aunt and left some numbers that may correspond to some of the Sana'a manuscripts that were put up for auction."

Abdullah Saud nodded. "I bought some of the documents a few years back. I suggest we go to my house. Perhaps some of my documents will complement yours."

Fouad's plane touched down at Najran airport. He walked through the walkway into the airport and saw a man in the uniform of the Najrani police force with a captain's epaulets on his shoulders approaching him.

"You must be Captain Jabir." Fouad extended his hand. "Thanks for picking me up at such short notice."

"And you are Captain Fouad. Any luggage?"

"No, just this carry-on." This is not the Sana'a airport, Fouad thought. The modern architecture was impressive. The European-style kiosks and the Southeast Asian nannies pushing strollers behind burqa clad mothers added an international feel that was a world apart from Sana'a. The two men walked through the exit into a blast of hot air. The sandy terrain looked like home. Jabir led him to an unmarked car and Fouad threw his bag onto the back seat. "We appreciate your cooperation with this case," he said over the top of the car.

"No problem. We're as interested as you are in this guy. Do you want to be dropped off at the hotel or shall we go straight to the station?"

"To the station. The less the delay the better." He opened the vehicle's door and got in.

Suddenly the door opened and Maryam's cousin Osama reappeared. "Hey everybody," he shouted, "I just heard on the radio that the Yemeni police and the Saudi police are working together on Salim's murder. The report mentioned that the prime suspects are a westerner and a Yemeni woman who may have crossed the border into Saudi. Two immigration officials claim they entered Saudi illegally and may be smuggling ancient documents. The two immigration officials said they could identify the suspects." As Osama finished his announcement he looked angrily at Rauser.

Rauser's heart missed a beat. *We need to get out of here without raising suspicions.* "Did they mention any names on the radio?" asked Maryam.

"No."

"Well, keep us informed; if it relates to uncle Salim's death we all want to know."

"Don't worry, I will," he answered, glanced at Rauser, turned and disappeared through the door.

Rauser and Maryam glanced briefly at one another. Then she turned to her aunt. "Thank you for your hospitality Um Faisal, but Abdullah invited us to see some manuscripts at his home. Please call if we can help with anything. We shouldn't be long." She turned to Abdullah. "Should we drive in one car to your place?"

"Put on an abaya to avoid suspicion while I call my chauffeur." Maryam nodded and walked down the hall and through a door.

Rauser was unsure of the direction events were taking. Getting out of this house was undoubtedly a good thing, but he wasn't sure Abdullah's place would provide adequate anonymity to hide them from the police.

Maryam stepped back into the hall. "What do you think?" she asked looking at him through the eye slits in her abaya. "Does this improve my looks?"

Rauser smiled. "Those things transform beauty into drab—and I guess that's the sad idea..." He saw her eyes narrow and presumed she was smiling.

The chauffeur arrived within minutes. He look Filipino. "Salaam, ya Yusuf," Abdullah addressed him. "Back to the house." He turned to the rest of them. "Everyone, I want you to meet Yusuf. He's my right hand man: drives my cars, fights at my side, manages my affairs."

"Salaam ya Yusuf," they all replied, nodding their heads.

Abdullah slipped into the front seat, turned around and caught Maryam's eye. "I have two large German shepherds who may at first seem a bit intimidating. They are well trained and won't bother you as long as I'm with you."

The drive took them through the center of Najran. The streets were a contrast to Yemeni streets because there were hardly any people; everyone appeared to own a car here. Rauser also noticed the lack of pot holes and garbage, which reminded him of his suburban commute in America. Yusuf wove through the the traffic and Rauser noticed a preponderance of Mercedes and BMWs. It always amazed him how a simple border, drawn arbitrarily by the colonial powers 80 years ago could, over time, result in such apparent differences between two countries, and all because of oil.

As they headed towards the outskirts, the boulevard widened. Palm trees graced the median at regular intervals. Fifteen minutes later they pulled up to a large stone wall with an ornate wrought-iron gate. Sure enough, as they entered the compound two growling German

Shepherds circled the vehicle. They stopped when Abdullah opened the door and ordered them to stand down. Rauser noticed their muscles twitching as they looked intently at Saud. These beasts were well trained, he thought.

"Let's go to the lab. I recently bought some new technotoys, but I hardly know how to use them. Maybe Dr. Rauser can help." The man's self-depreciation impressed Rauser. The lab was not unlike that in the House of Manuscripts in Sana'a. Among other things it contained manuscript presses, a black-light, spectroscope, and several cabinets filled with various chemicals and solvents. A black safe stood along one wall.

"What do you do here?" Rauser asked. He was amazed that a private citizen would have such an extensive lab.

"I bought a few of the Sana'a manuscripts, as well as one from Turkey. I heard they might be palimpsests. I'm trying to analyze them to see if there's any important historical data underneath – it's my new hobby."

"So which manuscripts do you have?"

"Let me look at the numbers." Abdullah headed toward a filing cabinet and opened a drawer. In the meantime Maryam dug into her purse, pulled out her phone and found the picture with the numbers on it.

Abdullah extracted a paper from a file, straightened up and began reading. "Codex Dam 01-27; Codex dam 02-32.2 and codex dam 03-15.5."

"Ya Salaam," Maryam's eyebrows rose. "Those are some of the same numbers Salim left us."

Rauser met her eyes. This was no coincidence. "Sir, who knows you have these manuscripts?" he asked.

"Anyone interested in tracking the auction of the Sana'a manuscripts," Abdullah answered. "I obtained some through Sotheby's in London."

"That means Salim might have known they were with you," Rauser said. "Have you looked at these manuscripts under a black light?"

"No, not all of them. I only just acquired the last two; actually, I borrowed them from a family member in Riyadh. He collects them as an investment. He didn't know they might be palimpsest; in fact, he didn't even know what palimpsests were till I told him."

"Shall we take a look at them?" Rauser asked. Abdullah walked towards a safe and twirled the dial this way and that. There was a brief hum, then he pulled the steel door open, reached in and extracted a leather case. He gingerly pulled a manuscript into the open and gave it to Rauser. Rauser placed it under the spectroscope and flicked on a switch. A screen lit up. He started twiddling with the keyboard and the manuscript came into view. He pulled up another screen, made various adjustments and there, under the dominant letters, the faint shadow of an older, handwritten text emerged.

"How does this machine work?" Maryam asked.

"It's like a digital camera," said Rauser. "The energy in the x-ray causes certain elements in the ink of the hidden text to glow. The computer picks up the unique florescence of these wavelengths and converts the data into images on the screen." Words began to appear on the screen. It was in the Kufic script and without vowel markings.

Maryam leaned towards the screen, her brow furled. Suddenly she smiled. "Guess what? I think the palimpsest is my father's favorite chapter in the Quran, from the chapter called 'Maryam.' It's all about Isa or 'Jesus' as you Christians call him. What's that over there?" she asked pointing to the bottom of the screen. Faint shadows of letters were barely visible but it appeared to be verse 33: *"So Peace is on me, the day I was born, the day that I die, and the … day that I shall be raised up to life again."*

"My Quranic teacher said this refers to Jesus," said Maryam.

"What's the word between 'the' and 'day'?"

"I'm not sure. It could be a smudge but..." Rauser paused and played with the computer to raise the contrast of the underlying text. "... I think it's the symbol for 'third.'"

"That ought to make Christians happy," smiled Abdullah.

"Yes," Rauser responded thoughtfully. "We would then have the Quran affirming that Jesus rose from the dead after three days."

"What does the modern Quran say in this instance?" asked Rauser.

Salim quoted the verse from memory: "So Peace is on me the day I was born, the day that I die and the day that I shall be raised up to life."

"I can see why someone interested in heightening the differences between Islam and Christianity would *not* want to put a number three in the text," Rauser said.

"Look at the screen," Abdullah exclaimed. Once again text scrolled down. "Look how this manuscript ends the chapter. It leaves out verse 35 in today's Quran. That also would make Christians happy. It would leave out the part that Allah didn't have a son." His face erupted into a broad smile. "This is amazing! I'm so glad you came to my place. Who would have known that the manuscripts I borrowed were actual palimpsests!"

"Would you mind if I download the picture from my phone to your computer so I can see it on your large screen?" Rauser asked.

"No problem."

"Let's also upload my phone video of the aunties singing onto your computer. I want to isolate the words. I also want some close-ups of your aunt's hands to compare them with the hennaed hand of Salim." They looked at the computer screen and listened to the singing, trying to find correlations with the henna designs. Abdullah jotted down the lyrics while the three of them listened. At the end of the song he acknowledged he was unable to catch all the words and began to replay the song again.

"Stop right there," said Rauser, "what did the women just say?" They scrolled back several frames: the words didn't sound Arabic.

"Perhaps this is a dead end. Let's move on and get back to the song later. What if we superimpose Salim's crude hennaed hands over your aunt's hands?" They downloaded the pictures from the cell phone and noticed the similarities. "Remember you thought it was a map back in Yemen. You still think so?" Rauser asked Maryam.

"Perhaps this is a map indicating where Salim thought the Hafsah Quran may be located." As they zeroed in on the henna design of Maryam's aunt's hand a line with three distinct dots emerged. "Perhaps this will clear up what we couldn't isolate in Yemen," Maryam said.

"The problem," said Rauser, "is that this is difficult to correlate with any modern maps. How do we know what the dots represent? Let's try correlating it with the words your aunt sang."

They stood around the video and listened intently to the singing. The Arabic dialect was strange. "This is the kind of Arabic Muhammad spoke," said Saud. They listened again and Rauser jotted down several place names: *Najran, Moni tes Hagias Aikaterines, Jabal Musa* and *Yerusalem.*

"Perhaps the song and the hennaed map are not related," Abdullah suggested. "There are four place names in the song but only three dots on the hennaed-hand map. Also, I have no idea what in the world *Moni tes Hagias Aikaterines* refers to; I don't think its Arabic or Hebrew."

"You're right," said Rauser, "it's a mixture of Greek and Arabic. *Moni tes Hagias Aikaterines* is Greek for *St. Catherine Monastery* and *Jabal Musa,* as you know, is Arabic for Mount Sinai."

Suddenly Rauser's eyes lit. "We know that Muhammad visited the monks at the Sinai monastery. We also know that one of the very few documents Muhammad ever signed with a handprint, an eternal peace treaty, was delivered to the monks there. I wonder if we're being directed to the monastery. Since there is an eternal peace treaty between Muhammad and the monks, what better place to hide the Hafsah Quran than in a Christian monastery. No Muslim would ever think of looking there! What if Hafsah's father, the caliph Omar dropped off the Hafsah Quran at the monastery for safe keeping? Some of the world's oldest manuscripts have been found at St. Catherine's Monastery, including ancient Arabic texts!" Rauser was ready to go... not only because trouble brewed in Saudi Arabia, but he felt he finally had a bead on the location of the Hafsah Quran.

19

Najran Police Station

"We just received a tip that Dr. Rauser may be here, in Najran." Captain Jabir slipped his cell phone into his pocket and looked at Fouad over his desk. "The individual stated that a western man fitting Rauser's description recently arrived at his home accompanied by two Yemeni women. I presume you have some idea who they might be."

Fouad smiled. "I do. Maryam and Salim's wife." *And now we have to get things into motion. I hope this guy isn't your typical lazy cop.* "All three are connected to the crime. Do you have any specific information on where they may have gone?"

"We do. It appears they're at the home of one of Salim's relatives. The caller gave us the address." Jabir motioned for another officer to join them. Once out the police department they sprinted to their car.

"They may be armed with weapons they took from the immigration office. I wonder if we should take a squad of armed police before we attempt to apprehend them," Fouad wasn't so concerned for his own safety as that of the safety of the Saudi captain. If the man was killed in this raid he would also be hauled on the carpet.

Jabir turned to the other officer: "Get three other patrol cars ready and meet us at the scene."

Fouad turned to Jabir as he closed the passenger door. "The woman is one of our officers." Jabir started the unmarked vehicle and drove off. "She's well trained," Fouad continued, "and may have joined the fugitive Dr. Rauser. We're not exactly sure of her status. She may even be a hostage along with her aunt. As a guest in your country, I would prefer to err in keeping your citizens safe… especially from our criminals," he added with a smile.

"Does this woman work for you?" Jabir pulled out into the traffic.

"No. She works for a joint Yemeni-American department which tracks terrorists."

Captain Jabir sped down Najran's main thoroughfare but didn't activate the siren. He looked over at Fouad: "Do Rauser and the woman have a relationship?"

"Not sure. We think they only recently met while Maryam was investigating Dr. Salim's murder."

"Could you describe her?"

"About 26 years old, 180 centimeters tall; she may still be wearing a Yemeni police uniform. Good looking." Fouad found Najran's wide streets, bounded by stately palm trees, and smooth flowing traffic soothing. The Mercedes passed several large glass office buildings, a modern mosque with an ornate minaret and several German car dealerships. The absence of billowing exhaust smoke from antiquated buses and the absence of pedestrians felt strangely odd. It was like driving down a sterile hospital corridor.

Jabir grabbed his car radio. "Block off all the roads to the following GPS location: 44.13229, 17.49173. Be prepared to apprehend armed suspect. Suspect is a white male accompanied by a woman who may be armed and dangerous. Woman may be wearing a Yemeni police uniform. There are innocent members in the house who are unaware of the danger. Proceed with all caution. Do not use sirens to warn the suspect. We'll try to take them by surprise. Do not do anything until I get there."

Fouad fidgeted with his phone; he didn't like receiving orders. He dialed Hussein's office number and got the answering machine: "Hussein," he intoned, "I think we're on Rauser's tail; call me when you get a chance."

"No one there?" asked Jabir.

"Oh, he's probably filtering the calls with the answering machine." He was right. Within thirty seconds Hussein called back.

"Hi boss. I heard you're on to something."

"Yeah, I'll let you know if we apprehend him. You on to anything?"

"Yes. Salim's bank account contains some Israeli contributions."

"You've got to be kidding! Where did the money come from?"

"A foundation housed in Jerusalem."

Fouad didn't answer for several seconds. This complicated things. "What did they fund?"

"Several trips."

"Where?"

"To Germany, the U.S. and Jordan."

"Any correspondence from Saudi Arabia?"

"Yes sir."

"Send them to me."

"Right away."

"Good job. Try to find more about that foundation." Fouad hung up the phone and looked out the window at what was now a suburban neighborhood. A minute later his phone vibrated. There was an email from Hussein entitled "RE: Contingency Re HQ." He opened the attached file.

"This is in regard to our previous conversation regarding the HQ, the PM's remorse and the perception of his chosen successor. If, as your palimpsests appear to indicate, the HQ gives unquestionable support to your thesis, we will do everything in our power to obtain the HQ, including empowering groups like AQ to ensure the balance of power in the Middle East is maintained. Thanks for your previous thoughts on this matter and let us know what you find."

The message was unsigned.

"Any helpful news from Yemen?" Jabir asked.

"It's all becoming a little more complicated than we thought. There may be other parties involved in this mess."

"Who?"

"The homicide victim who triggered this whole investigation received money from an Israeli foundation. We don't have diplomatic relations with Israel and they classify us as an enemy state. I wonder how legitimate that money is."

"There are always back channels," Jabir said as he slowed the car.

Fouad's mind turned back to the email Hussein had sent him. 'HQ' must mean 'Hafsah Quran.' The initials PM could refer to the 'prime minister' but that didn't fit the context. 'AQ' was a group – probably Al Qaida. His mind swung back to the initials PM. Perhaps these referred to the 'Prophet Muhammad'. The implications were disturbing. If the Saudis were ready to empower Al Qaida to ensure they got their hands on the Hafsah Quran it meant that everyone felt the stakes were extremely high. "We're a block from the suspect's home," Jabir interrupted his thoughts. "I'll call our informant and set things up."

Jabir punched a number into his phone. "Osama, this is Captain Jabir. We're a block south of your house and would like you to meet us. We're in an unmarked white Mercedes at the end of your street." Jabir hung up the phone. "He's the guy that called in the suspects; says he's related to your inspector Maryam."

"Really? He would turn in a family member?"

"Perhaps they had a falling out. In any case, I'm hoping he'll give us the layout of the home. Maybe he can help coax the suspects into the open."

Osama appeared within two minutes. He wore a large white Saudi robe, matching gold-trimmed caftan, traditional sandals. He strode to the white Mercedes. Fouad noticed another white Mercedes pull up two blocks down the street to seal off the other end. He hoped no one would be killed. Not only would it create a mountain of paperwork but it would close down the other part of the investigation: the discovery of the Hafsah Quran and Muhammad's last will and testament.

"Salaam Aleykum," Jabir extended his arm in greeting through the opened car window.

"Aleykum Salaam."

"Are you Osama?"

"Yes," the voice sounded strained and flat. The man seemed to be fighting to control some kind of inner rage by masking the intonation of his voice. His face was expressionless.

"Thank you for your call! We would appreciate any help you can give me. Have you just come from the house?"

"No, I was at the mosque."

"Where are they now?"

"Their car is still in front of my mother's house. I just passed it when I came here."

"Can you coax them out of the house? We don't want to barge in the door and hurt innocent bystanders."

"Sure let me try." Fouad noted the man's cold responses. It was as if Jabir had communicated with a machine. Would the robot do as he was told?

Jabir pulled out a writing pad. "Before you go, could you draw the layout of the house in case things go wrong? We hope we don't have to go in, but just in case."

Osama quickly sketched the layout. Another officer appeared at the car window. Jabir gave the man a quick nod and looked at Osama: "I'll need about three minutes to look over the drawing and confer with my officers. In the meantime try coaxing them out of the house. You think you can do that?"

"Sure," Osama replied, and walked toward the house.

"Osama," called Jabir to the receding man, "If you need help, walk outside and pretend to make a phone call. If they're gone, just come back and let us know."

"Salaam Aleykum,' Maryam responded. She put one hand over her ear and closed her eyes. Concentration etched her face as she listened on her cell phone. "So you're not sure when they may come?" There was a pause followed by, "OK, I understand; thanks." Maryam looked up and into two sets of concerned eyes.

"Something wrong?" asked Rauser.

"That was my aunt. Osama convinced the police we're the ones they're looking for. She thinks they'll be here in a few minutes." Turning to Abdullah she continued, "You have no need to get yourself involved in this. I know we look suspicious, but we didn't kill my uncle and our only concern is finishing his work and tracking down what he believed was an ancient Quranic manuscript. I'm sorry, but you know the Saudi justice system; we'd prefer not to get arrested and we don't want you to implicate yourself in our mess. We need to move. Can we borrow your BMW? Feel free to tell the police we stole it."

"Nothing like a bit of excitement!" Abdullah said with a wink and a smile. "Perhaps I can help you." Then, with a nod of his head he added, "Come with me to the back of the house; I have a way to get you out of here."

20

Abdullah's Home

Abdullah darted into the dining room. "Come on Yusuf, this is the emergency I warned you could happen. Get everything together and meet me at the hanger. We're leaving immediately."

He turned to Rauser and Maryam. "Follow me. I have a helicopter. We'll be out of here in minutes." As soon as they stepped into the courtyard the two German Shepherds came running. He held up two fingers. "Protect," he commanded. Immediately the dogs flanked them with a menacing growl.

Rauser noticed the elegant pool bounded by pink and white bougainvilleas, a volleyball court and, down the sidewalk, a large metal camouflaged structure. Must be the hanger, he thought. Maryam grabbed his arm and propelled him even faster to the hanger.

Yusuf caught up with them and was carrying two helmets, two Kalashnikov assault rifles and several spare magazines of ammunition. The two dogs had followed them into the hanger. The Philipino nodded to Abdullah and headed for the helicopter. It sat on a flatbed rail car. The tracks holding the rail car led through the back wall and out of the hanger.

"Get in," Abdullah commanded. He strode to a control panel on the wall and flicked a couple of switches. Two large doors that formed part of the back wall slid open.

"Get in before it starts rolling," Yusuf urged. Rauser and Maryam climbed into the machine. Maryam looked at Rauser with questioning eyes. Rauser shrugged. "If you say 'A', you've got to be ready to say 'B'", he shouted.

"My aunt said she saw police up and down the street."

Yusuf climbed in the pilot seat, put on his helmet and signalled for Rauser and Maryam to buckle up. The engine roared to life. "Is Abdullah coming?" Maryam yelled, struggling to be heard over the engine.

Yusuf adjusted several dials. "Of course." The rail car began rolling through the open doors and out of the hanger. "He wouldn't miss an adventure for anything!" Rauser felt helpless as the helicopter began to roll out the hanger. It was as if everyone else was deciding his fate. He looked at the floor and saw the guns Yusuf had laid between the seats. It had been a long time since he had shot an automatic weapon. When he looked up he saw Saud running beside the moving rail car flanked by his two German Shepherds.

"Watch out!" Maryam pointed at the hanger door. They could see Fouad reaching for his holster. Another officer was close behind.

Instantly the two dogs veered from Abdullah's side and rushed the intruders. They raced across the hanger with teeth bared and lunged. Jabir drew his pistol and fired. The lead dog squealed in mid-flight and rolled several times before crashing limp against the wall while the second dog flew through the air, mouth open, homing in on Jabir's pistol.

Fouad had anticipated the dog's move. He jerked Jabir to one side. The animal flew past the captain and smashed into the wall. It tried to recover but Fouad fired into it at close range. The beast squeeled and dropped to the floor. Fouad pumped another bullet into the animal before looking up.

Sweat poured down Rauser's forehead. He turned his eyes to the front of the helicopter and saw Abdullah jump in, fasten his helmet and look over his shoulder. "Haven't had this much fun in a long time," he grinned. He turned on his helmet microphone and turned to Yusuf. "Fly low enough to avoid radar; head east."

Two shots rang out and the window next to Rauser's head shattered. Instinctively he doubled over, his eyes wide with fear. Three more shots rang out. "Get out of here!" Maryam yelled, "Or we'll all be dead!" While the engine revved Abdullah grabbed one of the Kalashnikovs and fired out the shattered window. A cloud of dirt sprayed up at Fouad's feet. The helicopter blades churned up a sandstorm. Rauser saw the two officers shield their eyes and scurry back into the hanger.

Yusuf deftly guided the machine over the compound wall, over the trees and past the last Najran suburb. Everyone sat silent, looking out the window. Rauser exhaled a long slow breath. He was relieved no one was shot. In silence they listened intently to the rhythmic hum of the rotors, wondering if anything had been damaged in the firefight.

They flew barely 50 feet above the desert floor, the wind rushing by the broken window. Then in the distance they saw water.

"Where are we going?" Rauser asked.

"That's the Red Sea." Rauser could barely hear Abdullah over the static and the sound of the rushing air picked up by the microphone. "If we fly several hours this low over the sandy terrain we'll get too much sand in the rotary system and wear out the parts; this fine sand is like sandpaper. We'll fly up the coast of the Red Sea, on the Sudanese side, refuel twice along the coast and then cross into the Sinai Peninsula. We'll need enough fuel to get back."

"Where are we going to stop?

"Our last stop will be Sharm El-Sheikh; we'll never be noticed among all the tourists." Then smiling at Maryam he added, "Maybe we can get you into a bikini and do a little scuba diving."

21

Regrouping in Najran

"Nasty creatures. I think they're both dead." Fouad rolled one limp dog over with his foot.

"Thanks for the quick thinking. I know I need to lose weight; at least I didn't lose it as dog food," Jabir answered gratefully.

Fouad looked up, as the chopper headed for the horizon. He was frustrated. Rauser had been within his reach only to slip away again. He was not going to let the slick American win. This was no longer just about catching a killer. This was about uncovering a conspiracy that could affect the beliefs of millions of Muslims. "We need to have that bird tracked." He pointed his chin in the direction of the receding chopper. "Can you arrange that?"

Jabir pulled out his phone, dialed a number and gave some instructions. "They'll call back in a couple of minutes; in the meantime let's look around the house." Fouad wanted to head directly to the airport but bit his tongue. He followed Jabir back toward the house, past the pool. What a waste of water, he thought. Just for one family.

They entered the house. Although all the ornate furniture impressed him, Fouad's attention was draw to the exquisite round carpet with the minute intricate design. It was worth more than everything he owned! He was still staring at it when he heard Jabir calling him. "Fouad, you have to see this!"

He found Jabir in a room down the hall. He walked through the door, then stopped dead in his track. "Ya salaam. This room is a copy of Salim's lab. He's the dead guy that started this whole investigation."

"Really?" Jabir seemed unimpressed. "I just heard from the airport. Someone is tracking the helicopter." Then he motioned towards the computer. "I noticed it was still on but I couldn't log in. I'll get our guys to hack into it and see if they can find anything useful."

"Tell them to look for documents relating to the Hafsah Quran and Muhammad's last will and testament."

"Are they after the original Quran? I never heard of Muhammad leaving a last will and testament."

"Neither did I, but our preliminary analysis indicates that your Minister of Religious affairs had a hunch Salim was on the cusp of discovering something big." Fouad watched for Jabir's reaction but the captain just kept nosing around the lab. There was nothing else of immediate interest. "How quickly do you think you can get a helicopter to follow them?" Fouad asked as they trotted back to the car.

Jabir turned on the siren. "Not sure. We're a small town and don't have our own police helicopter. It would have to come from a larger police force. This could take several hours to arrange and then it would have to get here. By that time the suspects would be long gone. However, we're tracking them. Let's see where they go. When they land we'll get the police there to intercept them."

Fouad looked out the patrol car window and ground his teeth, a habit which helped him keep his mouth shut when about to say something he might regret. I'm no longer in charge here, he told himself, but I can put plan "B" in place. He pulled out his phone.

"Salaam aleykum Hussein. Any news?"

"Yes sir. I've been digging into the nature of the manuscripts. They seem to have attracted more attention from non-Muslim scholars than Muslim scholars. Most of the interest comes from scholars located in Germany, the U.S. and, oddly, Israel.

"Why Israel?" Fouad asked out loud, wondering if Mossad was involved. Those devious devils would undoubtedly love to get their hands on the documents, not for their historical significance but to use as bargaining chips with their Muslim neighbors.

"Not sure," Hussein replied. "I'll keep looking."

"Bring all the documents you have and join me here for now. I'll arrange a flight for you. You can work with the Najran guys while we track the chopper. I'll meet you at the Najran airport ASAP."

"Did Rauser escape in a helicopter?"

"Along with Maryam and a rich Saudi; I'll tell you more when you get here." Fouad redialed Sana'a and made the necessary requisite for Hussein to fly to Najran. Then he texted the head of the tech department and asked him to send any new documents from Salim's computer to his cell phone and to give hard copies to Hussein. After pressing the 'send' button, he turned to Jabir: "Any news from the airport?"

"They're tracking them." Jabir sported a determined look. "We're gonna catch these guys. No one tries to kill me and gets away without scars." They sped through Najran with lights flashing and siren blaring. It was nice to see Jabir fully engaged, Fouad thought. If they could get the military involved the fugitive chopper would be intercepted within minutes. Jabir pulled into the airport and they bounded up the stairs to air traffic control. "Any indication where the helicopter went?" Jabir asked the man who met them at the door.

"We saw a brief blip on the screen going east; we presume it is the aircraft you asked us to follow."

"How far can you track it?"

"Not far. We've notified the Air Force. They can follow them all the way to Israel if need be."

"Any likelihood they can fly under radar?"

"Easy in the mountains around here. However, when he emerges from the mountains, and if he keeps going east, he'll have a more difficult time, especially if he gets near the Red Sea. There the navy will snag him unless he flies lower than 50 feet."

"Hmm. Let's see what happens..." Fouad turned to his Saudi counterpart. "Could you get permission for our plane from Sana'a to land?" he asked. Jabir nodded, and so did the chief air traffic controller.

"Do you know anything about the owner of that chopper?" Fouad asked.

"A bit. His name is Abdullah Saud. Somehow related to the royal family. He travels a lot. Never runs out of money. I think he has investments in the Emirates. He has a passion for history and teaches the subject as a guest lecturer at different madrassas in the city.

"What about the pilot?"

"Man's name is Yusuf. Philippino. Came as a migrant laborer. Strange, but somehow they became friends. Yusuf often joins him on trips abroad. He functions like an administrative assistant." Interesting, Fouad thought. Might explain why the Saudi was willing to fly Rauser out. Maybe they knew each other through their common interest in history.

The captain's cell phone rang and he walked away. At the same time Fouad felt his own phone buzz. "Salaam Aleykum, ya Hussein."

"I'm on my way to the airport. It looks like I can be in Najran in a couple of hours. Should I be prepared to fly on immediately after we pick you up?"

"Maybe, we'll see. The Saudi Integrated Radar Defense System is tracking them. We'll wait to see where they are heading before we make any decisions."

"How did you get the big guns involved so quickly?"

"My Saudi counterpart arranged it. Good guy. Call back when you land here."

"Tamam. OK."

The Saudi Captain was talking excitedly with one of the air traffic controllers. He turned, smiled over his shoulder and motioned for Fouad to join them. "We think we've spotted them going west; they seem to be headed for the Red Sea. If they're like some of our other terrorists, they'll quickly scurry across the Red Sea and disappear in Sudan's porous coastline, and possibly head up the coast to Egypt. We'll notify the navy."

"Should we notify Interpol?" Fouad asked. "Our office thinks there may be an Israeli connection."

"No point as long as they're in our air space. In Sudan Interpol has no clout. Maybe we should contact the Egyptians. If they're trying to get to Israel they're going to have to fly over their airspace in the Sinai."

"Good idea" Fouad said. "It'll be interesting to see where they lead us."

"No need to hang around here any longer," Jabir said. "Let's go to my office. We might even get something to eat on the way. The guys will call me when something interesting happens."

Fouad felt himself relax over their lunch of fresh bread, soft cheese, honey, and helwa washed down with several glasses of tea. As the small talk turned to family and kids, Jabir's phone rang. Fouad listened in to the conversation. "So are they in Sudan?" There was a brief pause, then: "So you'll let me know if you catch a trace of them again?" followed by another pause. "O.K., thanks for the update." Jabir ended the call and looked at Fouad. "They managed to get into North Sudanese airspace, and landed on the coast. The military is keeping a close eye on the spot and will notify us when they see something depart from there."

"Do you know what town they landed in?"

"There is no town where they disappeared, and the helicopter flew under radar when they got near the coast. The navy's best guess is they landed just north of a place called Dunqunab. They probably needed to refuel." Jabir then added with a smile, "The Sudanese coastline is well known to us as the launching pad for human trafficking. Many Sudanese are smuggled by pirates from their coast to Middle Eastern construction projects where they're used as cheap labour."

"I would guess our fugitive's final destination may be Israel," Fouad responded.

"The navy will let us know if they spot a helicopter taking off and heading up the coast. My guess is that if they want to get into Israel they'll stay in Sudanese airspace for as long as possible, refuel at another camp and then land somewhere in the Sinai dessert."

"In that case our hands are tied until they either land in Egyptian or Saudi Airspace" said Fouad. "And since that will probably take a while I wouldn't mind if you dropped me off at a hotel so I can get a shower and cleaned up."

"Sure." Jabir stood up and paid for the meal. "There is a nice hotel just two blocks from the police station we use regularly for people who come to help us out. You O.K. if I drop you off there? We get a corporate discount which I'll pass on to you."

"Sounds good. Make sure you call me when anything develops."

"Tab'an. Of Course!"

Foaud was glad to get cleaned up. A leisurely shower was followed by prayers and a nap; three hours later he woke up to the phone ringing beside the bed. It was Jabir. "You need to come to the office. We have tracked them up the coast and your hunches are correct. They seem to be heading towards Israel. If so, they will probably use Sharm El Sheik as their jumping off point. We may be able to intercept them there. I've already sent a patrol car over to pick you up."

"Great, I'll be down in the lobby." Within minutes the patrol car arrived. They made their way to the central police station, a sandstone building on the outskirts of town. Faoud climbed the stairs, went up to the captain's office. Jabir was on the phone. Fouad looked around the office, one ear listening in on the conversation. He walked over to the neatly displayed pictures on a desk by the wall that showed a smiling Jabir at the Eiffel tower, another one by the Niagara Falls, and one with Jabir and, presumably, his wife on the Great Wall of China. This guy obviously had a better salary than he did.

Jabir's conversation drew him back to the present: "You mean you're in Sharm Al Sheik now..." followed by a pause. "Great.... Aleykum salaam." Jabir hung up the phone and turned to Fouad. "One of our men is on his way to Sharm Al Sheik right now. He'll get there ahead of the slow-flying helicopter. We're to contact him once we're certain they're heading there."

"Will he try to arrest the suspects if they land there?"

"He can't, but his Egyptian counterpart can. He'll alert them right away."

"Nothing to do but wait," Fouad said. He looked at his watch just as the muezzin sounded the call to prayer.

"Are you a praying man?" Jabir asked. Fouad nodded, and the two walked to a prayer room together. They completed their prostrations and were on their way back to the office when Fouad's phone buzzed. He looked at the screen: "*Landing in ten minutes*".

"My deputy is about to arrive," he said. "I would like to meet him at the airport. Could you lend me a car and driver?" He arrived at the airport just as the Air Yemen plane turned into the receiving gate.

"Salaam Aleykum ya Hussein. Welcome to Saudi Arabia," Fouad greeted his assistant as he came through arrivals.

"Thanks boss." Hussein looked around, "nice, clean airport." They walked out the airport and to the car. "Kind of lonely out here," Hussein commented. "They sure put the airport far from the town."

"Yeah, this isn't Sana'a. How was your trip?"

"Fine."

"Did you get any information on the money trail?"

"It leads to a private foundation that was listed as one of the main donors for the museum that houses the Dead Sea Scrolls."

"Interesting. I wonder why they would want to help out the Yemeni House of Manuscripts when we're on Israel's enemy list."

Hussein shrugged. "Maybe they're interested in old documents," he said as he followed Fouad to the car.

"Or maybe they're paying for Salim's flights out of the country so they can meet him at 'academic conferences.' Perhaps he's a spy." Fouad's voice had a hard edge.

"That could be true." Hussein handed Fouad an envelope. "This is what we pulled out of Salim's computer. You should read it."

Fouad stepped into the car and told the driver to head back to the police station. He opened the envelope, unfolded the printout and began reading:

Implications if the palimpsests regarding Jesus Christ as the Prophet Muhammad's (PM) successor are verified by the Hafsah Quran (HQ): Undermine the legitimacy of Sharia inspired governments/nations; these nations will have to address the reality that their foundational ideas as coming from PM are human political fabrications and have no divine foundations and therefore the political legitimacy of these governments will face erosion; countries affected include all Middle Eastern Countries, North African nations as well as parts of India, Pakistan, Indonesia, Malaysia and southern Philippines. Responses from these nations may include:

- *Attempt to undermine the credibility of the HQ and its assertions (best approach would be to blame Israel and Christians for attempting a 'divide and conquer strategy' as they attempt to control the growing influence of the Middle East);*

- *Create fear by keeping existing blasphemy laws in place and incarcerate/execute anyone asserting the legitimacy of the new 'heretical HQ' find;*

- *Empower clandestine Al Qaida and ISIS groups to do the dirty work by asserting this is just another attempt to undermine Islam and shame the PM;*

- *Secure a common response through the member nations in the Organization of Islamic Cooperation;*

- *Eliminate the documents "accidentally".*

Responses by Non-Islamic nations:

- *Vatican or Russia (via the Orthodox Church) would assert their role as the legitimate prePM heir to the hearts and minds of all those affected, attempting to sway all Muslims in their direction; the means the Orthodox and Catholic church would use to spread their view to the world of Islam would be multi-media (internet, television radio, etc.).*

- *Nations with active Christian missionary efforts (especially U.S. and Southern Africa) would exploit the findings and present themselves as the only legitimate monotheistic expression of Allah's will on earth. Possible mission strategies would include nurturing fear among Muslims of going to hell should they continue to follow the PM—this fear could be exploited to sway people from supporting any Islamic inspired government and orient people towards the West and Christianity.*

"Ya Allah," Fouad muttered under his breath.

"I know," replied Hussein, "it's all I could think of on the way here. We could be opening a Pandora's Box."

Fouad let out a long, audible sigh. "Let's put together the pieces we have so far." He began counting up and down his fingers. "We have a Yemeni curator working in a lab receiving money from a Jewish foundation. In comes Rauser who meets with Salim. Salim ends up dead. It just so happens that Rauser arrived from Germany where Salim's friends and Rauser's academic rivals are also killed. Salim leaves a note before his death regarding his meeting with Rauser which reads, *"Don't get caught discussing something you'll regret."* Then there is the email trail among the pseudonym group stating that they were going to leave Rauser out of their next publication, thus endangering his tenure. We have the Saudi Minister of Religion telling Salim that any untoward documents with respect to Islamic history could trigger an untimely death. There's the email exchange between Rauser and Salim with the pictures of the mutilated bodies. Finally, we have this latest document that hints at global disequilibrium should the Hafsah Quran support Salim's hypotheses regarding its alleged contents."

"Odd conglomeration of data, boss."

Fouad nodded and continued. "Then Rauser and one of the primary investigators join the widow of the deceased and disappear, force their way into Saudi Arabia and connect with an extremely wealthy member of the royal family who has an interest in ancient Islamic documents, has a lab in his basement, and seems to have international connections. They fly off together in the direction of Israel—from where the money originated."

"So... now what?" Hussein looked at his boss.

"We need to find out more about the Saudi local. Why was he prepared to stick his neck out for Rauser? Is he part of the larger Saudi connection? What is driving this guy? Perhaps he's related to Maryam as well." They arrived at the police station and made their way to Jabir's office. It was empty.

"Where do you think they may be heading?" Hussein asked. Fouad walked to a regional map hanging on the wall and looked at it. It was then that he remembered the map hidden in Salim's henna that had remained unanalyzed.

"Hussein, did tech find any maps?"

"Yes, it looks like the one on Salim's hand."

"Were there any specific place names on the map?"

"Yes, but only two made any sense to me."

"What were they?" Fouad asked impatiently.

"Najran and Jerusalem. I don't remember the one in-between." Fouad bit his lower lip. Was Najran a point of departure and Jerusalem the end point? If it was, they should contact the Palestinian authorities. If it wasn't... Rauser could just be hiding behind some sand dune.

22

Flight from Najran

Even with their earphones on they could hear the wind blasting through the helicopter's broken window. They had decided to continue following the clues on the manuscripts and were now headed to St. Catherine's Monastery. Their refueling stops at the coastal towns in Sudan had raised Rauser and Maryam's curiosity about Abdullah and his connections. "These are just work camps," Abdullah had assured them, "catering to small aircraft working for Sudanese oil exploration companies."

Rauser wasn't sure how much of this was true but realized it really didn't make a difference. Sitting back in the helicopter he was tired of the noise and wondered how long they were from the monastery. "How far to St. Catherine's?" he shouted over the wind rushing through the broken window."

"We have to refuel in Sharm El-Sheikh before heading into the Egyptian Sinai. That'll take maybe a half hour."

Rauser noticed Maryam lean back in her chair and look at him. "You know anything about that monastery?" she asked.

"I once spent a month there researching an article about some ancient manuscripts. The place is truly one of kind. I hope the librarian I knew back then is still there. He's an American. Loves ancient manuscripts; a true scholar."

"You think we'll find anything there that'll help us find what Salim was looking for?"

"I wouldn't be surprised. There was a fire there in 1971 which exposed a cellar underneath the chapel. Later, when the monks did a renovation they found hundreds of manuscripts, some dating back to the third century. There were documents written in Arabic, Syrian, Slavonic, Latin and Hebrew. If there's one place that I would hide a manuscript, it would be St. Catherine's Monastery."

"Why?"

"Because it's dry, warm and isolated. You don't have to worry about mold and theft, the prime destructors of ancient manuscripts."

"Is there any reason Hafsah or Omar would ever visit the monastery?"

"We know the Caliph Omar passed it when Jerusalem capitulated to his army. Salim seemed to have surmised that Hafsah's father Omar hid the Hafsah Quran there. That, combined with your family's songs, make me think the place is worth checking out." They fell quiet. Rauser gazed out the shattered window. Could they get into Egypt's Sinai without drawing too much attention, he wondered. Would flying to the monastery by helicopter make them too conspicuous? People normally took the bus or chartered taxi. He looked at the sun-scorched terrain below and the bluish gray haze shrouding the distant hills. It reminded him of the way the sun shimmered off the Yemen desert. Suddenly he felt the helicopter begin to descend.

"We're landing in a few minutes," Abdullah announced. "Stay in the helicopter; we'll refuel and get on with our trip."

"Last stop," thought Rauser when suddenlty the window shattered across from him. The helicopter suddenly lurched to one side, accelerated rapidly, and began to gain altitude. "What's going on?" he yelled. There was no answer. He saw Abdullah frantically manipulating the controls while Yusuf screamed something in an unknown language.

An officer shouted at Fouad, Jabir and Hussein from down the hall and motioned for them to come. "You'll never guess what happened," he said excitedly, "There's a firefight in Sharm El-Sheikh with an Alouette helicopter, the very one we were tracking!"

"Did it go down?"

23

Flight to

St. Catherine's Monastery

"Rauser, grab a weapon and fire back," Abdullah yelled as he veered the helicopter away from the gunfire. "Careful near the windows. The bottom of this thing can take a bullet but the windows can't."

Rauser grabbed a weapon and brought it to his shoulder. He knew it was stupid to fire randomly into a center of tourism, so he fired a burst out the window in the direction of the ocean. No point endangering innocent lives.

"We're going straight into the Sinai," the Saudi shouted from the front seat. "They'll never find us in the desert; it's like Afghanistan – a big rocky sandbox in which to hide," he added with a smile. He pushed the control stick forward and the helicopter swerved into the desert.

Just then another shot rang out. The bullet bored through the Alouette's floor. Yusuf screamed again, bent double and fell unconscious, held in place by his seatbelt. Abdullah's eyes darted between the gauges and the increasingly inhospitable and darkening terrain. The chopper lurched unsteadily towards the mountainous desert, leaving the fancy hotels behind. Someone had decided they were dangerous enough to kill on sight. Who had given that command? "Take a look at Yusuf," Abdullah shouted, "he appears to have lost consciousness."

Rauser nodded, then turned to Maryam. "You keep an eye on the guys below." He lay the machine gun on the floor of the chopper, unbuckled his seat belt, moved the pilot's seat as far back as he could, and did a visual inspection on Yusuf. There was a deep wound on the

Philippino's arm; the blood had already soaked the jacket's sleeve. There was also a blood stain spreading across the lower trouser leg. "Give me something to use as a tourniquet," he shouted at Maryam. She grabbed the bungee cords used to hold down several boxes of ammunition and passed them forward. Rauser fastened one around Yusuf's arm and pulled the other tight around his upper leg. The flow of blood slowed noticeably. "Where's the first aid kit?" he yelled at Abdullah.

"Under Yusuf's seat." Rauser reached past the puddle of blood, extracted a military-looking box from under the seat and gave it to Maryam. "Find the scissors." She fished them out and handed them to him. "Hold Yusuf while I try to fix him up." He cut into the sleeve fabric with steady hands, revealing a mangled mess of skin and blood. He looked into the wound. "The bullet went right through his arm!" he yelled at Maryam.

Suddenly he envisioned himself back with his father, assisting as the old man patched up people in Yemen suffering from gunshot wounds – usually the result of tribal altercation. He pointed at the pressure bandages. "Better open those two and place one on each side of the wound. Apply steady pressure." Maryam applied the pressure as Rauser grabbed a roll of tape, wound it tightly around the bandages and removed the tourniquet. "Let's treat the leg," he hollered. He bent over Yusuf's leg, cut away the fabric and pulled open the wound.

"Pinchers." The command reminded him of his father giving orders to an assisting nurse. Maryam rummaged through the first aid kit and handed him a pair of pinchers. He dug into the wound, glad Yusuf was unconscious. The pain would have been unbearable.

The pinchers touched something hard. "I got it," he yelled, and pulled out the lead, raising it like a trophy. Maryam handed him another pressure bandage. He grabbed the tape and wrapped it tight. "That should do for now; let's hope he didn't lose too much blood." Rauser took a deep breath, and squeezed back into the back seat.

"Good job," Abdullah shouted. We're getting close to the monastery—but we're not going to make it. One of the bullets must have nicked an oil line; we've been losing pressure slowly. We're going to ditch within five minutes." Rauser looked at his watch. He'd lost all track of time while attending Yusuf.

Suddenly Abdullah hit the power switch. "No more oil," he muttered. The engines went quiet as the chopper's blades went into autorotation. Rauser saw Abdullah work the directional pedals to counteract the lack of torque effect and work his cyclic control stick while the chopper began a slow, perfectly silent descent. It landed at a slight angle on the side of a sloping dune. Abdullah opened the door, got out and removed his helmet. The others followed after him. The Saudi reached back into the machine and grabbed two of the AK 47s. "Take one of these," he said as he handed one of the weapons to Rauser. Then he unbuckled Yusuf, slung the AK 47 over his shoulder and wrapped one of Yusuf's arms around his neck, pulling him out of his seat and through the door. "If we can get to the monastery they may allow Yusuf to take refuge there." Rauser grabbed one of Yusuf's arms while Abdullah grabbed the other and slowly they walked away from the downed helicopter, Yusuf dangling between them. Rauser looked down at Yusuf's bandaged leg -- it dragged like an unmanned plough leaving a scar in the dirt. This is not good, thought Rauser, but suddenly he didn't care. The gunshots and the adrenalin now triggered painful memories which flooded uncontrollably over him.

Ruth, his wife, had also died in a hail of shrapnel. She had just left the room—said she wanted to go for a walk to think about what they should do—wanted to pray while she walked the beach. She never made it to the beach. The car bomb had gone off minutes after she had left the hotel. He had run down the stairs and into a dust covered street. People were screaming and yelling; chaos everywhere. He never really found her; they only found parts of her. She was killed instantly. After the funeral he had told God that he needed time to process the death. He was still processing.

He looked up. The orange sun created an eerie silhouette of Maryam. She was carrying one of the AK 47s. Around them lay nothing but mountains of rock, pebbles and sand. No one spoke as they trudged towards the mountain. Finally Maryam broke the silence. "Just think, this is the place where Allah gave his ten commandments to the Jewish people."

"I can see why," said Rauser, sweat beading on his forehead. "This forsaken place yells, 'Don't come near or you'll die." The thought of God speaking again reminded him of his Ruth. She too had gone to hear God speak. She wanted guidance about what they should do: go to China or stay in the Middle East. That's why she had gone to pray.

They'd had a great marriage and often prayed together. Their first year of university had been pure bliss and they were married by the third. Those early years had been the best of his life: long walks, biking and exploring downtown Chicago for the best cheap diners. The shortage of money was no object to their happiness; they had each another. After graduation his ROTC commitment had sent them to Saud Arabia. For him, the Middle East was home, but Ruth felt far from home. She wanted him to request a placement in China, where she had grown up. It was the oppressive ways the Middle East treated its women that had kept her from enjoying the rich culture. The bomb went off while they were on vacation in Lebanon trying to discern what God would have them do...

Rauser heard the faint noise of an engine and snapped back into the presence. He looked around and noticed a vehicle approaching them in a dark brownish cloud of dust. It would pass them tangentially on a road. "I'll take care of it," Abdullah said. He lowered Yusuf to the ground and ran towards the road waving his arms. Rauser and Maryam gratefully flopped onto a rock in the rapidly falling darkness and watched the energetic Abudullah run towards the dusty cloud.

Jabir briefly looked up from the phone: "They damaged the helicopter." One hand cupped the telephone's mouthpiece. All the men in the office were looking at him. A few seconds later he whispered again: "One of the windows was broken – maybe both."

"Did it go down?" Fouad probed frustrated. The Egyptians had fired at the suspects based solely on a hunch he'd relayed via Jabir. If Maryam was killed and proven to be innocent he would have a major problem back in Yemen. He needed to get back into the action.

With his hand still over the mouthpiece, Jabir whispered: "They're not sure."

"Which direction did it go?"

Jabir relayed the question and held up his hand as he listened intently. Fouad focused on the phone like a tiger about to pounce. What's taking them so long? Why can't Jabir use the speaker phone! "It was headed north. The military are keeping a close eye on it. They're somewhere in the Sinai Peninsula."

"Is the Egyptian military involved?"

"Yes." He had to make a decision. The prey wasn't just hiding behind the next sand dune; it had moved to its next hideout. He turned to Hussein. "Here's what we should do. You go to the Sinai Peninsula and I'll go to Palestine.

"Why Palestine?"

"Three reasons: first, my gut tells me that's where I should go, and second, the henna map indicates three points, the last of which was Jerusalem. Since Najran proved correct, I'm willing to believe that the third is correct as well, especially now that we know the direction Rauser is heading."

"And the third reason?"

"The money came from Israel. My gut tells me they have a sugar daddy in Jerusalem."

24

Omar's Neighborhood

Omar vowed that today he would confront those haunting demons of the past. He was determined to walk the street of his youth without losing control of his anger and lashing out at the first Israeli he saw.

The day started off well. The old man at the desk had appeared happy when Omar booked his room, one of the more expensive ones in Jerusalem's old city. He had slept well, took his time eating his breakfast, signed the bill, re-tucked his kaffiyeh so it sat on his head at a rakish angle, got up and headed out the front door. He waited for the right bus and took it to East Jerusalem. The trendy shops outside of the old walls and the convoys of busses filled with tourists hadn't changed. As he looked out the window he noted how they crossed the invisible border between east and west Jerusalem. Suddenly roads were not as nice and the houses had water storage containers on their roof. The Palestinians never knew when the Israelis might turn off their water.

Emerging from the bus he surveyed the Jewish pedestrians hurrying down the sidewalk, their black fedoras and dark clothes adding a sense of sobriety to the old neighborhood. The neighborhood had been invaded. His stomach turned when he saw the Israeli security patrol walking towards him, their automatic weapons slung over their shoulders, eyes scanning the crowd. Their eyes met momentarily but he looked away. "Racist pigs," he muttered under his breath. They were the ones who had destroyed his life.

He hated Jerusalem. He hated the soldiers and hated his childhood memories. He would never have come back if Siddiqi hadn't asked him personally. "Don't think about the explosion," he kept telling himself. But the more he tried not to, the more the memories flooded back. His hand automatically felt for the non-existent Yagil. "I need to stay focused," he whispered, and his hand dropped to his side.

As he turned into his childhood street he wondered if anyone would recognize him. He was surprised to see old Mr. Abraham, the eccentric Jew, come shuffling down the street. That kindly man had always treated him with respect. He looked somewhat haggard, yet smiled and nodded in his direction. The old man clearly did not recognize the Arab with the moustachless beard and long robe as the same kid he had spoiled with candies from the market. Omar was tempted to greet the old man but decided to stay true to Siddiqi's directives.

Suddenly he felt confused. Had he taken a wrong turn somewhere? Home should have been right here! Was his memory fading? This had to be his street! Then it struck him: The cursed Jews had bulldozed his home and built a three story apartment building on the spot! There were no Palestinian homes left—he was the only Arab in the area!

His eyes rested on the second floor balcony. It was the ear locks dancing under the kippahs on each child's head – each bob of the ridiculous strands of hair triggered a wave of anger that threatened to explode from him. "Stay focused before you do something stupid," he whispered to himself "they're not the killers." He closed his eyes, grabbed the street sign, sweat now beading on his forehead. "One ... two... three... four... five..." he counted through clenched teeth and released the sign. It was a trick Siddiqi had taught him to cool down and regain his composure.

Just look straight ahead, he said to himself; don't let them get to you. After five paces he silently quoted the Quranic verse that Siddiqi had given him in preparation for this mission: *When you meet in battle those who do not believe, turn not your backs to them.*

His memories returned. Home had been filled with laughter, hugs and a never ending supply of food streaming from the kitchen. He could almost smell the fresh pita bread from the former bakery next door, and feel his father's encouraging pats on his head. *Why, O Allah, have you allowed this injustice and pain? When will you finish testing me?*

He came to the end of the street and leaned against the bus stop. He was exhausted. His right hand grabbed for the box around his neck; again he felt nothing. "I'll never come back here again," he mumbled.

His childhood had ended when the Jewish settlers had insisted they owned his family's home. "You have no ownership papers," they had alleged. His father had shown the certificate dating back to the Ottoman Empire, but they said it was invalid, and had taken them to court. The Jewish judge had sided with the settlers. They needed ownership papers from the state of Israel because Ottoman certificates had no legal standing in modern Israel. Trying to get an Israeli land certificate had been futile; they had met one time delaying tactic after another. The subsequent legal battles had sucked up most of the family finances—and were never concluded. One day as he came home from school—he was in seventh grade—he heard an explosion. He had run down the street to see what had happened. Old Mr. Abraham had intercepted him. The man had grabbed him in a bear hug and tried to turn him away from his house. "Son," the old man had said with pain in his eyes, "I am so sorry."

He had torn himself free and rushed towards the acrid-smelling dust cloud. His mother lay unconscious, crushed by the supporting beam that had held the second floor rafters. Her head lay in a pool of blood. There were screams from his brothers and sisters. Mr. Muhammad, their neighbor, was yelling over and over that Allah had punished them for collaborating with the enemy. "Traitor, traitor, traitor," the man had shouted. He never found out what Mr. Muhammad had meant with that accusation. Perhaps it had been his father's friendship with Mr. Abraham.

Several ambulances had come. They took everyone else to the hospital. He was left him standing alone on the sidewalk. Mr. Abraham had come after the last ambulances had left and offered to take him to the hospital. It had been the first time he had ever seen the inside of a hospital. Everything had seemed strange: the smells, the clothes and the hushed tones people used in the waiting room. Eventually a doctor had approached Mr. Abraham and whispered something in his ear. Mr. Abraham had then taken him to the corner of the waiting room, sat him down and told him that his family were all dead. He remembered screaming from shock and the scowls it precipitated from everyone in the waiting room—especially from the men in the black fedoras.

After the mass funeral he had moved in with his uncle and aunt. They never stopped reminding him of the sacrifice they made to feed him and buy him clothes. Finally the uncle found a madrassah that had taken him in as an orphan. That is where he had learned to hate. He grew to hate Allah who had allowed his family to be destroyed, the Jews who had ensured they never got ownership papers to their own house, and his Muslim neighbors who had destroyed his family honor by calling them traitors. "Don't trust anyone," he had resolved, "Only yourself."

Omar's thoughts were interrupted when the bus pulled up. He dropped the fare into the bin and noticed the Jewish mothers pulling their children a little closer. He smiled. Their fearful reaction made him feel powerful. He found a seat on the bus, next to a Jewish lady. He returned to the Arabic quarter and went to his hotel room. He pulled out his phone. There was a text from Siddiqi: "Faizal Abbas will help you. Look in the old Arabic Quarter behind the Golden Gate hostel. He recently returned from the hajj. The house has green and white markings."

Now we wait until Siddiqi gives the 'go-ahead.' I wonder who this Faizal Abbas is and if he works for Siddiqi? He glanced out the window. There, on the next ridge, he could see the Dome of the Rock glistening in the sun. His father had once taken him there to pray. Lining up with hundreds of men, every knee bowed and every forehead on the ground in humility before Allah had been exhilarating. He always imagined himself kneeling as one warrior among a thousand, all in reverence before the divine general, who had only to give the order, at which immediately he, along with the hundreds around him, would rise up and conquer the enemy. If only life had turned out like that.

He went back down to the lobby, stepped outside, and sauntered towards the Damascus Gate. As he walked down the ancient steps he glanced at the age-old doors and noticed the bullet holes. He was proud of the way his people had fought during the 1967 Six Day War. Pressing his way through the hawkers yelling and clapping for his attention, he pushed his way through the crowded, narrow streets and into the first restaurant he saw. A young man led him to a table near the back of the restaurant. He ordered a falafel and freshly squeezed orange juice. Next to him two students, their sharia textbooks piled on the edge of the table, were arguing.

The most argumentative one was dressed in jeans and a t-shirt. "I hate suicide bombers," the man exclaimed, "they just terrorize in the name of Islam; they do not build up Islam. They destroy it!"

"Why do you always focus on the darker side of Islam?" the other responded.

"We need to be honest about our history or we'll just repeat its mistakes," the student in the blue jeans responded. "There never was a 'Golden Age'. If Muhammad, praise his name, couldn't usher it in, why trust the likes of Siddiqi and his *Palestine Islamic Jihad* movement to do any better?" A tremor shivered up Omar's spine.

The student sitting furthest from him swallowed a piece of meat from his kabob and went on: "The Islamists tell us that if we change our ways and apply the laws of Allah we will once again be blessed with wealth and prosperity. Ludicrous. If we lost the war in 1967 because Allah was angry with us, then why did Israel win? Was Allah demonstrating his pleasure with the Israelis? If our declining standard of living is due to Allah's displeasure, then is God more pleased with China? Their standard of living is going up all the time and most of them are atheists!"

Omar feared the blasphemous morass that lay beyond the arguments. If Muhammad could not inaugurate the ideal state, then who could? He had to leave this den of blasphemy. He left half of his food uneaten on his plate, paid his bill and slipped into the narrow alleys of the Arabic quarter. The noise of the hawkers, tourists, and shopkeepers irritated him. "I'll head to where Faizal is supposed to live. It'll help me be on time when Siddiqi gives the order," he thought. He passed the spot where an Israeli soldier had apprehended him seven years ago for throwing rocks. That was the last time he had been in Jerusalem, other than for legal hearings and his prison sentence.

It was while he was in prison that Siddiqi had written him. Siddiqi had gotten his name from his Hamas section leader. The letter had promised that if he needed any help to contact him. Initially he had been skeptical. Yet there was no one else to help him so he had let fate take its course.

Siddiqi was there when he walked out the prison gates and had embraced him like a father. "Son," he had said, "you are the future of Palestine. It is men like you who know how to suffer and yet stay true; your generation will bring greatness to Palestine." They had gone into East Jerusalem and celebrated his release with a houseful of PIJ supporters. There had been plenty of food and the celebration had been exuberant. The men had even carried him on their shoulders around the living room. It was the first time in his life that he had felt like he could make a difference in the world.

Siddiqi had become his adopted father. They had traveled together, studied the Quran together and waged jihad against the Israeli oppressors. It was through Siddiqi that he had learned of the holiness of Allah: "Heaven will never be heaven if sinners are admitted," had been Siddiqi's mantra, "so never compromise." Between themselves they had vowed a "No Compromise Covenant", and this had become their motto. He relished this memory.

"Yagil," he whispered, "within a few days I'll have the package controlling a billion Muslims in my hand. Now that is power!" His hand reached for the box around his neck but once again fell limply at his side. What, exactly, would this document say that made Siddiqi think it would give him almost unlimited power in the Muslim world, he wondered.

26

St. Catherine's Monastery

Rauser and Maryam could see the vehicle's headlights come to a stop. There was a long pause, then they saw the lights turn and wobble towards them across the desert floor. Abdullah pulled up beside them and rolled down the window. "Did you order a taxi," he grinned.

"How did you get the car?" asked Rauser. "What happened to the driver?"

"My father always said, 'carry a big wad of cash along with a big stick and you'll be prepared for anything.'"

"So what did you do? Threaten the driver and then leave him stranded?"

"No, no no," Abdullah replied with a smile, "I made a little small talk, told him our helicopter had engine trouble, and then asked him to give me a fair price for his nice car. I mentioned an exorbitant amount which I then shoved under his nose without dickering. He was very pleasantly surprised to get that amount for this old crate, wrote a bill of sale on the back of a piece of paper and gave me the keys!" He hopped out of the car and opened the passenger door. Maryam and Rauser slowly lifted Yusuf into a sitting position. The man stirred and mumbled something in what Rauser figured was Filipino. They gently sat him in the front seat and buckled the seat belt around him. Rauser and Maryam put the guns in the back and then slid in the back as well. After carefully examining Yusuf's wounds, Abdullah slid behind the steering wheel and put the car into gear.

Rauser had to smile. He liked Abdullah's audacity. "So is the poor sucker you bought this beater from going to be stranded in the desert?"

"He asked for a ride back to Sharm El-Sheikh, but I told him we were planning on staying at the monastery. I gave him a second wad of money so he could call a taxi."

"Nice..." Maryam nodded sagaciously. Rauser glanced out the car window and took in the darkening landscape. His mind drifted to what happened here thousands of years ago. He found himself imagining the Old Testament Israelites encamped as they awaited the Ten Commandments. He looked at the peak of the mountain and imagined lightning and thunder rolling over it, and Moses walking down the mountain, his head glowing like a light bulb because he had been in the presence of Jehovah. That must have been a sight, especially if Moses came down at night... His thoughts were interrupted by Yusuf's groaning.

"When we get to the monastery, let me talk to the monks," he said from the back seat. "If Father Constantin is still there, I'm sure he'll do anything he can to help us." Half an hour later and they pulled up to the monastery's main gate. Rauser stepped out of the vehicle. The building loomed dark, a few lights were shining from the enormous corners. The tourists had long departed.

He knocked hard on the door. It took time, but eventually a youngish man in a monk's robe opened a latch. "Al deir makful," he said. The monastery is closed.

"Aaref," Rauser said. "I know. I'm a long-time friend of Father Constantin, the librarian. I've come to visit him." The door opened a crack and Rauser slipped inside. He nodded at the man. "I know the way," he said, and quickly found his way through the maze of alleys to the library, with the doorman in tow. He knocked on the door. It cracked open.

"Dr. Rauser, is that you?" a bearded priest, his black smiling eyes complemented by his black robe and black hat, grabbed his hand in both of his. He pulled open the door a little wider. "I didn't know you were coming again to our monastery. You here to study?"

"No. This trip wasn't on my agenda; it unexpectedly fell into my lap. I'm really glad you're still here."

"The pleasure's mine." Father Constantin opened the door wide to let Rauser in. That's when he looked down and noticed Rauser's bloody pants. "You look a little worse for wear."

"I have an injured man in the car – it's his blood. Do you think he could stay here for a few days?"

"Sure," said the priest with a concerned look in his eye. "Let me get Father Justin. He knows a bit about medicine."

"Thanks; I'll get the injured man. Where should I bring him?"

"Take him to the infirmary. I'll meet you there." Father Constantin closed the library door and disappeared down one of the alleyways while Rauser returned to the Land Rover. The other two were standing around the front hood. He noticed a bag at Abdullah's feet. "What's that?" he asked.

"I had Maryam buy some burqas from a gal packing up her wares at the edge of the parking lot. She was just boxing up her wares when I noticed her. We may need to disappear suddenly."

They carried Yusuf through the alleyways to the infirmary. Father Constantin was waiting for them with another man whom Rauser presumed to be Father Justin. "What happened?"

"Yusuf had an accident," Abdullah replied. "It may be best," he added softly, "if he remained out of sight for a few days. There are some unsavory characters interested in him."

Father Constantin looked at Father Justin who just shrugged. "I think that can be arranged. It wouldn't be the first time."

They placed Yusuf on one of the beds. Father Justin asked about the wounds and Maryam gave a quick synopsis. As Maryam talked, Father Justin cut the bandages and began washing the wounds. When Maryam had finished talking he looked up. "I think I can take it from here," he said. He glanced at Rauser. "Don't feel you need to stick around."

Rauser turned to Father Constantin. "Do you think my friends and I could stay in the guest house for the night?"

"Not a problem. Its low season and the middle of the week. Why don't you go get your stuff and we'll get things set up. Meet me in the priests' dining room and we'll eat together before you turn in."

25

Arabic Quarter, Jerusalem

Omar had spent the afternoon walking the streets of the Old City. Now he sat back on his knees, turned his eyes towards heaven and uttered an addendum to his evening prayers: "Allah", he intoned, "please use your servant this evening and continue to heal the wounds of my past. Help me enter the *Well of Souls* and guide my eyes to your revelation." Leaving the prayer room he walked through the alleys of the Arabic quarter towards the home of Faizal. Every now and then he looked up at the cameras that monitored everyone and everything. Most of the kiosks and hawkers had packed up their wares and gone home, leaving just a handful of sellers eager to make a last-minute sale. A group of college students sporting short skirts and bare shoulders passed him; he averted his gaze.

One block from the Church of the Holy Sepulcher he noticed an old man with a crisp, new white and black taqiyah draped from his head which contrasted sharply with his old, brown suit. The man shuffled towards him talking under his breath. They were about to pass in the darkened alleyway when the old man grabbed Omar's hand and looked directly in his eyes. "Young man," he said, "follow the way of peace." He then dropped his hand and slipped into an alleyway. Odd fellow, Omar thought. Could this be a message from Allah? His pace slowed. Perhaps this is Allah's affirmation that I'm on the right path. I could be averting a potential world war against the truth of Islam by ensuring these ancient manuscripts don't fall into the hands of pagans and infidels.

He trudged on, his eyes constantly moving from the cameras to the fur capped Hassidic Jews going to dance at the Wailing Wall. He paused for a moment to verify the address of Faizal's home and stopped in front of a wall marked with green, white and red paint. "May Allah grant me strength," he prayed as he raised his fist, knocked twice, and shouted the Arabic greeting of peace: "Salaam Aleykum!"

Rauser had enjoyed a refrehing shower. He slipped into the clean pair of pants and t-shirt which father Constantine had left on the bed, headed for the priests' dining room, and placed himself next to Constantin. He was surpised to see that Maryam and Abdullah were already there. A simple fare of breads and cheeses graced the long communal table. "So, my friend," what brings you here under these circumstances," asked Father Constantin while offering him some tea.

Rauser looked his old friend in the eye. "We're looking for a document that we've been led to believe may be in this monastery. It's an old version of the Quran, perhaps the oldest ever penned."

"You mean the Hafsah Quran?" Father Constantin leaned back in his chair.

"You know about it?" asked Rauser surprised.

"Of course. But you know this place—it knows how to hold its secrets. The Codex Sinaiticus only came to light in the 19th century. Could the Hafsah Quran be here? I'm not going to say 'no.'"

"Is that the same as 'yes'?"

Constantin smiled. "Our sources indicate that Hafsah never came through here, but it's highly likely that her father Umar did. His relationship with the Christians around Palestine was close. Tradition states that he came through by camel accompanied by a servant while on his way to Jerusalem when the Orthodox Patriarch was ready to hand Jerusalem over to Umar's army. The Patriarch didn't want Jerusalem destroyed, and insisted on making the agreement with Umar himself. The tradition states that Umar walked in through the gates of Jerusalem, holding the rope of the camel upon which sat his servant."

"How does this relate to the Hafsah Quran?" Rauser asked sipping his tea.

"I'll get to that, my friend. First let me give you some background information that will help you in your search. My hypothesis is that Umar was a misguided Muslim-Christian or, in other words, a Messianic Muslim. This explains why Uthman, the editor of the Qur'an in use today, tried to talk Umar out of coming to Jerusalem. Umar turned a deaf ear to Uthman and went to Jerusalem anyway. The question is, why did Uthman try to prevent Umar from going to Jerusalem, and why did Umar insist on going?"

"Perhaps they had different views on the importance of Jerusalem?"

"I think that's right," the priest responded. "Uthman manipulated the way the Muslim community came to view things. They suddenly came to see religious differences as being of fundamental importance, whereas the earlier Muslims saw only socio-economic differences. That's why Umar wanted to keep Jerusalem intact while Uthman was ready to raze anything and everything related to Christianity or Judaism, including the city of Jerusalem itself."

Rauser processed Father Constantin's theory. He had heard the term Messianic Muslim before but never in a historical context. "But that still doesn't answer the question about the whereabouts of the Hafsah manuscript..."

"My guess is that it is hidden somewhere else, some place that both Umar and Hafsah would have considered religiously significant.

"You mean Jerusalem?"

Suddenly Abdullah Saud joined the conversation. "Umar commissioned the Dome of the Rock, though it was actually built about 150 years later by the Caliph Abd al Malik." Abdullah paused momentarily. "I personally think the place should be called 'Umar's Martyrium'."

Rauser and Maryam were nonplussed. Father Constanin smiled broadly. "Go on," he encouraged the Saudi royal.

"Well, if you look carefully at the layout of the Dome of the Rock you can see that it was not designed to be a mosque. Mosques are built in such a way that they force people to pray in the direction of Mecca. The Dome of the Rock doesn't meet that condition. Architecturally it was designed to be a martyrium, a place to bury important people. In fact, it is modeled after another famous martyrium, the Church of the Holy Sepulcher. Both places were designed to commemorate deaths. In the case of the Church of the Holy Sepulcher we know whose death and resurrection it celebrates." Rauser raised his eyes in surprise at the Muslim's affirmation of the death and resurrection of Jesus Christ.

"You mean Jesus Christ?" Maryam asked.

"Right. Ancient martyriums allowed people to walk around the tomb of the deceased. In the Church of the Holy Sepulcher you walk around an empty grave."

"So why might the Dome of the Rock be a martyrium? Who's the martyr?" Rauser wondered aloud.

Father Constantin picked up the thread of the conversation from Abdullah. "Umar was probably one of the most devout followers of Allah after Muhammad. He couldn't really build a martyrium for Muhammad in Jerusalem—he was already buried in Mecca. But he could build a martyrium for another reason."

"Like what?" asked Rauser

"The revelation of Allah."

"A martyrium for the first Quran?" Maryam's eyebrows shot up.

Constantin paused, reached for the pita bread, tore off a bit, chewed on it and took a sip of tea. Suddenly Abdullah's eyes lit up with excitement. "Of course! That's probably where we get the Muslim tradition of burying old Qurans from!"

Father Constantin looked at him with his eyes a twinkle, adjusted his robe and nodded. "That's right. Think about it," the priest continued. "After Muhammad died, Hafsah found herself in possession of the best collection of the very words of Allah. Now imagine Caliph Umar and his daughter sitting over a meal and talking about the document in her possession, the only thing she had that would be of interest to future generations. If I was Hafsah, or her father, I would want to ensure that Allah's latest revelation, the Quran, would be enshrined forever. I would therefore commission the biggest martyrium I could afford." Father Constantin took a sip of tea and briefly paused. "The purpose would not be to commemorate the life of Muhammad, but to commemorate God's new revelation to humanity. You need to remember that for the Arabs it was as if an Arabic renaissance had taken place. For the first time in history they had a prophet of their own who had given them Allah's words, much like the Jews had received them from Moses and the Christians from Jesus. Just like Jesus, who was God's embodied revelation for the Christians, Arabs finally had a revelation from God in their own language."

Abdullah had been listening intently, his eyes never leaving Father Constantin's face. It was as if he was enraptured. "If I was Umar," he said with shining eyes, "I would build something that both celebrated these words, drew people to pay respects to these words and safeguarded them for eternity. I would build something beautiful, worthy for God himself. I would decorate the walls of this building with words drawn from the memory of this Arabic prophet, peace be upon him, in order to truly focus people's attention to his revelation."

Rauser leaned back in his chair and looked at the Arab. Obviously the man was on board with Father Constantin's hypothesis. He, however, had his doubts. "Why Jerusalem?" he asked. "Why not Mecca or Medina or some other Arabian city?"

Father Constantin took another sip of tea, nodded, and continued thoughtfully. "Because Jerusalem is the center of God's revelation throughout religious history. Remember, this is before Mecca became a dominant religious place of pilgrimage. I believe Umar was a Muslim-Christian, a believer in God, and probably a follower of Jesus.

According to the Jewish narratives, which Umar must have known, God began the creation of the world on the temple mount. Abraham, the father of all Arabs, sacrificed his son there. The temple of God's Shekinah glory was in Jerusalem, and Jesus is coming back there at the end of the world. Do you know the title Muslims have for Jesus? They call him the "al-Kelima" or "The Word'. This means that the martyrium Umar commissioned, one that predated the final edited version of the Uthman Quran, would be identified with the new 'Word'. If you go inside the Dome of the Rock what do you see? Words, words and more words, and if you compare them to the carbon dating of the oldest Qurans they may predate the text of today's oldest Quran." Rauser was impressed with the logic of Father Constantin's theory. Nothing the old monk mentioned contradicted the clues Salim had left: the map on Salim's hand had indicated Jerusalem, and the song sung by Maryam's aunt had also mentioned al-Quds, Jerusalem. They would have to go there.

He glanced at his watch. He knew the monks had a tradition of going to sleep at midnight. "Father Constantin," he said, sliding his chair backwards a few feet, "I want to thank you for sharing your hospitality and understanding of Islamic history with us this evening. The three of us have had a long day, and if it's O.K. with you, I think we're ready to turn in for the night."

Constantin smiled and nodded. "I will show Ms. Maryam and Mr. Saud the way back through this maze, and then I'll return to pick you up."

Left alone, Rauser began to look around the dining room. His attention was initially drawn to the Byzantine icons hanging on the walls. He scrutinized each one until he came to a table under one of the icons. Looking down his attention was drawn to three large old coins used as paperweights on top of a stack of paper. He picked one up, turned it over and noticed the symbol: a cross emblazoned in the center of the coin with the letters MHMD, inscribed around the edge. He examined the other coins as well. *I wonder why they're here.*

Constantin opened the dining room door behind him. "You find the old coins interesting?"

"Fascinating." Rauser looked up. "When were these minted?"

"During the time of the first caliphs."

"Where did you find them?"

"While renovating the floor of the old mosque here in the compound."

"If you add the missing vowels between the consonants inscribed around the edge of the coin you end up with 'Muhammad.'"

"That's another reason I strongly suspect Muhammad and the first two caliphs may have been Arabic followers of Jesus. These coins were minted before Islam became an anti-Christian religion. It was before Uthman's editorializing of the Quran, before Muslims were encouraged to shape their identity as 'anti-Christ' instead of as 'Arabic followers of Jesus.'"

"Who would have dreamt that the cross and the name of Muhammad would ever have been minted on the same coin," Rauser mused. "It's fascinating! What if Muhammad really did see himself as a follower of the cross."

"At this point it's just a theory."

"So I guess I should go to Jerusalem if I want to test it...?"

"That's right."

"We're planning to leave early tomorrow morning." Rauser put the coin back on the paper. "I'll let you know if your hypothesis is correct, but before I do, I'd like to take a few pictures of them with my cell phone."

27

The Dome of the Rock, Jerusalem

"Ahlan we sahlen. Welcome." Faizal said. "Siddiqi told me you would come." The skinny little man looked like he would blow over in a stiff breeze.

Omar looked around nervously at the little courtyard. He had seen enough cameras in the old city to know he would have been filmed entering this place. He suspected that cameras were pointed into the private courtyard as well. "How will we avoid being intercepted?"

"We can get almost the whole way by walking from roof to roof," Faizal answered. "When we get close to the wall we go down through my uncle's home and then slip in through the Omar gate. It opens directly into the Old City."

"How are you connected to Siddiqi?" Omar was trying to piece together the pieces of Siddiqi's puzzle.

"Siddiqi has helped me financially ever since my father was imprisoned for inciting terrorism. He gave a rousing sermon in the mosque..." Faizal suddenly grinned. "It was a good one."

"So now what do you do?"

"I clean the Dome of the Rock. I sweep, mop and empty the garbage. It helps pay the bills." Omar nodded. That explained why Siddiqi had directed him to Faizal and why Faizal felt obliged to help.

"When can we go?"

"Whenever you're ready."

"How will we get in?"

"As the janitor I have keys." Faizal patted his pocket. They climbed the stairs to the roof. Omar was surprised when Faizal interrupted the silence. "Where around here did you grow up?"

"What makes you think I grew up around here?"

"Your accent. Over the years I have heard every possible accent as I clean the mosque. I try to guess where people are from. You grew up in east Jerusalem."

"That's right." A few hours ago he was walking in his old neighborhood where no one recognized him, and now, within a few minutes, this janitor had pinpointed his birthplace. He should be working for Palestinian Intelligence, Omar thought.

"You must have visited the mosque before."

"Once. When I was a child."

"Just once?"

"Yes." Omar was uncomfortable with the small talk, especially with someone he didn't know.

"You must be very well connected to get a personal pass to come here to pray by yourself. This never happens."

Janitor, you have no idea how well connected I am.

Faizal opened the door to the roof balcony. Stars blinked overhead. Omar could hear the noise of the traffic down below as he followed Faizal from roof to roof, never sure where one home finished and the next one began. He noticed the black outlines of numerous crosses, minarets, and domes silhouetted in the night lights of Jerusalem. They came to the edge of the wall encircling the Dome of the Rock. Faizal opened another door and turned on a light. They walked down a staircase into the living space below. There was no one there. They entered another courtyard. Faizal opened the front door and Omar found himself looking at the Omar Gate. He scanned for cameras but couldn't see any. They crossed the street and walked through the gate.

He followed Faizal up the broad stairs and stopped. Omar took a deep breath, as his mind took in the immensity of what could happen in a few minutes. The anticipation of what he might find caused his heart to beat faster. By morning he would be holding the original Quran: the very words of Allah.

Spotlights illuminated the great Dome of the Rock, and Omar glanced at it before following Faizal past the large marble columns and towards the door. The janitor held the door open for him. He heard it close behind Faizal.

As soon as his eyes adjusted to the light they were drawn to the great golden cupola. The elaborate red and gold floral decorations meticulously interwoven with Arabic inscriptions awed him, and the stylized representation of vegetation made him feel he was entering paradise. He noticed the exotic golden breastplates and crowns depicted in the stunning tile work. He had entered the home of royalty. Then the initial sense of awe at all this opulence gave way to a feeling of waste. What a waste of money, he thought. We Muslims can be so stupid. If we all stayed focused on empire building instead of wasting money on extravagant buildings we would have attained world domination long ago.

"The Dome of the Rock is a replica of the Church of the Holy Sepulcher," Faizal said, interrupting the silence. "The dimensions are almost identical: the size of the dome, the pillars and everything are almost a carbon copy of the original church just a few blocks from here, the one built centuries before the present church."

"It's time we built our identity in relationship to Allah's revelation, not based on differentiating ourselves from Christians and Jews," Omar said. *Where did that come from; you never talk with such conviction-especially with strangers!*

"That's a good point," Faizal responded. "I'm always amazed at how closely Christian and Jewish groups work together in Jerusalem. Why can't we get along with them?"

"We shouldn't try to get along with them," Omar responded hotly. "We need to bring them under our rule. We honor their prophets Moses and Jesus, but they don't honor the seal of the prophets."

"Would you like me to show you around the building? I noticed you were looking at the rock," Faizal asked.

May Allah guide me to the Well of Souls. Omar forced a smile. "That would be greatly appreciated."

"I have worked here for 20 years. My favorite part is The Rock. You see this hole?" he said pointing to a small hole in the southeastern corner. "This rock is also known as the "Pierced Stone", or "Adam's Naval", because it has a small cave underneath called the *Well of Souls.*" Omar wanted to ask how one might get to the Well of Souls, but Faizal just kept on talking. "That small hole connects the cave to the stone which lies over the cave. Most Jews believe this is the spot where the Holy of Holies was located in the Jewish temple."

"Amazing," mumbled Omar, torn between wanting to know more and wanting to get on with his mission. "Can you tell me more about the *Well of Souls?*"

"The *Well of Souls* has a rich history. The name comes from the Jewish belief that voices of the dead could be heard along with the sounds of the Rivers of Paradise from this spot in the Holy of Holies. What probably happened was that voices of the worshippers up in the temple reverberated in the cave. These mistaken echoes were presumed to originate from the souls of the dead."

"Why is it called the *Well of Souls?*"

"Because the souls of the dead were believed to be below the rock in the cave or 'well'. They also believed that God's final judgment of the living and the dead will take place from this spot. Many believe the Ark of the Covenant was hidden there when the Babylonians attacked Jerusalem." The evolving history lesson generated both anxiety and exhilaration in Omar. He felt torn between the anxiety of going into a place believed to be inhabited by the souls of the dead and the exhilaration of being on the cusp of finding the Hafsah manuscript.

"This may seem like a strange question," he asked, "but how does one get into the *Well of Souls*?"

"The door in the corner leads down to the *Well of Souls* but it is locked each evening for security reasons."

"Would it be possible for me to spend the rest of the evening praying there?"

"That's... highly unusual," Faizal said slowly. Omar noticed the hesitation in the man's voice. He hoped Faizal would follow through with his request. If he didn't he would have to force the janitor's hand. Allah had directed him here, and a true mujahid never lost focus of his goal: obedience to Allah, regardless of the opposition. "I wonder if the people who called you indicated this was my desire." Omar hoped that Siddiqi had convinced him.

"They said this might be the last week of your life," Faizal answered. "They said that you are a famous mujahid and that I should make every effort to grant your request to spend the night in prayer. Do you mind if I stay here as well?"

"I prefer to be alone."

"You must understand that although this is not technically under Jewish control, they control everything that goes on here. If I'm caught leaving you here alone all night, I may not have a job tomorrow." Was this janitor attempting to block Allah's will? Omar felt his neck muscles tightening and the tension building in his heart. Trying to control his anger he grabbed for the box around his neck but his hand sliced through the empty air. He was so close to finishing his mission and this skinny little janitor was not about to stand in his way.

"Leave me alone! If you don't want to obey those who asked you to give me my final request, I'll ensure you won't have a job in the morning," he blurted threateningly.

"OK," Faizal mumbled. "I'll see you in the morning," and hurried off. Omar watched him scurry off in the direction of the door which led to the Well of Souls. After Faizal had disappeared Omar felt the urge to pray. *Allah, help me to get through that door and into the Well of Souls; may my hands be worthy of your words.*

28

The Well of Souls

Omar looked around to see if he was alone. Satisfied no one was looking he took off his shirt, grabbed his small backpack and took out the zanjir. He closed his eyes. "Allah," he prayed, "thank you that you allowed the zanjir to make it through customs." Within minutes he was in a state of self-hypnosis; his head bowed, his eyes closed. "Allahu Akbar, Allahu Akbar, Allahu Akbar," he moaned. The beat of the zanjir's chords slicing into his back matched the rhythm of his chant; rivulets of blood streamed down each side of his back.

He wasn't sure how long he had flogged himself but something made him stop. It might have been a noise inside the building. Or had it come from the outside? He stood up, put the zanjir back in his bag, wiped his back with a towel, pulled out a clean shirt and zipped up the bag. He looked around, but the place was empty. He put the bag by the nearest pillar and headed for the door leading to the Well of Souls. He turned the doorknob but it didn't open. He pulled his lock-picking tool from his pocket and within minutes it swung open. He stood silently for a minute, thinking he heard something in the darkness down the stairs. Don't get paranoid, he said to himself. Just finish the job.

He took two steps and stopped again. He *had* heard something. Could that be the sound of the restless souls of the dead? What if the spirits assaulted him? He waited, listened and thought. Don't be a coward! Suppressing a rush of emotion he forced himself to walk as soundlessly as possible down the stairs. Focus! He was on the cusp of holding the very words of Allah. Who would have thought that in the very place where the Jews hid the ark during the Babylonian exile Hafsah's Quran was hidden? Two religions which had battled each other for centuries had used the same hiding spot for their most valued artifacts!

The bottom of the stairs emerged into a simple cavern. A thin line of light descended from the mosque above through the hole Faizal had called "Adam's navel". It cast eerie shadows off the cave walls. He wondered where the ancient Quran might be hidden. In a hole under the carpet? Behind a false door? He saw the light switch near the bottom of the stairs and turned it on. A single bulb hanging from a cable in the center of the room lit up. At the far end of the cave was a cupboard with a bookshelf to one side. Next to it was a niche indicating the direction of Mecca. He dropped to his knees, feeling the gravity of Allah's true presence. He sensed the holiness permeating the cave. "Allah," he prayed, "cover my sins and I turn to you repentant."

He looked up and opened his eyes and noticed a shadow twitch to the side of the cupboard. His gaze froze on the shadow, but it no longer moved. Getting up slowly he approached the cupboard, peered around it and saw Faizal shivering with fright. "What in God's name are you doing here?"

Faizal stepped out of the shadows. He was holding a broom. "I came down here to do some cleaning," he answered glancing at the stairs, "I wasn't expecting anyone."

Omar sensed the scrawny man was lying. "You tried to keep me out," he hissed. He felt his neck muscles tighten. "You're a liar," he spat out in a low, seething whisper.

"Forgive me." Fear radiated from Faizal's eyes. "You're right. I'm a liar. No one is supposed to come down here without permission from the imam. Forgive me. I don't want to lose my job!"

"Where is the secret compartment?" Omar demanded.

"What are you talking about?" The man's voice expressed both anxiety and surprise.

Omar felt anger spread from his head to his chest. He was on the verge of losing control. He pointed an accusing finger at Faizal: "Don't pretend you don't know. If you want to live, tell me the location of the secret compartment with the Hafsah Qur'an."

"I don't know anything about a secret compartment," Faizal squeeked. He tried to move from the cupboard towards the stairs.

Omar's anger erupted. "You lying son of Satan!" He looked around for a weapon, swiped the books off the bookcase, grabbed a hold of the piece of furniture and swung it towards Faizal. Suddenly an excruciating pain seared through his head. The bookcase dropped with a clatter from his hands and he dropped to the floor like a butchered goat.

29

The Vision

As he hit the ground Omar felt a shock course through his veins–it was as if he had been electrocuted. Then he saw another body lying face down at the feet of a man holding a broomstick with a metal handle. What was *that* man doing lying down? Where had he come from? Why was there glass from a broken light bulb at his feet? The man crumpled on the floor looked familiar. He had been clubbed! Omar sprang to his feet in a panic and ran up the stairs. Halfway up, he looked back from the top of the stairs. Faizal was bending over the man lying on the floor and weeping. "Oh Allah, forgive me, forgive me," he cried. But his lips were not moving.

The jinn are in this cave! Omar ran up the rest of the stairs and noticed his feet were not touching the ground. He ran faster than he had ever moved in his life. Within a split second he passed through the door and to the edge of the foundation stone. *I've got to get out of here!*

He saw the exit and sprinted. He was running, but not panting. The outside air was cool. He looked down. Strange, he thought, I'm moving but my feet don't feel anything. He rose from the ground and found himself looking down on the rooftops of the old city. Bizarre, he thought, but continued running. This is crazy–how can I run in the air? *What has happened to me? I feel more alive than ever but this is not real!* Stores, homes and streets passed by below. He headed towards the graveyard where his parents lay buried. He didn't know why. Perhaps he was possessed—the jinn taking over. He descended slowly and approached the gate and saw the chain. The gate was locked. He reached for the chain but his hand went right through the metal. He walked effortlessly through the gate.

"What am I going to do here?" he suddenly thought, and looked around with questioning eyes. Under a lamppost a young man was sweeping the day's leaves from graves. "May I borrow your broom?" he asked, "just for a few minutes, to clean my parent's grave?" The young man acted as if he didn't exist. Perhaps he was deaf. Omar reached out to touch the man's shoulder, but his hand sliced through thin air as the young man suddenly walked away. Grabbing one hand and then the other a mind-boggling thought passed through his head. What if the solid nature of his body had evaporated? What if he could no longer touch things, hold things or be seen? The sweeper... he should have seen me and loaned me his broom!

He sat on the side of his parents' grave, put his head in his hands. He wished he could cry, but he couldn't. "Father, I wish you would tell me what to do... I'm so tired," he whispered.

"Go back son. I'll meet you in the *Well of Souls*. I'll help you find peace." He looked up. The voice was father-like, but not his father's. It dawned on him that the body of the man lying at Faizal's feet may have been him. If it was he needed to return, to recapture his body.

He started running again, flashing like an X-ray through each tombstone. He ran through the gate and once again floated through the air. He no longer moved his feet; it was as if his thoughts propelled him forward. He saw the roof tops of Jerusalem. As he re-entered the *Dome of the Rock* the word "death" entered his consciousness. Maybe he had entered the realm of the dead... He traveled past the foundation stone, through the door and down the stairs to the Well of Souls. Faizal had moved the body and it now faced upward. He saw the face; it was his own. He was very pale. He was dead. How can I be dead? I'm thinking, moving, experiencing. I must reunite with my body. He tried but passed through it like smoke through the air.

He became aware of a growing brightness entering the room. It made him squint. Coming down the stairs was a man of light. "Come," the man said, and turned around. But the words did not come from his lips, they came from inside Omar. The invitation was not a command—yet it was impossible to refuse. He stood up and began to climb the stairs after the man. "I am in the presence of Allah," he thought, then wondered if the thought was his or if it came from the man of light. He sensed the man of light had limitless power, but also sensed it was controlled by limitless mercy. As he climbed the stairs the impact of love emanating from the light released deep wells of emotion within him. Cathartic tears welled up in his eyes and began to flow freely. This man loved him more than any love he had ever known. His love was mysterious, unshakeable, selfless and all embracing. It uncovered his every shameful secret. His life lay exposed in a flash of insight. The guilt over all the killings was lifted off him and waved off to a distant galaxy. His hatred for the Israeli military changed to compassion for their fears as a hated minority in a sea of angry Muslims. Shameful scene after shameful scene crossed his mind, and each was hurled into space and replaced with an overpowering balm of love. The searing light was both scalpel and salve. It cut and healed.

Suddenly a question filled his mind: "Do you want to be free from your guilt and shame forever?" To say 'no' was ludicrous. Anyone who could experience this kind of holy love would forsake all to be able to relish this security for eternity. "Yes!" he heard himself shouting. "What can I do to obtain this love?"

"Nothing," was the answer.

Nothing? Nothing! That made no sense at all. Seeking to hold on to this incredible presence Omar cried, "I'll give you my life!"

"Your life for my love?" the man asked.

"Yes!"

"Then I will put my words in your heart," the man said. He reached across and touched his lips. Suddenly Omar became aware of his body.

30

History Revealed

The cold, damp floor and the cave's dark cool air penetrated Omar's consciousness. He opened his eyes and looked around. He was lying on his back. Just then the cave began to rock gently. Instantly he was fully awake, on high alert. He had felt this type of rocking before, during the earthquake when he was a child. He heard something fall in the pitch darkness and wished for light. He felt claustrophobic. Would the cave collapse and leave him trapped? "Ya Allah," he pleaded, "Save me." Dust and pebbles fell from the ceiling. Then the swaying motion ceased and he breathed a sigh of relief.

"Are you O.K.?" A man's voice cut through the darkness. Faizal's voice. He remembered trying to crush the man with the bookcase. Thank God he was alive.

"Yes," he answered. "That must have been an earthquake... What happened to me?"

"You fell," the janitor said hesitantly.

"I have a splitting headache!" Faizal didn't reply. Omar tried to remember the sequence of events prior to the earth tremor. He had had a vision of a man of light who had offered to put words in his heart. What had that meant? He felt strange, and the darkness felt claustrophobic. Then, suddenly, a beam of light fell through Adam's navel – the hole in the foundation stone – and he breathed a sigh of relief. The lights had gone on upstairs. But why did they not go on in the cave? He turned to Faizal.

"Thanks for helping me," he began. His thankfulness appeared to put Faizal at ease. "Forgive me for my anger," he added spontaneously, surprising himself. With the exception of Allah he had never before asked anyone for forgiveness. Something had happened to him.

"I should have let you down here; forgive me for not being more helpful," Faizal replied.

"You have nothing to be apologetic about." Omar sat up and shook his head. "I think I've had more sense knocked into me than you'll ever realize."

Faizal looked relieved and glanced up the stairs. "Perhaps you want to know some of the other stories pertaining to this place?"

Omar got to his feet rubbing his head and remembered why he was here. "That would be great."

"Let's go up to the foundation stone. You need to see the mosque's layout to understand it. There are hidden symbols with multiple meanings." Sensing he was about discover the event that led to the construction of this holy dome, Omar followed the skinny Palestinian upstairs to the edge of the foundation stone in the middle of the Dome of the Rock. He looked up at the dazzling ceiling mosaics. "Look at the building's layout," Faizal said. He pointed in four different directions. "It is shaped like a cross. If you draw lines down the center, you'll find the foundation stone right in the middle of the cross. In fact, this place is shaped like a crucifix, just like many ancient churches were." He grabbed a pen and paper from his pocket and sketched the exterior of the building and all the pillars, finally connecting the pillars to reveal the hidden cross.

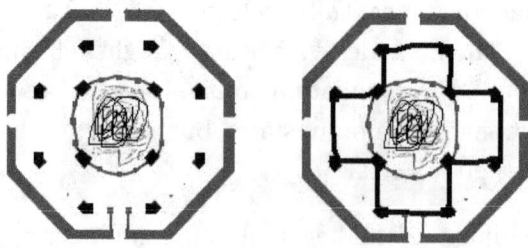

"Are you saying this place is a church?"

"Its dimensions are the same as the original church of the Holy Sepulcher, where Jesus is said to have been buried."

"So if Jesus is not buried here, what is buried?"

"Some say the Caliph Umar came here when he commissioned the building of this place. Stories have circulated for centuries that an artifact honoring the prophet is buried under the rock. It is believed that when the prophet went to heaven from this rock he saw Isa the Messiah. When he came back he told Umar and Hafsah that they were to ensure this place would always honor Isa bin Allah." Omar had never heard the term 'Isa bin Allah.' It implied Jesus was the son of God–and that was heresy!

Faizal pointed upward, "Read what it says up there," he said. Reading the Arabic calligraphy that circled the dome Omar read the text: *'O People of the Book! Do not exaggerate in your religion nor utter aught concerning God save the truth. The Messiah, Jesus son of Mary, was only a Messenger of God, and His Word which He conveyed unto Mary, and a spirit from Him. So believe in God and His messengers, and say not 'Three' - Cease! It is better for you! - God is only One God. Far be it removed from His transcendent majesty that He should have a son. ... Whoso disbelieveth the revelations of God will find that lo! God is swift at reckoning!'*"

"I once had a vision in which a man of light came to me and I asked him if Jesus was who the people of the book claim he is, the Son of God," Faizal said hesitantly.

This Faizal had also had a vision of a man of light!

"The man of light," Faizal continued, "answered as follows: 'It depends on how you read this verse. It commends Jesus as being 'the Word' of Allah. That is like saying he is a 'walking Quran.' And if he is a 'walking Quran' then he is Allah because he embodies Allah's presence as a visual representation to humanity.'"

Omar was quiet. If Faizal had a vision of the man of light, was he the answer to the man's promise to put his words in his heart? Skeptically

183

he probed: "Well, that's no different than Muhammad, peace be upon him. He showed us the best way to live our life before Allah in the Qur'an and hadith."

"Yes, but there is a hadith, quoted by the wife of Muhammad, peace be upon him, saying the following: *'O Allah! Wash away my sins with the water of snow and hail, and cleanse my heart from all the sins as a white garment is cleansed from the filth.'*

"That's just a hadith. Can you point me to a verse in the Quran that points out that Muhammad, peace be upon him, considered himself a sinner?"

"According to Surah 48:2 God considered Muhammad, peace be upon him, as a sinner. In it God says: *'Know thou therefore that there is no god but God, and ask forgiveness for thy sin, and for the believers, men and women. God knows your going to and fro, and your lodging.'* You see, Muhammad, peace be upon him, was considered a sinner by God — God told him to ask for forgiveness, while Jesus never sinned, as both the Bible and the Qur'an affirm. Since Jesus never sinned, he more accurately represents God in human form. Do you think it is possible for God to appear in human form?"

"I think that Allah can do anything," Omar responded slowly, fearing where the logic might lead.

"In that case" Faizal continued, "Allah could have revealed himself to us through Jesus. Look again at the verse on the wall overhead." He pointed upward. "It says that Jesus is the 'Spirit of Allah.' If he is the walking 'Word of Allah" and the 'Walking Spirit of Allah', and if he was conceived of a virgin and never touched by Satan or sinned, then who was he?" Omar felt a tremor go up his spine. He remembered a conversation he once had in prison with a Palestinian Christian. They had shared a cell for a week. Every time the man had been dragged back to their cell after being tortured on the infamous slanted chair, he would pray, "Father, forgive them for they know not what they do."

"Don't you want them all to die like dogs?" Omar once asked that fellow prisoner. "They deserve to rot in hell!"

"I deserve to rot in hell as well, but that's not how Jesus, praise be upon him, looks at us. The Spirit of Jesus that I feel living in my heart ever since I asked him to forgive me has changed me. He tells me that my response to them should not be more hatred but a willingness to extend forgiveness, even if they don't ask for it." The memory of the conversation had never left him. He marveled how anyone could have such an attitude in the face of such cruelty.

He turned to Faizal. "What about the verse that says we are not to say, 'Allah is three.' That is *shirk*, polytheism, the unforgivable sin."

"True. Jesus said that as well. Jesus said 'the Lord our God, the Lord is one,'" Faizal replied.

"How do you know that?"

"I've read the Injil, the Gospel."

"So who was Jesus? A man? A god-man?"

"I can only answer that question from experience. The man of light, whom I now know was Jesus, showed me my life, my guilt and all the shameful things I have ever done. He laid everything bare. But when I looked into his eyes all my sin was totally absorbed in them, and I was never the same again. I am at peace, even as my father sits falsely accused in a filthy Israeli prison cell for something he never did. I am totally convinced that Jesus will bring all things to a righteous conclusion." Omar was quiet. This man had had a vision just like his. They stood quietly beside the rock. He longed for the peace and love that Faizal had described and which he had felt in the presence of the man of light.

"So how do you put it together? Is God one or three?" His voice wavered as he voiced his heart's question.

"I can confirm what the Quran says: that Jesus is the Word of God to this world and that the Spirit of God is in him. I am not here to try to figure out what Christians have struggled to define over centuries. I do know that the Injil teaches that Jesus was fully Allah and fully man. They call it 'incarnation'".

Omar's voice was low, as if he was talking to himself. "If you believe that Jesus is the 'Word of God' and the 'Spirit of God' and if he was born of a virgin, like we do, is that the same as affirming something like the ...." Omar couldn't bring himself to say 'trinity' or 'incarnation.'

Faizal remained quiet. The silence lengthened until it became uncomfortable. Finally he spoke. "Let me show you around some more and tell a bit more of the building's history."

Suddenly Omar remembered his quest. "I've heard that an ancient Quran is hidden in this place. Have you ever encountered that story?" Before Faizal could answer Omar's phone vibrated in his pocket. He looked at the number and saw it was Siddiqi. "I have to take this call," he said apologetically and turned his back to Faizal. "Salaam Aleykum."

"Aleykum Salaam," answered the voice on the other end of the phone. "Do you have the manuscript?"

"No not yet. I'm with Faizal right now." Omar glanced over at Faizal who was gazing over the foundation stone.

"What do you think about keeping the documents instead of selling them to the Imam?" The question caught Omar by surprise. Siddiqi had never before asked him for his opinion on an operational matter.

"Why?" he asked.

"We could use the money for our cause."

The idea's implications troubled Omar. "I don't know." he answered hesitantly.

"Think," Siddiqi countered. "If Uthman succeeded in using the Quran to unite his army against his enemies, perhaps we could use it to unite the ummah against Israel. We would finally have the necessary resources to push the infidels into the sea."

"But we can't use the manuscript any way we want," Omar was aghast. "We don't know if it may assert things that may counter our cause."

"Like what?"

"Well, say it states that Muhammad actually went to heaven on buraq from somewhere in Saudi Arabia? It would remove our religious claim on the Dome of the Rock. And that just might empower the Israelis to bomb it without fear of consequence from the Muslim world."

"We wouldn't tell people that. We would control the book! We could tell everyone what it said without giving them access."

"The truth would come out, and if it didn't support our cause, we would never again be trusted." Omar paused. "When do you need the manuscript?"

"The imam called and he was hoping to get it within the next few days. I told him I'd contact you and see how things were going."

"Call me in twenty-four hours," Omar responded. "I'll know something by then."

"Tamam. O.K." Omar ended the call and turned back to Faizal.

"I'm sorry," the janitor said, "but I couldn't help overhearing your conversation. Are you looking for something here?"

"Yes," Omar hesitated. Then he decided to tell him the truth. "Do you know anything about the Hafsah Qur'an?" Simply saying the sentence felt cathartic. There was no more need for pretence.

The man looked puzzled. "I thought you were here to pray and now you say you are here for the Hafsah Qur'an? Which is it?"

"I'm sorry…" Omar paused for moment. "The truth is that we think the Hafsah Qur'an is hidden here."

"How can I know you are speaking the truth?"

"You cannot. But when I lay unconscious in the Well of Souls, a man of light touched my soul and, well, I don't think I can lie any longer…."

Faizal nodded and looked him in the eye. "I've never heard anything about Hafsah's Qur'an being here. What makes you think that's a possibility?"

The question stirred feelings of guilt in Omar. "A scholar in Yemen mentioned that he thought the Hafsah Qur'an was buried here. After all, it was named after her father for centuries."

"I don't know anything about the Hafsah Qur'an being here," Faizal said pensively. "You may search the entire building, but I don't think you'll find it. If it had been here someone would have found it by now."

"The scholar said it may be in the *Well of Souls*," Omar probed.

"So that's why you went down there." Faizal looked as if he had just solved a crossword.

"Yes."

"Feel free to go back down and look. But remember that the Man of Light will be watching you. And make sure everything is the way it was before the early morning prayers, by 4:00 a.m. I'll get you a flashlight. The lights are out down there."

"Thank you. I'll wait till you get back," Omar said sincerely. He walked down to the stairs to the *Well of Souls*, and reflected while he waited. I wonder whose souls might be down here. The thought made him uneasy. He was glad when Faizal returned.

"I'm going home now," Faizal said. "It's past midnight."

"Thank you for everything." Omar looked at him. "Could I have your phone number? That way I can contact you should anything arise." Faizal hesitated, then gave him a number, turned and left. Omar could hear his footsteps growing faint, and then a door open and close.

Omar descended the stairs. He had determined he would examine the cave systematically, beginning at the bottom of the stairs. He began a methodical, counter-clockwise examination of the walls, beginning with the column at the bottom of the stairs. He tapped its entire length to see if it was solid or not. He inspected each section of the wall, pressing his hands against the stones, hoping to find a loose rock leading to a hidden chamber. He rubbed his index finger through each crack, trying to locate anything unusual. Finally he found himself facing a diagonal, plastered wall in the direction of Mecca. He tapped against it looking for any hollow points. He inspected it centimeter by centimeter but found nothing.

Finding himself back at the foot of the stairs he shone the flashlight up at the ceiling. Faizal's broom stood in a corner, and he used it to poke it in some of the darker pockets. Some loose dirt cascaded into his eyes.

In a corner of the floor there was a spot where the carpet lifted easily. He pulled at it, and about four feet of it peeled back. He saw a crack in the bare floor running from the wall under the rest of the carpet. It was too straight to be natural. He kneeled over it and started tapping every few centimeters. It sounded solid until he came to the crease where the carpet folded back. Hollow, he thought and tapped again. There was a light resonance. He tugged at the carpet, but it was proving difficult to move. He looked at his watch. He only had another hour before the first people would be coming for prayer. He replaced the carpet in its original position, then started pulling it up along the length of the edge. Once it was pulled loose he could roll it up like a long tube. The length of the crack was laid bare. In fact, there was a second crack at right angles with the first crack. He tapped where they intersected. Hollow. He took the broom and began knocking gently on the ground, beginning where the cracks intersected and radiating outwards, towards the walls. Within minutes he had established the perimeter of the cavity beneath the floor. *I've got to lift this slab.*

He rubbed his nail along the crack to try to scrape away some of the dirt, but nothing lifted. Must be cemented, he thought. He looked around, but there was no other object he could use as a tool. Maybe upstairs, he thought and climbed the stairs. Then he heard the voices.

Odd, he thought. Faizal had said there would be no one here till early morning prayers. He looked at his watch and saw it was 3:40 a.m. I'll put the carpet back down and clean up, he thought. Tomorrow night I'll return with some tools.

31

The Tunnel

Abdullah had insisted they leave the monastery at 4 a.m. in order to get away from prying eyes. "They'll be watching," he had warned.

Father Constantin had lowered them down the massive back wall by rope, a circumstance necessitated when two policemen had shown up at the front gate asking for them. "This is the way everyone came and went two hundred years ago," the monk had joked. Once on the ground they had made their way separately to the hidden Land Rover.

"The police are looking for four people. If they only see a single person walking around early in the morning they're less likely to pay attention," Abdullah had advised. Twenty minutes later they had all met at the Land Rover and were driving the vehicle over the rough topography. With the headlights off the rocky terrain that towered darkly around the Land Rover made Rauser feel like an ant negotiating an unknown sandbox. He was glad Abdullah's cell phone had an inbuilt GPS.

Maryam, quiet up to this point, spoke up from the back seat. "Do you think they'll find Yusuf?"

"The monks won't resist the police, but they won't help either," Rauser answered. "If they do find him, it'll be a while." He turned to Abdullah. "Beside the GPS, what else do you have in the backpack? Anything that'll help us get over Israel's security fence?"

"I grabbed some basic tools and some camouflage netting from the helicopter. It'll do." The doughty Arab flashed a broad, white smile.

The rapidly rising sun quickly dispelled the darkness. Hours passed and the terrain changed. Abdullah struggled to keep the vehicle from getting stuck in the undulating sand dunes. Then they started seeing lights in the distance. Israeli border surveillance posts, Abdullah explained. At one point he stopped the vehicle in order to perform his prayer. Maryam had joined him. Afterwards Abdullah pointed to what looked like a blank area on the GPS screen, "There is a tunnel here where we can cross. According to my contact, these coordinates correspond to a dry river bed that crosses the border."

"What do we look for?" Maryam asked.

"An old olive grove and a few palm trees. Our contacts use the tunnel to smuggle people in and out." Rauser wondered about the term "our contacts," but decided not to ask. By this stage it didn't matter any more if his contacts were terrorists or not. Undoubtedly Interpol had them all listed as terrorists by now.

The four wheel drive progressed steadily over the dry river bed. Then Rauser noticed some straggly olive trees at the top of the river bed. Several minutes later they pulled up to the copse of trees, and Abdullah turned off the car. Rauser looked around. The Israeli security fence was about a kilometer away. There was nothing to suggest a tunnel anywhere near.

"We're not very far from the security fence," Rauser pointed out.

"Indeed," Abdullah replied. He turned to Maryam, "Where's that camouflaged netting?" Maryam handed him the netting and Abudullah threw it over the Land Rover. They headed different directions among the trees. Suddenly they heard Maryam give a yell.

"Did you find the hole?" Abdullah shouted.

"Come on, take a look," she shouted back.

Sure enough. Maryam was standing beside the entrance, a faded desert-brown piece of tarp kicked to one side.

"Put on those burqas I bought at the monastery," Abdullah said. "I'll call my taxi contact on the other side."

192

Rauser struggled to find the eye slits. "If my students could see me now I'd never hear the end of it," he joked. "How do I look?"

"No worse than a few minutes ago," Maryam replied, a twinkle in her eye.

"You look better," Abdullah joked. He too had slipped into a burqa. He walked to the hole and lowered himself into it. Rauser and Maryam followed. They could feel the air cooling as they descended.

Rauser looked into the mute darkness ahead. He could see about six meters and was surprised how high the tunnel was; he could walk through it if hunched over.

"Anyone have a flashlight?" Maryam asked.

"Sorry; can't think of everything," Abdullah answered. "Let's go."

Abdullah led the way, followed by Maryam. Rauser saw her stretch out one arm to touch the tunnel's dirt wall as she hunched over and started walking. Smart, he thought, and copied the motion. Before long the darkness became oppressive; he could almost feel it tangibly. Did animals ever get trapped in here? He had heard that these caves sometimes collapsed. "Oh, sorry," he heard Maryam saying. Then he bumped into her. "Why are we stopping?"

"I think there's been a bit of a cave-in." Abdullah's voice sounded exaggeratedly loud in the narrow confines.

"How bad is it," Rauser asked from the back.

"I think I can get over it. Be patient." He and Maryam waited. They heard some grunting sounds followed by, "This stupid burqa!" Rauser smiled. A few minutes later Abdullah's voice sounded again: "It's not too bad. Just a few meters of fallen dirt; have fun."

Maryam moved ahead. He heard her grunting. Suddenly a couple of choice expletives followed by, "Crap, I hit my head." Then, "Shit! I just tripped over my dress." Then, "Those bloody jihadists! They should invest in some lights." After a brief pause she shouted again: "Your turn, Rauser! Don't get lost."

Rauser took his time. Several times he had to brace himself against the wall to keep from falling as he inched his way up the invisible mound, stooping as low as he could. He stepped on his burqa and fell. "These burqas are impossible," he mumbled. Then the mound sloped down and he found himself on level ground. He took a step forward and bumped into Maryam. "Let's get out of here," he grumbled. They continued on in the darkness. Some twenty minutes later the tunnel took a turn. They could see a light ahead and some time later found themselves at the bottom of a hole. A harness with a rope on it dangled down the middle.

"We will have to wait here for about twenty minutes," Abdullah said. "It will take that long for my contact to get here. In the meantime, let me make another call." He dialed a number. "We should be there this evening," Rauser heard him say. There was a pause, followed by, "that would be a terrible mistake. You're not ready for nuclear weapons." A few more grunts followed. Rauser could see consternation spreading over Abdullah's face.

"Any problems?" he asked.

"Nothing another phone call won't fix." Abdullah pushed a speed-dial button, turned his back to Rauser and cupped his hand over his mouth. Rauser couldn't make out the conversation.

33

The Jordan–Israel Border

Fouad finished reading the front page story, folded the Jordan Times and set it aside. *Shoot-out in Sharm El-Sheikh* the headline shouted. He was impressed: the journalist had already figured out who the owner of the downed helicopter was. He looked over the crowd in the restaurant as he sipped his coffee. The flight from Najran had landed at midnight and he had slept in, right through his morning prayers. He sighed, put the empty cup on its saucer, and returned to his room. He knelt on the carpet.

"Ya Allah," he prayed, "I'm struggling. Did Uthman really change your word or are Salim's conjectures false? What is the truth about your prophet? Should I be involved in helping to find the Hafsah Qur'an? Please… let me live a life that is faithful and honours you." He got to his feet, stretched, and turned on the television. He flipped through the channels until he came to Al Jazeera. The reporter was interviewing a monk. The caption below read: *Suspects of downed helicopter believed to have hidden in ancient Sinai monastery.*

"Has anyone fitting the description of the Yemeni fugitives entered the monastery?" the reporter asked.

"Our policy is to allow the police to freely investigate," the monk responded. "They have searched the monastery and found nothing." The camera panned over the monastery before the news anchor promised to update viewers as the story unfolded. "Now turning to the recent tensions in Gaza…" Fouad turned the television off.

That monk was hiding something, he thought. The man did not look the reporter straight in the eye. There was no way anyone was going to turn the monastery up-side-down looking for fugitives. That would be a political P.R. disaster. He lowered himself into a chair by the window and looked down at the bustling traffic. Let's prioritize, he thought. He reached for the print-out Hussein had given him and reread it. Should this change my course of action, he wondered. The political instability that the Hafsah Quran could unleash was only hinted at. In any case, it had not been found, and doing so probably required the know-how of the late Dr. Salim—or of Rauser. The best means of advancing his case of catching Salim's killer or finding the Hafsah Qur'an was to nab Rauser. He pulled out his phone and called Hussein.

"Good morning boss! Where are you?"

"At the Shepherd Hotel in Amman. I saw an interview on Al Jazeera with one of the monks at the monastery about what I presume are our suspects. You think Rauser and his gang are there?"

"We suspect so but have no evidence."

"Were you able to search it thoroughly?"

"We did our best. The place is like a maze: little alleyways, chapels, libraries, a mosque; very confusing."

"What did the monks say?"

"They told us we were free to look around. One came with us. He opened all the locked doors."

"Did you ask him if he saw any suspicious foreigners?"

"'Who's suspicious?' the monk asked me and pointed at all the tourists and people swarming the place. He left me feeling it was a stupid question. I didn't probe any further."

Fouad could understand the monk's need for religious neutrality. They would have to work around that. "If they're in there, they'll have to come out. Stay in the neighborhood, interview the locals. Someone must have seen them. Keep a lookout on all possible exits."

"Boss, one more thing. We found a man unconscious in their infirmary. He may have been the pilot. He looked Malaysian or Filipino or something like that."

"Ah, that's good. Make sure he gets all the medical attention he needs, and interrogate him as soon as possible. Bring in chaps from immigration if you need to lean on him."

"O.K., Sir. What are your plans?"

"I'm off to al-Quds, Jerusalem."

Rauser looked over at Maryam, sound asleep next to him in the tunnel. She had removed the headpiece of the burqa to facilitate breathing. Other than the sound of her steady breathing, all was quiet. He looked passed her at Abdullah Saud. The man was sitting quietly with arms propped up by his folded legs. Interesting chap, Rauser mused.

"I noticed you were pretty interested in Father Constantin's theory regarding the Hafsah Qur'an" he said quietly to the Saudi. "How far did you get in your analyses of your documents?"

"I've tried to compare them with some other ancient ones I've been able to get my hands on, although I've never analyzed them as palimpsests… at least not yet," he said with a smile. "I was hoping to do that soon. That's why I got all that new equipment."

"What other documents have you examined?"

"I got permission to see the Topkapi and Tashkent manuscripts. Cost me a bundle, but they let me photograph them. That enabled me to compare my version with the same verses in those Qur'ans."

"What did you find?" Rauser probed. It intriqued him to learn that someone had actually got permission to examine individual pages of these two revered Quran's, both of which were presumed to be Uthman originals.

"The Topkapi manuscript differs from some of the pages I bought from the Yemeni trove. The curator in Istanbul dated it to the 8th century, so it's younger than my Sana'a pages. The Samarkand manuscript in Tashkent had paleographic and carbon dating applied to it. They are quite certain that it dates back to around 150 years after Muhammad's death, so it's also younger than mine. The Tashkent Qur'an shows that somewhere along the way changes were made. Some of the word choices were different from my Quranic pages."

"Does this bother you?"

"Yes, a lot. It leaves me with one of three choices: the oldest Qur'ans we have today are different from the original, or today's version is different from the original, or the original was different from today's version *and* the versions that lie in Tashkent or Istanbul. In any case we have no consistent proof that the Qur'an we use today is the same as that spoken by Muhammad. If the changes are substantial it could undermine the credibility of Islam altogether."

This man, thought Rauser, is coming to the same conclusions Salim was. Salim had found palimpsests proving that Uthman's political agenda dictated which verses were to be deleted from his Quran. If Abdullah knew that all the changes the third Caliph introduced pertained to undermining the Christian teaching that Jesus was the Son of God, how would he respond? "Is that why you're interested in finding the Hafsah Quran?"

"Yes. We need to identify which is the true Quran in order to ensure Muslims properly follow Allah and his commands. Also, it would be great to discover that my pages are copies of the Hafsah Quran," Abdullah smiled. "If I can find the Hafsah Quran and compare my pages, they would be worth millions."

Rauser smiled back, but decided to probe a bit deeper. "What if we find this original Hafsah Quran and it proves to be much more in line with the revelations of Moses and Jesus than with today's version of the Quran?"

"Then we have a major problem," Abdullah said, and stood up. "Listen," he paused for a minute and held up his hand for Rauser to be quiet. "I think our ride has arrived."

Fouad got out of the taxi at the Allenby/Hussein Bridge and looked up at the large archway spread over the two-lane road that marked the border between Jordan and Israel. People were queued up like a long line of cattle between fences waiting for Israeli immigration to let them through. The line barely moved. A mother holding her young son's hand reminded him of his own mother. She had looked just like that. She used to take his hand, lead him to the bedroom and hide him under the bed to protect him from his abusive father. His becoming a policeman had had something to do with the fact that even as a child he had wanted to do something that protected the vulnerable from evil men who inflicted pain because they loved no one but themselves.

The long, boring wait gave Fouad time to call Hussein for an update. "I'm at the border. Traffic moving as slow as a lame camel. Any new developments?"

"I found out they bought a car. Paid for it in cash."

"How do you know it was them?"

"The fellow who sold it to them accurately described Abdullah Saud."

This was good news. "What kind of car was it?" Fouad asked.

"A brown Land Rover."

"Has it been located?"

"I asked the Egyptians to put out an APB."

This was also good news. The trail had not gone cold and Hussein was working well with the Egyptians. "Great. Did you get the license plate?"

"Yes, sir."

"Text it to me."

"O.K. boss."

"Check the hospitals. See if anyone with bullet wounds shows up."

"I'm on it."

The line moved forward. "Gotta go. It's almost my turn to get interrogated by immigration."

"O.K. Ma' salami. Go in peace." Hussein was doing good work, Fouad thought. He hoped his 'Jerusalem plan' would be as fruitful as Hussein's chase.

He hated border guards. They were cops who couldn't make the grade.

34

Jerusalem

Rauser was the last out of the hole. No sooner had he surfaced when Abdullah's friend hurried them off to an old black Toyota Corolla. The man's black robe blended marvelously into the darkness. He kept looking nervously around. "Never know who is looking," he said uneasily.

Rauser climbed in the back seat and closed the door. The man handed Saud a plastic bag. "Had the wife prepare some bread. Thought you might be hungry." He pointed to a thermos on the floor. "There's the coffee."

They drove northwards for several hours, along the Sinai road running parallel to the miles and miles of security fence along the Egyptian border. Every couple of kilometers they could see the silhouette of an observation tower. An hour into the drive an Israeli helicopter followed them for several minutes. Their chauffeur became panicky. "Get down! Get down!" he hollered, his knuckles white from gripping the steering wheel. It was only after the helicopter had left that the three fugitives fell asleep.

It was the slowing of the vehicle that woke Rauser. "Where are we?" he asked.

"Abu Ghosh," the driver replied. "This is as far as I can take you. I'm unwanted in Jerusalem. Take a bus from here. It's less than an hour to Jerusalem." They got out of the old Corolla and looked at the bus station. It was a small affair, with a single bus waiting to be boarded.

"So sorry I couldn't take you all the way," the man kept repeating, "May Allah bless you on the rest of your trip. I have given Mr. Abdullah enough shekels for three bus tickets."

"Maryam," Abdullah whispered through the burqa, "here's the money. Buy the tickets." As she left he turned to Rauser. "I feel like a pervert, dressed like this."

"If we're caught we'll probably get charged with some moral infraction," Rauser whispered back.

Abdullah stepped off to one side and dialed a number on his phone. "Find out what happened," he muttered "and have everything ready by tonight. Call me if there's a problem."

"Anything wrong?" Maryam had returned with the tickets.

"Nothing that won't be smoothed out by tonight. Let's get on the bus." Maryam suggested they sit together at the back.

"Excuse me sir," the woman on the other side of the thick slab of bullet-proof glass said to Fouad, "but our two countries do not have diplomatic relations. I'm afraid I cannot let you into Israel without the necessary clearances." She slipped his passport back through the slot.

Fouad smiled politely. "Ma'am, I realize that." He reached into his pocket and slipped his Yemeni Police ID through the slot. "You have every right to send me back to Yemen. However, we believe some Yemeni and international criminals may have entered Israel. I'm part of a team tracking them. Would it be possible to speak to one of your officers?"

The lady looked at his police I.D. "You can verify this?"

"Yes ma'am."

"One minute." She reached for the wall-phone next to her chair and within a minute a man appeared. He motioned for Fouad to make his way to a side-door, met him there and led him to an interrogation room. Fouad noticed the picture of the Israeli prime minister on the wall and the web cam fastened to the ceiling. This was going to be recorded.

"Please have a seat." The officer pointed to a chair. "You apparently said you were tracking a criminal. Could you provide details?"

"Perhaps you saw on the news this morning the story about a helicopter that crashed near St. Catherine's Monastery. We are trying to find the people that were in that chopper."

"Other than this ID card can you verify your position at the Sana'a police force?" the officer asked.

Fouad had to smile. Typical immigration, he thought. Meticulous. "The Sana'a police department will verify my identity." He jotted down a number. The immigration official took the paper and walked out of the room.

Fouad was pleasantly surprised at how respectful they were treating him. He would have to convince the Israelis to let him continue to pursue the case by stating there was a substantial threat to the safety of their citizens. He might have to exaggerate a bit.

Fifteen minutes later the immigration officer returned to the interrogation room. He was accompanied by a policeman. "Your story checks out Captain," the officer said. "I've brought in Sergeant Mosley to see what we should do next." Sergeant Mosley was a husky man with a short black beard and wire rim glasses. He wasted no time getting to the point.

"So Captain Fouad, what can you tell us about that helicopter crash?"

"We've been following an alleged murderer from Yemen to Saudi Arabia, and have reason to believe he was on board that helicopter. We believe the suspect killed an esteemed museum curator in our country. He may also be responsible for the death of several academics in Germany."

"What does this have to do with Israel?"

"We believe the suspect may be heading in this direction."

"Based on....?" The policeman's voice trailed off into skepticism.

"The suspects apparently left the monastery by vehicle. The Egyptian police have already put out an APB. We're hoping you would do the same."

"That car would never get over the border without our knowledge." Fouad looked quietly into the man's eyes, smiled, then pursed his lips.

"Perhaps you could give me the license plate number." Sergeant Mosley took a pen out of his breast pocket and slid over a writing pad. "Also give me the names of the suspects, a description and any other information."

Fouad opened his phone and found Hussein's text message. "This will take a few minutes."

"Not a problem." He nodded his head for the immigration officer to exit the room with him. "Take your time Captain. We may be a few minutes," he said as he closed the door behind him. Fouad heard the lock turn. He spent the next fifteen minutes writing the the essence of what he knew about the case. Then he looked over the paper, made some minor corrections, and waited. Another twenty minutes passed before the two men returned.

"Sorry to keep you waiting Captain. We had to see what legal options were available to us, should we need your assistance inside Israel. You can appreciate that we don't often have police officers from Yemen offering to help us out."

"I understand." Fouad was not surprised. The fact that they had acknowledged he was 'helping' was a good sign.

The officer lifted the writing pad off the table. "We will look over your statement and get back to you shortly. Would you like a coffee while you wait?" Fouad nodded and the two men left the room. Within minutes the immigration officer was back with a coffee. The insipid liquid made Fouad miss the rich, mocha flavored coffee from home; no one could brew coffee like the Yemeni. He let his mind wander. This case is good for me, he thought. It's forcing me to become more of a team player. Playing ball with Jabir and now with the Israelis. It's also stretching me religiously. When this is all over I'll have to take some time to learn more about Islam and the formation of the Quran. But who should I ask? Finding someone to trust with my questions will be difficult in Sana'a.

It took some twenty minutes before the men came back. "Captain Fouad, some good news. It seems that the Egyptians found the car. The suspects may have entered Israel. The Egyptians found a tunnel near the abandoned car, something we were able to verify from our end."

"What is the plan?" Fouad asked.

"We have asked immigration to expedite your entry into Israel. We may need you to help identify the suspects." The immigration officer placed a legal document in front of Fouad. "Captain, if you sign this *Temporary Protection Group* document we can grant you entry into Israel as a refugee. This will allow you to work here for three months, much longer than you probably want." The man smiled. "It will also allow us to keep you under the radar screen. We will place the immigration entry stamp on a separate piece of paper which you must keep with your passport. That way your documents will not be compromised."

Fouad smiled as he picked up the pen. "I never thought I'd be applying for refugee status in Israel," he said. "Don't tell my boss."

"We won't," the official said, and stretched out his hand. "Welcome to Israel. Now let's get you to Jerusalem as quickly as possible."

Sitting in the back of the bus wearing a burqa made Rauser feel conspicuous. There was only one other woman on the bus. She was also wearing a full burqa. He noticed the driver repeatedly looking in his rear view mirror. No point mentioning that to Abdullah and Maryam; they were both asleep.

Twenty minutes later they hit the Jerusalem traffic and the driver no longer looked in his mirror; negotiating the large vehicle through the helter-skelter traffic took all his attention. Rauser shook the other two awake as they pulled into the central bus station on Yafo Street. "Better call your contact," he told Abdullah. "We'll be in the Old City in about fifteen minutes."

Abdullah pulled out his phone, cupped his hand over it, and whispered some directives. Then he nodded at Maryam and Rauser, leaned across them and whispered, "Everything's set for the Dome of the Rock. My man will bring a change of clothes for all of us. Women are only allowed to pray in front of the Dome of the Rock, so we're all going to become men".

"You O.K. with Maryam and an infidel, entering the mosque?" Rauser asked.

"I don't mind. Muhammad, God bless him, encouraged women to pray with men. All this extreme segregation just caters to radicals." The bus pulled into the the station and the three burqa clad figures walked to the Jaffa Gate. A skiny, bearded man wearing dark trousers and a polo shirt met them carrying three plastic shopping bags. His eyes shone with an infectious kindness and his quick smile radiated peace.

"I'm Faizal," he said, nodding politely. "Are you here for the evening prayers?" He glanced at each of them. All three of them nodded and followed Faizal through the crowded markets and through a door into a courtyard. Faizal closed the door behind them and he gave them each one of the bags. Then he led them into the house. "You may want to change in the bedrooms down the hall," he said and pointed to a series of doors.

"Thank you," Abdullah said. "I can take it from here."

35

The Dome of the Rock

Abdullah's passion for the history of the Dome of the Rock was contagious. He rambled on and on about the place. The three of them, dressed like Arab men in white flowing robes and kufiyya, followed him around the Temple Mount through the Al Aqsa mosque, the Dome of the Chain, and the Dome of Ascension. Rauser was enjoying himself. His previous attempt to visit the place years earlier had been thwarted by political instability; the temple mount had been locked down.

By midnight they had covered every inch of the area, except the interior of the Dome of the Rock itself. They were standing on the steps of the mosque gazing at Jerusalem's evening lights. "I've saved the best for last," Abdullah said. "Let's go in and see if we can find the Hafsah Quran." He looked at the Palestinian guard standing in front of the Al Aqsa mosque, his back towards them. "It's late enough that there shouldn't be any suspicious eyes inside." Rauser wondered how they would enter the mosque at this time of the night—but Abdullah just pushed one of the doors open and stepped inside. Maybe he had told Faizal to leave it open. He glanced in the direction of the soldier; the man had not moved. He joined the other two and pulled the door closed behind him.

"Let me have a quick look around," Abdullah said. "I'll be right back." Left standing in the vestibule, Rauser's attention was diverted to a figure in a white robe and moustacheless beard. The man emerged from a doorway. Rauser could see that there was a staircase leading down on the other side of the door. He presumed it was the Well of Souls where the man had probably prayed. *I thought everyone was gone by now.*

The white robed figure nodded politely to Rauser while brushing some dirt off his hands. As he walked past, Rauser noticed light colored, fresh dirt in the man's hair as well. Odd, he thought. Within seconds the silent figure had disappeared through the exit. Abdullah returned. "I think everyone has left," he said. He turned to Rauser and Maryam. "Come on, let's take a look."

Rauser took a few steps towards the central nave, then stopped. He looked up in awe. "What's it like for a non-Muslim to be in the third most holy site in Islam?" Abdullah asked.

"It's absolutely amazing," Rauser whispered. He couldn't take his eyes off the ceiling. It was as if the golden mosaics in the ceiling drew his soul up into the heavens. He looked across at Abdullah, a grin on his face. He lifted his gaze once more to the intricate, gold tile-work above him. "Everyone should be allowed in here, just to experience the feeling of insignificance in the presence of such beauty. I wonder," he added thoughtfully, "how all this beauty impacted the first generation of worshippers in this building."

"Let me show you something." Abdullah was still in his tour-guide persona. He grabbed Rauser's arm, led him to the foundation stone and pointed to an imprint in the rock. "What do you think about that? The hoof print of Buraq, the horse Muhammad rode to heaven."

Rauser looked at the stone. It looked like a pagan object of worship to him. Just a large rock an animistic tribe would worship. Odd that Islam would give rocks—this one and the one in Mecca—a central role in their faith and worship. After all, the Qur'an specifically forbade worshipping the creation. He turned his gaze back to the beautiful ceiling. "I love the beauty of this place," he said quietly. "It's wonderful to actually see and experience it."

"How does it speak to you?" Maryam asked.

"Although I have lectured about this place several times I do have some new feelings actually standing here," he answered with a smile. "In my imagination I can see what took place here 1200 years ago."

"Well Professor Rauser," Maryam smiled, "give me the abridged university lecture. It's your turn after Abdullah gave us the outside tour."

"You sure?"

"I love history."

Rauser glanced at Abdullah. "Go for it Dr. Rauser. I'd love a free lecture from a world expert." Rauser wondered if the man was serious.

"OK then," he said. He stepped forward into the center of the nave. "It is hard to escape the conclusion that this place was designed to be a place of ecumenical unity among the world's monotheistic religions. As you know, this was the Jewish temple mount, the place where Jehovah met with his covenant people." Pointing to two large pillars he continued: "It's also a historical fact that those two pillars once had Christian crosses on them. Those pillars were probably originally taken from destroyed churches, but that still begs the question why those crosses were not removed until centuries later..." Rauser walked to one of the walls and pointed at one of the mosaics. "Look at the gorgeous palm leaves and plants in the beautiful tile work. Such pictures are perfectly acceptable in churches or synagogues but are anathema to orthodox Muslims, who consider such depictions as blurring the line between Creator and creation, thus leaving people open to worshipping the latter."

"Dr. Rauser," Abdullah raised his hand like a student, a whimsical smile on his face. "Could you tell us about the shape and design of the building?"

"Look at the four central pillars holding up the central dome," Rauser was in his lecturer mode. "They represent the four camps of the people of Israel in the desert as they camped around the tabernacle." He pointed to the other eight pillars. "Count the total number of pillars. There are 12 in total, and they represent the twelve tribes of Israel and the 12 apostles of Jesus. Now look at the building's layout: it's in the shape of a cross. It was originally designed by a Messianic-

Muslim as a place for Jewish-Christian-Muslim worship. 'Believers' they called themselves. This gorgeous building celebrates the tribal history of Israel, the cross of Jesus Christ, and Muhammad's journey to heaven." Rauser surprised himself with the finality of his final statement, and feared he may have overstepped the theological sensibilities of his audience of two. There was a momentary uncomfortable silence. Finally Abudallah spoke up.

"Where do you think the Hafsah Quran might be buried?" he asked quietly.

"I'd start with Father Constantin's hypothesis: the Well of Souls," Rauser answered.

"That's what Salim also thought," Abdullah stated.

Had he heard Abdullah correctly? Rauser looked at Maryam. Her head was turned in his direction; he could read the question forming in her eyes: *How did Abdullah know what Salim believed? The man knew things about Salim that no one else knew. How?* Rauser directed his gaze at the Saudi prince. "You sure about that?"

"So I heard." Abdullah shrugged his shoulders and glanced from Rauser to Maryam.

"From who?" Maryam probed.

"Oh, I have my sources," he answered cagily.

"What sources?" She was beginning to sound like a cop interrogating a suspect.

"That's none of your business."

"What do you mean, 'none of my business?'" Maryam raised her voice. "Everything about my uncle is my business. I've come all the way from Yemen because it's my business." She paused, looked Abdullah in the eye and slowly enunciated her next six words: "Tell me," and she paused, "who are your sources!"

Maryam's intensity had no effect. He calmly looked her in the eye. "The time for interrogations and religious lectures are over." He reached into his robe and pulled out a handgun.

"Are you crazy?" Maryam exclaimed. "Put that away!" Rauser looked at the man with shock. He felt betrayed.

"Each one of us wants the Hafsah Quran." Abdullah said. He looked Rauser in the eye. "No, I never betrayed you. You asked me to get involved. I joined you, but for my own reasons." The gun was pointed at Maryam. *The guy is nuts, thought Rauser. I should've recognized that when he helicoptered us out of his compound.* "You came looking for me," the Saudi bastard prince continued. "I didn't ask to be involved in your quest to find the Hafsah Quran." Maryam and Rauser were too stunned to answer. Their eyes stared down at the revolver. "I risked my life for you. I helped you escape death several times. If I'd wanted you dead, you would've been dead by now. The gun is just to help us all stay focused."

"On what?" Rauser asked.

"On finding the Hafsah Quran."

Rauser took a deep breath. He felt Maryam's hand on his arm. "Why?" he asked.

"We all know that the Hafsah Quran is the most important document in the world. It was hidden by those who understood its priceless value, something all the great Caliphs understood. Salim was about to betray this trust. He was going to hand over our heritage to infidel German academics, men who mock the God we serve. Salim was the worst of infidels. The Hafsah Quran needs to be protected by those willing to lay down their lives for the advancement of Islam." He paused briefly and looked directly at Maryam. "I was glad," he said deliberately, "when Salim was eliminated."

"Tell me it wasn't you." Her eyes drilled into the man. "Tell me you weren't involved in the death of my uncle!"

"He was the greatest traitor Islam has ever seen. The Muslim world had tried to quieten your family but he insisted on divulging our greatest secrets." To Rauser's ears Abdullah started to sound like the patient, zealous fanatics who had set the car bomb that killed his wife; the quiet, obsessive types who never succumbed to baubles and trinkets; men who could bomb innocent women and children without remorse.

"My family had the guts to stand up for truth," Maryam snapped. "You people justify any means for your extremist end."

Abdullah chuckled coldly. "True believers have a thousand years of practice to ensure our ends are met. We may no longer use assassins drugged on hashish, but our reach is long." He paused to make sure Maryam heard his next words. "If you had listened carefully to your father, you would've understood why you're not called 'Hafsah' but 'Maryam.'"

"What do you know about that?" she spat out.

"Everything. Your father named you Maryam because he no longer believed in the Hafsah Quran. Your name was his testimony that he had shifted his allegiance from the Quran to the son of Maryam, the prophet Isa, or Jesus." The anger flared up in Maryam's eyes, but Abdullah just grinned. "Do you know how your father was charged as a heretic? It was my mosque that bankrolled the court case against him. We would not normally take up a case like that, but he was a dangerous man. He had to be chased out of Yemen and exorcised from the Middle East. He was not only undermining our Islamic beliefs, he was blaspheming the Creator. And that would open the nation up to Allah's judgment. We are blessed that Yemeni judges are paid so little and fall so quickly."

"You're a crook!" Maryam snapped.

The man's cold, calculating fanaticism sent a chill up Rauser's spine. You couldn't negotiate with this kind of man. You either killed him or tried to escape from him. He measured the distance to the nearest door; it was far from where they were standing. He looked for anything that might serve as a weapon; the shiny marble surfaces offered nothing.

"Salim's death was predestined by Allah or it could not have succeeded," Abdullah said quietly. "It proves my men are doing the will of Allah." Maryam opened her mouth to speak but no words came.

"Such fanaticism is not the true way of Islam," Rauser said.

The response was dismissive: "You Westerners worship a weak God." Abdullah turned to Maryam. "Turn around and put your hands on your head." Maryam didn't budge. Abdullah cocked the pistol, "Stubbornness does not lead to longevity." She looked at the gun, then turned around slowly. Abdullah walked up behind her and laid the cold barrel against her neck. "Your family was chosen for the awful responsibility of keeping the truth of Islam. You failed in your duty. You opened Allah's revelation to the infidels' microscopes." He jammed the pistol into her head. "Salim failed the Quran, he failed Muhammad, peace be upon him, and he failed in the eyes of Allah. He deserved to die."

"You're nothing but a dog!" she cried. Rauser coud see the hatred etched in her eyes. This is not going well, he thought. He briefly caught Maryam's eye. He could see quiet desperation there.

"There's no one here to help you Dr. Rauser." The man had noticed his searching eyes.

"Do you really think," Rauser said mockingly, "that killing an old scholar is a heroic act?"

"Oh, I don't normally pull triggers." Abdullah chuckled. "People line up to do that. Salim put a price on his own head when he chose to work with the Germans. The only reason we spared his brother is because he chose to go to France to do his heretical scholarship. He was no longer desecrating the land of the prophet. But Salim worked secretively among us, like a scorpion. Scorpions are poisonous. They need to be crushed before they kill. Now that he has been eliminated, you and I may be able to work together to correct this evil that he was ready to unleash."

"I will never help you," Rauser sneered

"You don't understand, Doctor. Think of the boost your career would receive if you find the manuscript! You'll become a living legend. You owe this to yourself." He turned to Maryam. "And you owe it to your aunt, and to your father, and to all the women that have been called 'Hafsah' in your family line."

36

Fouad in the Old City

The last hour had seemed surreal to Fouad. Discussing Salim's case with this Israeli police officer had destroyed many of his stereotypes: these people weren't all arrogant, condescending or dismissive of Arabs. In fact, if he was honest, he'd have to admit he was enjoying his interaction with them. The self-deprecating humor and probing questions of the officer assigned to him left him feeling that he could easily work with him. He was amazed how quickly the man had honed in on the important variable: the Hafsah manuscript. His gut told him this man could be trusted.

As the car sped through the Jordan River valley, into the hills, and then merged into Jerusalem traffic, Fouad was surprised at how modern the outskirts of Jerusalem looked. They eventually parked just outside the Jaffa gate. The officer had led him through the maze of alleys to the security room in the heart of the Old City. A smiling lieutenant opened the door and greeted him. "Salaam Aleykum and welcome to Jerusalem, or as you might prefer, Al Quds," and firmly shook his hand.

"Aleykum Salaam," Fouad replied, happy the officer spoke Arabic. After introductions all around Fouad scanned the little room. It was jammed with screens tracking everything in the Old City. "You can't pick your nose here without someone watching," he commented, amazed at the high resolution screens.

"We like it that way," the Israeli officer said. "With these fanatical settlers of ours going in and out to pray at the wall and Islamists trying to provoke them, you never know when the lid could blow off." Fouad nodded.

"Now that we all know each other," the lieutenant continued, "I think we also realize we're all after the same information. I suggest we keep this little joint venture out of the media for now. Once we make some arrests or get our hands on the manuscripts we can work jointly on our press releases." He looked at Fouad. The Yemeni captain nodded, pleased that they offered to involve him with any media fall-out.

"Captain Fouad, thank you for providing us with the information on the Land Rover and its occupants. That has already opened up several different fruitful directions of inquiry. For instance, we learned that one of the passengers who travelled on a bus from Abu Ghosh to Jerusalem carried an expensive bag with the name "Saud" embroidered on its side."

We're making headway, Fouad thought. "Using some back-channels we contacted the Saudi police in Najran. They kindly gave us the cell phone number of one Abdullah Ibn Saud. We've been able to trace a few calls from this number with a man named Siddiqi. For those of you who don't know, Siddiqi is on our terrorist wanted list."

"Were you able to listen in on any calls?" asked Fouad.

"Yes. Siddiqi apparently arranged permission for Saud and his friends to spend the night in the Dome of the Rock. It also appears that Saud may have arranged to have someone killed in the old city.

"Who is Siddiqi working for?"

"Palestinian Islamic Jihad."

"Has the hit taken place?" Fouad wondered who Siddiqi was trying to eliminate.

"Not that we're aware of."

Fouad gestured to all the television screens. "Have your cameras picked up Rauser, Abdullah Ibn Saud or Maryam?"

"Unfortunately not."

"Any ideas of where they might be?" probed Fouad.

"They are probably wearing disguises," the lieutenant suggested with a shrug. "The phone calls were too short for us to triangulate their position."

Fouad smiled—nice to hear the famed Israeli's also got outsmarted once in a while. "Any other news?"

"In one of the calls Siddiqi mentioned that the safe house was ready."

"Any idea where that might be?"

"It appears to be right here in the old city. We're trying to establish a location."

"Let Maryam go," said Rauser. "What you want is that manuscript. She can't help with that. I'll do what I can to help you find it."

"I may need her later," Abdullah smiled. "I'm planning on getting out of here alive."

"I'm never going to help!" Maryam snapped defiantly.

Abdullah turned towards Rauser, lifted the pistol and fired. Rauser ducked automatically. The bullet hit the pillar behind him, ricochetted, and lodged into the foundation stone. This guy is truly nuts, he thought. I can't believe he'd pull the trigger in here! Maybe someone heard the shot.

"Don't try to run or scream Rauser. The next bullet won't miss. Yes, I need you. I will keep you alive if you cooperate. If you don't—well, my informants always do... " he added menacingly.

All I have is Father Constantin's hypothesis which this lunatic now confirms was also Salim's hypothesis, Rauser thought. I have to stretch this out as long as possible. Someone has to show up! "I'll show you where it might be, but I need tools to make accurate measurements,"

"Wrong answer." Abdullah turned to Maryam and pulled the trigger. The bullet grazed her thigh. She bit her lip suppressing a scream and grabbed her leg. Blood oozed through the fabric.

"Rauser," said Abdullah motioning with his pistol, "go and stand by the rock." Rauser stalled. "Get going Rauser," Abdullah barked. "You want to be a dead hero?" He pointed the pistol in the direction where he wanted Rauser to stand.

Rauser moved slowly to the edge of the rock, his fists clenched. He was angry; he felt helpless. As he turned around at the rock he saw Abdullah Saud grab some plastic ties from his pocket. He pushed Maryam around and tied her hands behind her back. Then he backed away and threw something at Rauser. "Bandage her," he ordered as the object flew towards. "And when you do, think about how your stubbornness is affecting her."

Rauser walked rapidly back to Maryam. He saw the muscles in her jaws flex; she was doing everything to keep from screaming. "Don't give in," she whispered through her teeth. "Buy time. We'll get our chance."

"She's fine," Abdullah ridiculed. "It's just a flesh wound." It looked like a bad scrape. Rauser applied the bandage tightly. Immediately the blood stopped flowing.

"Back to the rocky tract," Abdullah ordered waving the pistol in the direction of the foundation stone. "How much time do we have left before morning prayers?"

Did he say 'rocky tract?' I've heard that term somewhere before. Rauser looked down at his watch: "It's 15:80."

"Hours have 60 minutes, professor. You can't take the pressure?" Abdullah's voice was laced with sarcasm.

Rauser never heard the man. His mind was racing, flipping the pages of his office Qur'an. It stopped at Surah 15, verse 80. "I got it!" he shouted spontaneously. "I figured out the meaning of one of the numbers on Salim's note. It's a verse from the Quran! It's surah 15, verse 80."

Abdulah was silent for a minute, then he quoted the verse in question: "'The Companions of the Rocky Tract also rejected the messengers.'" He looked at Rauser. "Why is that important?"

"The 'Companions of the Rocky Tract' that rejected the messengers' were the Hebrew people," Rauser said excitedly. "Whether one looks at the Bible or the life of Muhammad it's clear that the Jews rejected their own prophets, as well as Jesus and Muhammad. The 'rocky tract' that was central to the Jews' rejection was *this* rock, the rock in the Holy of Holies: the foundation stone."

"What does all this have to do with the location of the Hafsah Quran?"

Rauser fell silent. He suddenly felt certain that if they dug under this rock they might find the Hafsah Quran. And if they did find it he'd be forced to give it to the mad Saudi.

"I knew you would cooperate, Dr. Rauser. Let us descend into the Well of Souls. We may well find the Hafsah Qur'an there." Saud waved the gun in the direction of the door. Maryam hobbled after Rauser and the three of them walked down the stairs into the dark cave.

"Turn on the light Rauser. Find the light switch."

Rauser looked around, found the light switch and flipped it on. "The light is broken."

"Don't be a hero," Abdullah threatened. "Turn on the light."

"Sorry man." Anger and frustration crept into Rauser's voice. "But it's true. The bulb must be broken."

37

The Old City by Night

Fouad knew the politics of the Temple Mount. An aggressive response by the Israeli security forces could spark a major international incident, something they were not likely to risk in the current political climate. "I can go up to the Temple Mount," he offered. "I'm a Muslim and have the liberty to enter the Dome of the Rock. Wire me. If the suspects are in there, I'll let you know."

The Israeli captain and lieutenant looked at him for a long moment, then nodded. "I'll have a soldier direct you to the Omar gate. You're on your own after that." He handed Fouad a pistol. "Be careful—and don't tell anyone you got this hardware from us."

Fouad was surprised the lieutenant had given him a weapon, and amazed that these men would integrate him, a Yemeni, into their patrol as an equal—without having to get permission from the highest authority in the land. No one in Yemen is going to believe this, he thought. His escort led the way out of the surveillance room and into a darkened alleyway. As they walked through the maze of the Old City, Fouad felt like he was back on night patrol in Sana'a. Every now and then a cat ran across an alleyway chasing some rodent. The alleys were devoid of human activity. The store-fronts were shuttered, the yellow streetlights reflected off the cobblestones. Suddenly two muffled gun shots echoed through the darkness. The sound appeared to come from the Dome of the Rock. Fouad's escort grabbed his arm and pulled him into the shadows. The man put his fingers to his lips and pointed to his earpiece. "The Lieutenant said to stay put," he whispered. He motioned for Fouad to crouch down.

Two minutes later Fouad's escort tapped him on the arm and pointed down the alley. A patrol of five soldiers was coming towards them. It stopped just short of the intersection ahead. Half the soldiers took up positions in the shadows on one side of the street while the other flanked the other side. They dropped to one knee. Everyone waited.

Minutes later the silhouettes of three people wearing long, white dishdashes came walking down the road. One of them was limping. He heard two of them arguing in heated whispers. As they came closer he recognized Rauser, followed by the limping Maryam, her hands tied behind her back. Abdullah Saud was last. He was holding a pistol, pointing at the two in front of him. Suddenly a command in Arabic punctured the darkness. "Drop your weapons. Now!"

Fouad saw the Saudi look up and down the dark alleyway. "If you shoot, I'll kill her," he yelled. His pistol was leveled at Maryam's head as he glanced from side to side.

I wonder why he's looking behind himself, Fouad thought. Is there another patrol back there? He was glad to be out of the glare of the street lamps. The Saudi could not spot them. "Open that door Rauser." Saud's voice sounded strained as it echoed down the dark alley. The silhouette of his pistol flashed briefly at a door that opened into the alleyway. "Hurry or I shoot Maryam."

They could see Rauser lift the latch. Nothing happened. The American looked over his shoulder and shrugged: "It's locked." Fouad was amazed at the man's composure.

A controlled voice from the other end of the alleyway broke through the darkness. "Why are you taking these people hostage? I would advise you to release them."

"Once you get your hands on me you Zionist swine, you'll never let me free. There's more at stake here than a few hostages."

"We are not here to hurt you. We know you're looking for the Hafsah Quran. We feel it may be best if we work together."

"I would sooner die than work with you. I'm not afraid to die." Abdullah's voice had a nervous shake.

Fouad could see Maryam clearly now. She carried herself with poise. "Maryam, this is Fouad." He could see Maryam glance in his direction. "I'm here to help. Are you hurt?"

"Don't answer the question!" Abdullah barked.

"Abdullah Saud," Fouad continued, "I too am a Muslim – from Yemen. We all want to work with you to find the ancient manuscripts."

"You are a lacky working for the Zionists." The voice was thick with disgust.

"Mr. Saud," the voice from the other side of the ally continued, "if there are any manuscripts, we can assure you that we will negotiate in good faith with mutually agreed upon authorities."

"Never!" screamed Saud followed by a shot fired in the direction of the patrol. A second shot rang out from the far end of the alley followed by Abdullah's scream echoing through the old city. His pistol clattered to the ground. Rauser dove to the ground and snatched it off the pavement.

"Everyone to the ground," an authoritative voice barked from the other side of the alley. "Hands over your head, palms on the ground! I want the man who picked up the pistol to slide it hard in this direction." Rauser gave the pistol a hard push.

Fouad's eyes followed the pistol as it slid down the cobblestones. Then he looked back at the group. Rauser and Maryam were laying face down. Saud was sitting up, clamping his right wrist with his left hand, cursing and yelling. Several shadows erupted out of the darkness and took him down. "Cowards! Hiding in the dark like rats! You haven't heard the end of this. You know who I am?"

"Shall we go see?" Fouad whispered to the Israeli officer. The officer nodded. By the time they arrived the patrol had handcuffed everyone. Within minutes two soldiers arrived with a stretcher. One of them stood in front of Saud, his arms akimbo. "You want to shut up and get a free ride or rant and walk?" The Saudi prince slumped down and folded himself in the fetal position. The two soldiers rolled him onto the stretcher and carried him out of the ally toward the Jaffa gate. Rauser and Maryam followed from a distance, handcuffed and guarded by an IDF patrol. They saw Saud loaded into the ambulance, the soldiers taking positions on either side of his stretcher. Within seconds the vehicle sped into the Jerusalem night.

Rauser and Maryam were led to another police car and pushed into the back seat. Rauser glanced up and saw Fouad hop in another police car. "Now what?" he thought as the police car raced, with lights flashing, to Jerusalem's central police station.

38

The Jerusalem Hostel

Omar paced nervously in his hostel room: fours steps one way, four steps back. He glanced once again at the book on the dresser. Faizal had given it to him after he had texted him with the request to walk him back to the hostel along the rooftops. The skinny janitor had arrived with a package under his arm and silently escorted him back in the cool evening air. Right after he'd thanked him on arrival, Faizal had thrust the package in his hands. "Meet the man of light,' he had said and disappeared.

He looked again at the cover: it repulsed, yet drew him. He sat down on the bed. Beads of sweat formed on his forehead. His eyes shifted between the Injil, the New Testament, and the Quran. "Don't open it" the inner voices screamed. Yet his heart wanted to see what was written between those black covers. The voices of his father, mother, teachers and that of Siddiqi rang through his head: "That's the distorted word of Allah! Don't be deceived by it." Yet something deep inside him drew him to it.

He stood up once more, lifted his eyes to the ceiling, bent his arms at the elbows, palms facing heavenward and prayed: "Ya Allah, will I really find the man of light in this book? I'll open it one time, and if I sense that you are not there I'll never open it again. But if the man of light steps from the pages, then I know this book is from you." He walked to the dresser and stood in front of the Bible. He extended his index finger and slowly, randomly opened the book to a random page. He bent down and read the first paragraph he saw: *Jesus shouted to the crowds, "If you trust me, you are trusting not only me, but also God who sent me. For when you see me, you are seeing the one who sent me. I have come as a light to shine in this dark world, so that all who put their trust in me will no longer remain in the dark."*

He closed his eyes. *This was the man of light he had seen; this was the man who absorbed his shame and guilt; this was the man who took Allah's punishment for our misdeeds. This man speaks for Allah.*

A floorboard creaked on the other side of his hostel door. He looked at his watch. It was 3 a.m., too early for anyone to be about. He slid nervously behind the door and waited. Had the Israeli's tracked him down? His heart beat in his throat. Ever so slowly he slid behind the door. The floorboard creaked again and there was a faint audible whisper. Suddenly the door flung open and a man in police uniform, pistol drawn, stood in the doorway. The cop swung the pistol to the right and then to the left. With the speed of a viper, Omar tackled the man from behind the door. His weight drove the man to the ground. The gun clattered to the foot of the dresser and Omar lunged for it, rolled over and shot the groaning man.

He expected a second man: cops always came in pairs. He dove behind the bed and leveled the gun at the door. A second man appeared in the doorway, aiming his handgun indiscriminately from left to right. Omar fired a single shot. The man staggered backward against the wall, grabbed his chest, and fell to the ground. Was there a third? His ears were ringing from the gun blasts in the confined space.

A woman began screaming hysterically in the next room. He peered over the bed. Both men were moving. He jumped and reach for the second man's gun. *I've got to get out of here!* He headed for the door. His ears were still ringing. Then he heard a voice coming down the hallway yelling "Where's Omar? Anyone seen Omar?" *Someone else was after him.* The woman in the other room was still screaming, but the corridor was empty. Omar dropped down behind the bed again and pointed the pistol at the door. Suddenly a silhouette appeared and he fired two quick shots in succesion.

The hysterical woman stopped screaming. He stood up. The third person was dressed in a white robe just like his. Siddiqi lay slumped on the floor.

225

Omar ran silently down the deserted corridor to the lift. Acting like a concerned hotel guest he lifted the emergency phone off the hook. "Quick," he shouted to reception. "There was a shoot-out of some sort. Two police officers appear to have been wounded. Call an ambulance." His voice carried down the hallway. Doors began to open cautiously, and people stuck their heads out to see what had happened. As the guests filled the corridor, Omar disappeared into the night.

39

Golden Gate Hostel

Rauser had never been imprisoned before. Sitting on the hard bench of his cell he went over the charges he would likely face: illegal entry into Israel, Salim's murder, and insulting Islam by entering the Dome of the Rock. Was this the end of the road for him? By the time the legal proceedings had finished in Israel and Yemen he would probably be an old man. A black wave of depression washed over his spirit and he put his head in his hands. "Father," he prayed, "I need a miracle." He looked up and saw a ray of light peak through the window. Dawn was breaking. His mind drifted to the immediate future. Even if the Israelis never charged him with the crimes done in Yemen and the illegal entry into Saudi Arabia, he would likely never get another visa for Israel: they didn't take kindly to infiltrators.

He wondered what had happened to Maryam. He liked her. She was smart, brave, beautiful and multicultural... and yet he knew she could never replace his Ruth. She lacked the one thing he needed now more than ever: the spiritual peace Ruth had had—and which he needed.

Then deal with the issue now! The thought came to him as a command. To disobey was not an option. He bowed his head again. "God," he prayed, "even if I never get out of here, I want you to know, I'm coming back to you. I'm not here to make a deal to get out. I need you more than a good job and tenure. I need your peace once again. Forgive me for having given you the silent treatment these last years." He stood up and took a deep breath. "All right God," he whispered, "now where do we go?" Slowly he exhaled. As he did it was as if the wall he had built against God flowed away. A deep peace, which made no sense under the circumstances, flooded into the depths of his being.

A voice sounded in his mind. "I've waited a long time to give you peace in your pain, son. It's been hard to respect your desire to grieve alone. I know what you're going through: I once lost a son." Tears welled up in Rauser's eyes. The voice now pierced his heart. "Ruth is doing well. She is waiting for you."

He was unsure how long he had sat there when he heard the lock turn, and a guard entered his cell carrying a breakfast tray. An hour later the door opened again. He was surprised to see Captain Fouad, along with an Israeli officer. "Rauser," Fouad announced, "how are you?"

"Oddly enough, I'm not doing too bad," replied Rauser. "How did you get here?"

"I always get my man," Fouad smiled, "even if they're American." I guess I'll be heading to Yemen as well, Rauser thought. "So what's going to happen to me now? Are you escorting me to Yemen?"

"No. You're free to go." Rauser couldn't believe his ears. He stood there, speechless.

"I didn't know you had bad hearing," Fouad joked. "It's true. You're free to go. Come on."

Rauser walked up to the Yemeni captain and shook his hand. "You mean I won't be charged with anything?"

"You're fortunate Maryam took off with you," Fouad replied. "We've compared her story with our data, and since my only concern is Salim's murder, and since all the data indicates you were not the killer, I have no more interest in you."

Rauser turned towards the Israeli officer with a questioning look. "We did a background check as well," the man said. "You have a number of important friends in Israel. They all vouched for your character and since your only crime is an immigration offence, and since you still had a valid visa, I too have no reason to make a mountain out of a molehill. I suggest, however that you stay away from Saudi Arabia for a while."

Rauser smiled at the reference to Saudi Arabia. "How did you discover that I am not Dr. Salim's murderer?" he asked as they walked through the police station.

"We recorded the phone conversations between Saud, Siddiqi and Faizal. When we searched Faizal's home we found Omar." The Israeli officer led him to the lobby. Rauser's heart skipped a beat: there stood Maryam, with sparkling eyes and a brig grin on her face. There was no need to say anything as he walked up and embraced her. She made no attempt to disentangle herself from his embrace. Finally, he pulled away, and holding her shoulders he looked her in the eye. "I don't know how to say this, but this last week with you has been one of the most exciting weeks in my life."

"You know," she answered with a twinkle in her eye, "You're not the only one who had a good time..." She paused, momentarily as if hesitant to offer up the next sentence. "Guess what? Fouad worked things out with my boss so I have three days off for having worked overtime."

"Fouad is getting soft." Rauser smiled. "Let's find a place to stay for a few days. I know a place called the *Golden Gate Hostel* in the old city in the Muslim Quarter. It's not much to look at, but they serve a great breakfast and the place has a real old-inn feel to it. It's been around for centuries." They left the station. Rauser hailed a taxi and asked the driver to drop them off at the Damascus Gate. As they walked down the steps and through the ancient doors accosted by sellers and assaulted by hawkers trying their best to entice them into their stalls, Rauser felt at home. The world seemed to be alive in a way it hadn't for a long time. His senses feasted on a myriad of little things: the colorful fruit stands shimmering with shiny oranges, apples and pears, the fragrant spices from the east stacked in neat little geometric shapes and best of all, the exotic girl fate had dropped into his lap.

They passed through the black wrought iron gate of the ancient hostel. A young Palestinian man sat behind the desk serving two blond backpackers in flawless English. Al Jazeera played on the television screen beside him. Behind him was a security monitor that projected images of the hallways that honeycombed the building. Instant coffee, sugar and creamers were set out for the guests.

"I would like two beds, one in the women's section and one in the men's dorm," said Rauser in Arabic. The concierge switched languages, slid some forms across the counter and asked them to wait while he checked the rooms. Rauser filled out the forms while Maryam prepared a cup of coffee. They sank into one of the large wooden chairs lining the vestibule, exhausted yet satisfied.

"Maryam, ever since talking to the monk at the monastery in the Sinai, I wonder if we should take one last look for the Hafsah manuscript here in Jerusalem." Rauser was pensive.

"You want to go back to the Well of Souls to finish what we started?"

"No." said Rauser.

"Why not?" She looked at him quizzically. "We never had a chance to search it."

"I don't think it's there."

"What do you mean?"

"The *Dome of the Rock* wasn't built when Caliph Umar came here, so the Hafsah Quran is probably not in a Muslim building. When the Caliph captured the city he did it without a fight. I think Umar may have made a deal with the Patriarch."

"So... where do we look?"

"In the Church of the Holy Sepulcher."

"You've gotta be kidding!"

Rauser smiled at the expression of surprise. "If we're going to look where I think we should look," he continued, "we will need to sneak into the church at night, wait till it is deserted, and then start poking around all likely spots."

"Excuse me sir, but your rooms are ready," the concierge interrupted.

Maryam turned to Rauser, "I don't know about you, but I'm exhausted. Let's rest, shower, and meet here at 8 p.m. By then we should be fit enough to spend a night in church."

He nodded. "I feel like I aged twenty years. See you at eight." He watched her as she followed the concierge out of the lobby.

We will need some small pry bars, he thought. He got up, slipped out of the hostel and into the tangle of shops, bought a small backpack, four small pry bars and returned to his room. Within mintues he was under the covers and fast asleep.

40

Church of the Holy Sepulcher

Rauser and Maryam stood in front of the two, seven meter high wooden doors. Rauser looked at Maryam. He noticed that she looked a bit tense. She had mentioned that she'd once visited the Notre Dame in Paris. What made her nervous this time, she'd said, was the fact that this was a place of pilgrimage, and she wasn't sure of the rituals. What was she supposed to do? What if she did it all wrong? What if it compromised her faith?

They stepped through the massive wooden doors and immediately faced a group of pilgrims kneeling in front of a large, pale stone, approximately three meters in length, and kissing it. "Why are they kissing the stone?" Maryam whispered.

"Eastern Orthodox Christians believe that Jesus was dressed for burial upon that rock; it's called 'the stone of unction.' They kiss it to show their appreciation for Jesus's death for them.'" No sooner had he given his explanation before he remembered his response to the Muslims' veneration of the foundation stone in the Dome of the Rock. Perhaps he had been too judgmental...

"Sounds a bit idolatrous to me," Maryam said. They walked around the kneeling pilgrims into the main rotunda. The massive expanse was packed with hundreds of people, mingling, going from chapel to chapel praying and lighting candles. In the middle of the rotunda was a small shrine. "What's in that little shrine?" Maryam pointed to the building.

"That's called the aedicule."

"What's an aedicule?

"In it a small chapel known as the Chapel of the Angels. It is the foyer to the cave believed to be the place where Jesus was buried and rose from the dead. People built a shrine on the spot, and the rest of the cathedral in which we are now standing was built around that original shrine." Maryam was silent and looked around at the people, the candles, the paintings, and the line leading into the aedicule.

"You want to go inside?"

"Should I? I'm not a Christian."

"That's O.K. This is not like the Dome of the Rock where only Muslim males can enter. Jesus invites everyone into his presence, anywhere, anytime." He paused for a moment. "I bought some gum before we left. You want a stick?"

"No." She looked at him with an odd look in her eyes.

"I think you should take one. We may need it chewed up later on." Maryam furrowed her brow into a question, but took a stick and put it in her mouth. They joined the queue that led to the aedicule. It took about twenty minutes before it was their turn. As they entered the place Rauser surreptitiously placed his gum in the door lock. Maryam's eyes asked the question: "What are you doing?"

Rauser just winked and answered. "I think mine was enough; you can continue enjoying yours." Once through the door they found themselves standing before a small wooden pulpit. They walked around it and entered another, smaller door less than a meter and a half high. It forced them to bow before entering the tiny room. There, in the semi darkness, illuminated by flickering candlelight, they could see a low rock ledge. Several people were kneeling in prayer and an Eastern Orthodox Monk stood at the end of the small little room. He motioned to the three kneeling pilgrims to move on when Rauser and Maryam entered the cave.

"Do I have to kneel?" whispered Maryam.

"Yes."

"But I'm not Christian."

"You don't have to pray. Just kneel out of respect. If you want to pray, feel free." Rauser knew she feared committing idolatry. "You can tell God anything you want." They entered the room and knelt down. Rauser reached for and held Maryam's hand as he bowed his head. Thoughts flooded back as he thought of his mother and father regularly praying with him before every meal and before he went to bed. *"God,"* he murmured, *"Thanks for looking after Maryam and me. I don't have much time – you see the monk here as well as I do. I would like to leave two requests: please help us tonight, and thanks for restoring my sense of peace with you. I'm glad the silence is over and my shriveled soul has found new life with you."*

"Time to go," whispered the monk. The two of them stood up and left the cave. As they approached the door of the chapel Maryam whispered: "Why did you put your gum in the lock back there?"

"Because we have to get back in tonight."

"For what?"

"The Hafsah Quran."

"Whatever you say professor," whispered Maryam, adding with a smile: "And now perhaps the great professor Rauser would be so kind as to guide me through the rest of the building." Rauser enjoyed showing her around this ancient basilica. He showed her the omphalos, believed by pre-Copernican peoples to signify the naval of the earth. They toured the Armenian section, where he explained the meanings embedded in the beautiful mosaics. He took her to the roof where the Coptic Monks lived. As they went up the stairs he showed her the tiny crusader crosses scratched in the stones by pilgrims over a thousand years ago.

"The actions of the crusaders must have pained Jesus deeply," he said. "Jesus never condoned killing."

"Why should we go back there?" she asked as he led her back to the main basilica. "We've already seen it."

"Once the pilgrims and tourists have left the real rituals begin. The Eastern Orthodox, Armenians, Catholics, and Coptics all get a chance to worship without the distraction of pilgrims and tourists. I've asked my Coptic friend if we could be his guests for the evening. Once they're done, we'll just stay and tell them we want some time alone to pray."

"And then what?"

"Then we'll search for the Hafsah Quran."

They walked back up to the roof and were greeted by an Ethiopian monk. "Hello Dr. Rauser, it's great to see you again. Can I offer you a cup of tea?" They drank tea, chatted, ate some dried nuts and fruits, and drank some more tea until it was time for the evening liturgy. They made their way back down to the rotunda, where the Coptic priest introduced them to some of his fellow priests. Following some brief instructions Rauser and Maryam joined the buzz of activity as groups of monks from each of the ancient churches worked efficiently to sweep the building, change the oil in the lamps and clean the candle holders. Then the worship began.

From twelve midnight till almost three in the morning Maryam and Rauser enjoyed the chants and prayers echoing through the rotunda. It was half-way through the singing and prayers that Rauser pulled Maryam to a kneeling rail in the Catholic area, right under a candle. "What have you got there?" Maryam asked him as Rauser pulled a book from his back pack.

"A Bible."

"A Bible? I thought we were going to dig?"

"Pull up the pictures you took at the crime scene of Salim's on your cell phone. Last night I couldn't sleep—my mind was full of the events of the past days. Suddenly something clicked: I realized there was a double meaning in the second list of Salim's numbers. Read the last set to me, will you."

"60:2:6-8."

If you count up the number of books in the Bible in the same manner that Muslims do with the chapters in the Quran, book number 60 in the Bible is the letter of I Peter. What we have in I Peter 2:6-8 is a verse that sounds a lot like the verse in the Quran, but which clarifies the Rocky Tract mentioned in the Quran even more. Listen: *"As the scriptures say, 'I am placing a cornerstone in Jerusalem, chosen for great honor, and anyone who trusts in him will never be disgraced. Yes, you who trust him recognize the honor God has given him. But for those who reject him, 'The stone that the builders rejected has now become the corner stone.' And 'He is the stone that makes people stumble, the rock that makes them fall.'"* "This stone," Rauser went on, "is considered to be Jesus Christ by Christians. Salim knew both passages dealt with the stone—and we kept thinking it must be a physical stone. My guess is that if Hafsah was a Messianic Muslim who believed in Jesus, she would want her manuscript buried under the stone that closed the tomb of Jesus: her spiritual corner stone."

"So do you think it's under the large stone where we knelt and prayed?"

"No. That stone has never moved. I think it's under the pulpit in the *Chapel of the Angel.* As a devout Muslim Salim believed Jesus was the Prophet of the Word. I therefore believe the best place to look is under the ancient pulpit that symbolically held the Christian *Word* or Bible."

When the last hymn was sung and the last monk had regressed for the evening, Rauser's friend approached them. "Rauser, I probably don't want to know what you want to do here before the pilgrims come again in two hours," he said. "Just don't get me in trouble."

"Father," answered Rauser, "Thanks so much for arranging everything. We will keep our noses clean and make sure yours doesn't get broken." The monk smiled, shook their hands and disappeared back up the stairs.

Stepping silently towards *The Chapel of the Angel*, Rauser opened to door. "The gum did the trick," he whispered. "Close the door behind you. We don't want company." He walked up to the ancient pulpit. "Let's move it and pry up the stone underneath. They carefully moved the pulpit, afraid that the iron clasps that kept the ancient pedestal together would snap. They held. After they'd moved it to one side Rauser pulled the four small pry bars from his backpack. Scraping the seams of the old marble floor tiles they worked furiously. "I feel like I'm digging my way out of prison," Rauser whispered laboriously. "I sure hope we find something."

They continued to dig and scrape until the seams between the stones were clean. Then Rauser wedged each of the pry-bars into the exposed cracks. "You lean on these two and I'll lean on the other two." They pressed with all their body weight against the pry-bars. Slowly the stone rose, and as it did they could see something square beneath it.

"You see that?" whispered Maryam, her eyes wide with surprise.

"Yeah, but this thing is heavier than I anticipated," Rauser grunted. "Put it down again. We need to jam it up. You have anything?"

"Your shoes," Maryam said, wiping beads of sweat from her forehead. "Take them off, and put them near your knees. When the stone slides up, nudge them into the cracks to jam it." Once again they threw their weight against the pry bars and Rauser slid his shoes into the cracks. The stone jammed half way up.

"Now what?" Maryam was breathing heavily.

"We'll reposition the bars and give it one more push." They leaned against the bars and saw the stone move. With a final shove, it shifted off to the side. There, in the hole, lay a gold box encrusted with jewels. A series of words were engraved on it in an ancient script.

"What does that mean?" Maryam asked in an excited whisper.

"They're proto-Arabic or Syro-Aramaic letters, a language that predated Arabic. It says, "The words of Muhammad, the servant of Allah."

"You probably want to analyze everything now Dr. Rauser," Maryam smiled impishly, "but we should think of the time. Don't the priests re-open this place to the public at 4 A.M. That's only half an hour from now. What should we do?"

"Put the box in the backpack and get everything back to normal. Let's put something in its place, though."

"What?" Maryam looked around the chapel for something to grab.

"Let's leave our shoes," Rauser said. "It's a nice symbolic gesture."

"What do you mean?'

"Just like Moses took off his sandals when he stood before Jehovah, we can take off our shoes in respect for Jesus and the true words of Muhammad." They slipped their shoes into the hole, replaced the stone, filled the cracks with dirt, and moved the pulpit back in place. Then they slipped out of the aedicule. When a new cadre of priests opened the doors at 4 a.m. they quietly slipped out of the building on stockinged feet.

41

Prison

Omar had run straight to Faizal's home. Unfortunately the Israeli Defence Forces were waiting for him when he arrived. By morning he had been thrown into a prison cell and by evening Siddiqi, whose bandaged body demanded the lower bunk, had joined him.

Sitting in silence and holding Siddiqi's sleeping head in his lap Omar entreated Allah: "Please," he beseeched, "save Siddiqi and take my life if you need to." His mind replayed the terrible scene over and over: the door bursting open, the men in the police uniforms and the shots. He would never forgive himself if Siddiqi died. He felt movement and looked down.

"Where am I?" mumbled Siddiqi.

"In prison." Siddiqi winced. Must be pain, Omar thought.

"What happened?"

"I'm sorry," Omar said through tear stained eyes. "Why did you come with the police?"

"I didn't come with the police. Those men were just dressed up like police."

Omar was confused. "Then who did I shoot?"

"Men sent by the greatest devil of all." Omar noticed Siddiqi's eyes narrow in hatred and his mind became a blur of questions. Who in the world would Siddiqi think was the greatest devil of them all? The Israeli's?

Siddiqi had other questions: "How did I get here?"

"After the shootout the IDF came and must have taken you to the hospital to get bandaged up. I was dragged in this cell to join you a few minutes ago. I spent the night in some other police station."

"He knows everything!" Siddiqi blurted.

Omar looked at Siddiqi's panicked face. "Who is 'he'?

"The devil's name is Prince Abdullah Saud, the imam from the blog. He's the one who bankrolled everything. He paid the janitors to photocopy and email me all of Salim's papers. He's the one who commissioned your hit on Salim and the Germans."

"You mean this was all about money?" Omar asked suspiciously.

"A month ago I wrote the imam and explained how the PIJ was struggling to sustain the fight in Gaza when he offered a way we could make some quick cash – with one caveat."

"And?"

"I had to swear on the Quran that I would never reveal his identity."

"Then what happened?"

"He explained about Salim. He asked if I could be counted on to eliminate the enemies of Allah and protect the honor of the Quran." Omar was silent. He knew the rest of the story. He understood the need to protect the honor of Islam and the prophet. He also knew the strain Siddiqi was always under to find funding. Still, he struggled with the price: three dead men in Germany and Salim.

"Then why did he try to kill me?"

"He was afraid I would keep the Hafsah Quran, that I wouldn't turn it over to him."

"You told him that?" exclaimed Omar.

"Not exactly. I suggested perhaps we could have a shared ownership. I thought he was committed to our cause." Siddiqi paused. "He had already sent a million dollars in our support. I never suspected him to be the devil he was; I thought he was one of us."

"So the policemen weren't policemen but his paid assassins?"

"That's right. He asked where you were and I told him."

An awkward silence filled the room. Siddiqi's body felt increasingly heavy. "How did you find out Saud was going to kill me?"

"Saud recruited some PIJ guys. I happened to run into them at the market. They told me about some rich guy who called them up this morning and promised them fifty thousand bucks if they eliminated someone."

Omar was quiet. "I can't believe my own PIJ family would sell me out for a few bucks," he said finally.

"The PIJ guys never knew it was you. They just knew it was some guy in your room." Omar needed to have one last question answered.

"Why didn't you stop the killing?"

"Omar," Siddiqi cried, "how can you ask that question! You're like a son to me! That night, when I couldn't get to sleep, I lay there thinking about the hit the PIJ were going to do. Suddenly I realized the statistical impossibility of a person having enough money to order a hit in the very same hostel where you were staying. I immediately went looking for you. Unfortunately I was too late. When I heard the shooting my heart broke." Omar didn't know what to say.

"Omar, I'm so sorry ... please, can you forgive me?"

Omar was silent before answering. *What would the man of light say?*

42

House of Manuscripts Yemen

"So what are you going to do with the manuscript?" Maryam asked. Rauser was quiet for a few minutes. His eyes roved over the old manuscripts being augmented in Salim's lab.

"I'm not sure yet. As I analyzed the document it struck me that perhaps Salim had a double meaning with the numbers 60:2:6-8. Instead of referring just to I Peter in the Bible, he also referred to the Surah 60, section 2 verses 6-8." Rauser reached for the Quran sitting on the shelf: *"There was indeed in them an excellent example for you to follow – for those whose hope is in Allah and in the Last Day. But if any turn away, truly Allah is free of all wants, worthy of all praise. It may be that Allah will grant love and friendship between you and those whom ye now hold as enemies. For Allah has power over all things; and Allah is oft-forgiving, most merciful. Allah forbids you not, with regard to those who fight you not for your faith nor drive you out of your homes from dealing kindly and justly with them: for Allah loveth those who are just."* Rauser closed the book and placed it back on the table. "I think Salim knew this manuscript could lead to a potentially disastrous situation between world political powers. He too was aware that the Hafsah Quran could hugely exacerbate the tensions in the Muslim world," he said.

"So should we keep it hidden?"

"Perhaps one day the truth of these manuscripts will come out but I think for the time being, the truth that needs to be revealed is not this manuscript but the sacred verses that guided Salim: that Muslims too must follow Jesus, the Word of God, who reflected God's love, and that in the light of that and of God's future judgment we would do well to love Him above all and our neighbours as ourselves. Surely that message is particularly pertinent for the Middle East at this time. When that message has been internalized then, perhaps, the world will be ready to face the truth of the Hafsah Quran."

"What about your quest for tenure?"

"There are more important things than tenure."

"Are you concerned about the Saudi government coming after the Hafsah Quran – or after you?"

"Yes. I'll deal with that when it happens."

Appendix A: Historical Facts

- "Hafsah" was one of Muhammad's thirteen wives. She kept detailed notes regarding the prophet Muhammad's revelations.

- According to local lore Muhammad commissioned the building of the Great Mosque of Sana'a, Yemen, around 630 A.D.

- During the renovation of the Great Mosque of Sana'a, Yemen, in 1972 and 2010 a large cache of Quranic documents dating to the earliest era of Islam were discovered. Several of the most ancient proved to be palimpsests, documents that were over-written, hiding a more ancient version of the Quran underneath. The complete publication of these palimpsests is proving to be much slower than anticipated, especially after some of the manuscripts proved to be variant versions of today's Quran.

- Caliph Uthman, (579–656 CE) sponsored today's version of the Qur'an when he discovered his army dividing over disputes regarding the memories of Muhammad's actual revelations (Note that Muhammad himself was illiterate). The result of Uthman's directive to burn all competing manuscripts of the Quran, including the one from Hafsah, Muhammad's wife, resulted in a strong backlash to his rule, including the accusation that he "obliterated the Book of Allah" (Ibn Abi Dawud, *Kitab al-Masahif*, p.36). Obliterated may refer to burning, ripping or, in the case of manuscripts, *washing the ink off*, which results in what are called palimpsests today.

- Palestine Islamic Jihad (PIJ) is a real organization. While the characters described in this book as being members of this organization are fictional, the real-life organization is dedicated to the destruction of Israel and the establishment of a Sharia inspired, Palestinian state.

- Regarding Shiite's in Palestine, see: Holy Land Studies. Volume 7, Issue 2, Page 183-199, ISSN 1474-9475

- All verses from the Quran are taken from standard translations with the exception of Quran 2:282-283, which include the author's edits. Those from the Bible are drawn from the English New Living Translation.

- The exegesis of the eighty-fifth chapter of the Quran, Surah Al-Buruj, regarding the terrible execution of many Christians in Najran by Jews is based on historical sources. Dhu Nuwas, the leader of the Jews, attacked Najran in order to eliminate the Christians. He had them dig ditches, threw them in, and then lit them on fire while still alive. The heroic and uncompromising stance of the martyrs quickly spread throughout the region resulting in Najran rivaling Mecca as a place of holy pilgrimage for pre-Muhammad god-fearing Arabs. This story was known to every child in the Arabian Peninsula, and Muhammad used it as an example to all Muslims to persevere in the face of great persecution. See Sheikh Safi-ur-Rahman al-Mubarkpuri 2002, *Ar-Raheeq Al-Makhtum (The Sealed Nectar): Biography of the Prophet.* Dar-us-Salam Publications, p. 33.

- Islamic hadith (tradition) mandates that old Qur'ans be wrapped and buried; burning is a last resort. The hadith also tells us Hafsah received her Quran back after Uthman was finished with it. This conflict of opinion gave rise to the questions posed in this book regarding the likelihood the Hafsah Quran may still be found.

- The U.S. administration included Yemen, Sudan and Chad as exemptions to the *Child Soldiers Preventions Act* because it would undermine U.S. aid to these countries and therefore reduce their influence in obtaining information on radical Islamist groups. By making these exceptions the U.S. was able to continue working in close partnership with the Yemeni administration in their anti-terrorist agenda.

- According to Yemeni Muslim law a heretic is not allowed to remain married to a Muslim. This may result in a court demanding the dissolution of a marriage.

- Islamic tradition indicates Muhammad is believed to have been killed by poison. See *Sahih al-Bukhari*, Volume 3, Book 47, Number 786.

- There was a fire at the St. Catherine's Monastery in 1971. Renovations in 1975 exposed a cellar underneath the tower on the north side of the monastery. When the monks went into the cellar they found hundreds of centuries-old manuscripts, some dating back to the fourth century. There were documents written in Arabic, Syrian, Slavonic, Latin and Hebrew. See the Sinai Monastery website: http://www.sinaimonastery.com.

- The Codex Sinaitic of the New Testament, one of the most famous New Testament documents, was discovered at St. Catherine's Monastery. http://www.sinaimonastery.com.

- One of the few documents upon which Muhammad placed his handprint was the peace treaty he made with the monks at St. Catherines Monastery in the Sinai Peninsula. It is known as the Actinama. See John Andrew Morrow. 2013. *The Covenants of the Prophet Muhammad with the Christians of the World.* Angelico Press / Sophia Perennis.

- Coins with a cross engraved in the center and the letters MHMD inscribed around the edge of the coin have been found in various locations. They date to the early Islamic era. See Karl-Heinz Ohlig. Karl-Heinz Ohlig & Gerd-R Puin. 2009. *The Hidden Messages of Islam.* Prometheus Books.

- The Greek Orthodox Patriarch, the defacto ruler of Jerusalem at the time of the Muslim conquest, and Caliph Umar were not hostile to one another. When the Caliph captured the city he did so without a fight. See Abu-Munshar, Maher Y. 2007. *Islamic*

Jerusalem and its Christians: a history of tolerance and tensions. Tauris Academic Studies.

- The dimensions of the Dome of the Rock are the same as the original church of the Holy Sepulcher, and both are designed as martyriums. See K.A.C. Creswell. 1924. *The Origin of the Plan of the Dome of the Rock,* British School of Archeology in Jerusalem: Supplementary Papers. London.

- Jews believe that the temple, and specifically the Holy of Holies holding the Ark of the Covenant, stood over the Well of Souls. The description of the ark and ritual in the Holy of Holies is taken from the Bible. (II Chronicles 5:1-8).

- The historical roots of the language of the Quran have been traced to Syro-Aramaic. See Christoph Luxenberg, 2007. *The Syro-Aramaic Reading of the Koran: A Contribution to the Decoding of the Language of the Qur'an.* Berlin: Verlag Hans Schiler.

Appendix B: Books of Interest

Gibson, Dan. *Quranic Geography*. Independent Scholars Press, 2011.

Luxenberg, Christoph. *The Syro-Aramaic Reading of the Koran - A Contribution to the Decoding of the Koran*. Berlin: Verlag Hans Schiler, 2007.

The Hidden Origins of Islam: New Research into its Early History. Ed. Karl-Heinz Ohlig and Gerd-R. Puin. Prometheus Books, New York, 2010.

Mondher Sfar, *In Search of the Original Koran: The True History of the Revealed Text*. Prometheus Books: New York, 2009.

Suyuti, *Al-Itqân fi'ulûm al-qur'ân*, ed. Said al-Mundarawh. 4 vols. Beirut: 1996.